LIGHTS OUT

THE GRID SERIES
BOOK 1

KAYLA JAMES

THE GRID SERIES BOOK ONE

Lights Out

KAYLA JAMES

Cover Illustration by Kayla James

Copy Editing & Proofreading by Kristen Hamilton @ Kristen's Red Pen

 Created with Vellum

This is for everyone who's ever been told 'you can't' or 'you don't belong' or 'you'll never make it.'

Tell those assholes to fuck off and watch this.

CONTENTS

PLAYLIST

Losing Hold by Esterly, Austin Jenckes
Do It Like A Girl by Morgan St. Jean
Ignite by UNSECRET, Neoni
I'm Coming For It by UNSECRET, Sam Tinnesz, GREYLEE
Dark Room by Foreign, Jonny T
Carry You Home by Circa Waves
In A Perfect World by Dean Lewis, Julia Michaels
This Is It by Oh The Larceny
You Need To Calm Down by Taylor Swift
I Wanna Be Yours by Arctic Monkeys
Legends Are Made by UNSECRET, GREYLEE
Fall Into Me – Acoustic by Forest Blakk
How Do I Say Goodbye by Dean Lewis
I GUESS I'M IN LOVE by Clinton Kane
Something in the Air by Steelfeather
I Found by Amber Run

TERMS

Balaclava: A mandatory head covering made of fire-retardant material. Worn under helmets.

Cockpit: The section of the chassis in which the driver sits.

DRS: Drag Reduction System. Adjustable rear wings that allow the driver to switch between two predetermined settings. Designed to boost overtaking.

Formation Lap: The lap that immediately precedes the start of the race.

Halo: A cockpit safety structure that resembles a horseshoe, surrounding the drivers head and is bolted to the chassis at three points.

HANS Device: Head and Neck Support Device. A mandatory safety device that fits over the driver's shoulders and connects to the back of the helmet to prevent excessive head and neck movement in the event of an accident.

Pit Wall: Where the team owner, managers and engineers monitor the race.

PROLOGUE
RYDER

A SYMPHONY *of crushing metal and squealing tyres fills the air. My body jolts, thrown against the constraints of my five point seat belt system as my car ricochets off a sidewall. Debris flies through the air when I explode through the gravel lining the runoff of the turn.*

My breaths come out in clipped spurts as the world around me stops spinning. With shaking hands, I unlatch my steering wheel and place it on the hood. Anger descends as I pull myself out of the cockpit and over the side.

Hands grab me when my boots hit the ground and I jerk back, ripping my helmet and balaclava off in quick succession.

"Ryder!" I blink rapidly into the blinding light, trying to focus on the blurring form in front of me. What the fuck is going on?

Freezing hands cup my jaw as the person steps closer. I can hear my race engineer, Tyson, calling out my name, but his voice is muffled by the one in front of me. I pinch my eyes closed and shake my head as the soft voice grows clearer.

"Ryder!" My eyes shoot open and I choke on an exhale when I'm met with emerald greens.

"Mum?" I whisper on a shaky breath.

"Ryder, you have to walk away."

"How are you here right now?"

"Please, just walk away," she pleads, clutching onto the front of my race suit. She looks over her shoulder and I reach out to touch her, only to connect with nothing but air.

"King!" Tyson barks in my ear.

"Mum." I step towards her, but she takes one back, shaking her head.

A figure appears over Mum's shoulder in the distance and rage floods my system as I watch my teammate clamber out of his destroyed car. He kicks the tyre and throws his gloves off into the rocks. Spinning to face me, he charges in my direction and we meet in the middle.

"You stupid son of a bitch!" My hands connect with his chest, sending him stumbling back.

"But this is pretty on brand for you, is it not? Saying you'll do something and falling short. Or hell, blowing the whole thing out of the damn water." I open my arms to the massacre of our cars around us as my voice raises.

"Fuck you. Maybe if you had even half the talent of your father—"

"Don't you fucking think about it," I growl.

"You know what I think? Ryder King, son of one of the best drivers in Formula 1 history never actually had what it

Pole Position: First place on the starting grid.

Qualifying: The knock-out session prior to the race in which drivers compete to determine the starting grid for a race.

Reconnaissance Lap: When drivers leave the pits to assemble on the grid for the start.

Retirement: When a car has dropped out of the race.

Race Engineer: The single point of contact between the driver and the team.

Safety Car: The course vehicle that is called from the pits to run in front of the leading car in the event of a problem that requires the cars to be slowed.

Tyre Warmers: An electric blanket that is wrapped around the tyres before they are fitted to the car so that they will start closer to their optimum operating temperature.

Team Principal: The person who is in charge of the team and its personnel.

Lights out and away we go!

takes." He steps farther into my space and my hands clench. "Everything you have has been handed to you. All because of who your papa is," he pauses and shakes his head, "But the truth is that the legacy of the King name—"

"Don't—"

"Crashed and burned when Rex did."

I shove him hard and he goes flying back. A hand grapples for my arm and my head twists, meeting Mum's pleading eyes.

"Please, Ry," she whispers.

Getting his feet back under him, he lunges for me as I move in front of Mum.

His helmet collides with my temple, sending me crumpling to the ground with blinding pain flashing behind my eyes.

The back of my head cracks against the gravel and my vision blurs, darkness creeping in from the sides. I blink, but wince at the sting.

I bring my hand up, brushing my fingers against my forehead and the warm substance pooling there. Pulling back, I squint at the crimson dripping from my fingertips.

My hand falls to the ground beside me as I struggle to stay conscious.

The sound of approaching sirens grow louder and a figure steps over me, shielding my eyes from the sunlight. My vision waivers as he removes his helmet and I choke on a gargled scream.

My father glares down at me, disgust, disappointment, and hatred burning through his hazel eyes. It's the last thing I see before everything goes black.

———

I jolt awake to a blaring alarm, eyes blinking into the darkness of my bedroom. Chest heaving, I run a hand over my sweat drenched hair and pinch my eyes closed as phantom pains torment my head.

It's been months since this twisted rendition of that day first plagued my dreams. Endless nights of hearing those poisonous words over and over as Mum pleaded for me to walk away. Of feeling the back of my skull crack. Of seeing my failure reflected in my father's eyes as he watches me fade into nothing.

They weren't there that day, but that's the thing about nightmares; they don't give a single fuck. It's a playground for all of your worst fears, insecurities, and vulnerabilities to bully the realistic and logical sides of your subconscious.

I groan, flipping onto my back after grabbing my phone from the side table. Turning off the alarm, I bypass the newest voicemail notification from Jace and click open my calendar.

Multiple red dots decorate each day. It's a grueling schedule and one my doctors probably wouldn't be completely on board with, but it's what I need.

I have two sessions a day with my trainer, one in the gym and one in the simulation lab. When I'm not there, I'm at home watching tapes from last season. The one I missed.

That day, almost a year and a half ago, I'd lost the final thing I'd ever cared about. Dad had died when I was still a kid. Mum succumbed to her cancer just before the season.

Racing was all that was left, but the two hits to the head did enough damage to take me out for the rest of that season and the next.

For months I've been on a mission to prove that I can come back. That I'm worth the investment. That despite the injuries and setbacks, I will clinch a fifth world championship.

An alert for an incoming message pops up and I immediately move to swipe it away, a habit I've built up over the last year when all I wanted was to be left alone. I freeze, my thumb hovering over the banner as my eyes glance over the message preview.

UNKNOWN (MAYBE: NIKOLAI MOROZOV)

Ryder King, you're a hard man to get a hold of.

The sheets rustle next to me and a slender arm drapes over my middle. She either ignores or doesn't sense my body tensing as she runs her hand up my chest.

"What time is it, baby?" *Yeah, no. I have never and will never be a* baby *kind of guy.*

My nose twitches at her morning breath when she presses up to kiss my jaw. I turn my head away from her advances and pull my phone to my chest.

"Time for you to go."

The blonde shoots up in bed, sheets pooling around her waist and leaving her fake tits on full display. She glares down at me and curls her lip.

"Excuse me," she screeches.

5

"Exactly." I return my attention back to my phone, ignoring her as she scrambles out of bed and around the room to collect her discarded clothes.

She was nothing but a warm body to scratch an itch. I'm a grown man with needs after all, but I don't have the time or patience for anything more than one night. It's nothing against the girls, I just have nothing left of myself to give them nor do I really want to.

That part of me died off long ago.

"You're such an arsehole," she cries, zipping up the ridiculously short skirt that caught my attention in the first place.

I grunt in response. What the hell does she expect me to say? I am an arsehole. No sense in trying to deny it.

She huffs and snatches her purse off the floor, stomping towards the bedroom door. With a hand on the knob, she turns and snarls, "Go to hell, Ryder King." *Already there, sweetheart.*

The door slams and a minute later so does the front door, but I couldn't give two shits. One? Maybe. Two? That's asking too much.

I pull up the text from Morozov and send off a reply.

RYDER:

> Nikolai Morozov, you're a man I never thought would have been looking for me.

NIKOLAI:

> I'm in London and we've got a meeting at the new Nightingale Racing facility at 08:00.

6

I shoot up in bed and stare down at the screen, heart hammering in my ears.

RYDER:

We do?

NIKOLAI:

We do.

FULLY THROTTLED ARTICLE EXCERPT

NIGHTINGALE RACING: A NEW DAWN
(FEBRUARY 3, 2024)

As of January 1, 2024, Nightingale Racing has been officially licensed as the newest Formula 1 team after the dissolvement of Reynolds Racing Group at the end of this past season.

Nightingale's founder and owner, Callum Brennan is a previous three time world champion, holding records in 2004, 2008, and 2009. After retiring from racing in 2010, Brennan trained with up-and-coming drivers at the Formula 1 driving school.

> *"It was always the plan to one day own a team. If I had to step into an already active one or start from the ground up, it didn't matter. So when Reynolds disbanded, I saw my opening," Brennan said in an interview.*

On January 16, 2024, he signed Nikolai Morozov, former Formula 1 driver, as Principal for the team. Morozov previously raced for

Arcadia Racing from 2012 until retiring after a career ending collision in 2022.

Morozov's first act as Team Principal was to sign four time world champion, Ryder King, as Nightingale's first driver. King officially signed with the team on February 2, 2024 following a year of medical leave resulting from an altercation on track during the 2022 season.

> *"We are building a team that everyone will underestimate. Not to say that the talent of Ryder King is to be put in question, because his four consecutive championships say otherwise. But it doesn't escape us that he has had an entire season off. You'd be inept to think that time away wouldn't affect the best of us," Morozov comments.*

Brennan and Morozov are tight lipped on who will be filling that second seat, but sources say that you won't see this one coming.

CHAPTER 1

BLAKE

My thumb taps against my thigh as I scowl at the alarm clock. I swear the red numbers are taunting me with every dragging minute.

Five.

I can totally last five more minutes.

I check the clock again after those agonizing minutes and groan, flopping back on my bed in defeat. It's only been *two* minutes.

Eight years and the excitement thrumming through my veins on race day never gets old. Well, it never gets old to *me*. Mama on the other hand?

"For being one of the top drivers on your circuit, you're one of the clumsiest people I know," she scowled at me one morning after I accidentally tipped over a shelf full of dishes.

Since then, I've sworn not to leave my room before her alarm goes off. Not that she needs her beauty sleep. I've heard her referred to as a MILF more times than I would have cared to and by people I'd like to forget.

Mama's a nurse, but the hospital she works at is in the city and the commute absolutely sucks. It's enough to have her contemplating injecting caffeine directly into her veins, but she swears she loves it.

She's always dreamed of being a nurse, and as of last year, she's fully certified. And damn, if anyone deserves to live their dreams, it's her.

She gave up everything for me. Some willingly and some not. Having a kid out of wedlock after only knowing the sperm donor for two weeks didn't live up to my grandparents' expectations for her. At eighteen, no less.

So off she went, taking anything she could fit in her car and driving until she didn't want to anymore. She ended up in a small town just outside of Atlanta, Georgia and six months later, she had a baby girl. Me.

She worked two jobs to put me through childcare and schooling, all the while attending night classes for her own education. While she may be starting her career a little later by societal standards, she's still killing it. *Not literally, obviously.*

Breanna Stone is my hero. Role model. Best friend. Inspiration.

She's the reason I push so hard with driving. She instilled the same determination in me that I've seen in her every day of my life. The kind of commitment to achieve my own dreams.

Beep! Beep! Beep!

I bolt upright at the sound of Mama's alarm and the shifting of her bed. I close my eyes and listen to the sound of her morning routine.

The shuffle of her slippered feet. Flip of a bathroom switch. Squeaking faucets and trickling water. A muted buzz from her electric toothbrush. Creaking closet doors and hangers as they scrape against the iron rod. Her footsteps grow clearer as she exits her room and heads down the hallway, pausing outside my door.

Tap. Tap. Ta—

I'm off the bed and swinging open my door before she can fully land the last knock. Her one hand is raised while the other holds the end of her dark auburn braid.

"You're ridiculous," she mumbles.

"You love me anyway," I sing.

She opens her hand in a 'stop' signal and shakes her head. "Nope. Coffee first. Over the top daughter second."

I giggle and follow her down into the kitchen where she beelines for the Keurig while I retrieve our cups from the cabinet.

"Why couldn't you have this same level of excitement for the first day of school?"

"Uh, because it's school," I laugh.

"Fair enough," she shrugs and screws on the top of her travel mug. "Okay! I'm outta here. Love you and good luck today." She loads both of her arms down with bags and kisses my cheek on her way out the door.

Taking the stairs two at a time, I rush into my room and

double—okay, triple—check that I have all of my gear and overnight bag.

Our small circuit preseason race today is only an hour away, but my best friend, Cassie, decided we should have a girls night in a fancy hotel before our schedules get crazy with me racing and her in school.

Thirty minutes later, I'm standing on the front porch with my bags at my feet and arms crossed as she full throttles it into my driveway.

Tires screech as she slams on the brake and sets out her kickstand. She hops off her bike and yanks the keys out of the ignition, rounding the front tire.

"I am so sorry! Collin decided to make a snack of my panties and I spent fifteen minutes chasing him around the house. For having only three legs, he's a quick fucker."

I shrug. "It's okay, we didn't have to leave until six anyway."

She stops mid stride and her jaw drops. Her mane of curly red hair sways in the light breeze and she sputters when a strand sweeps into her gaping mouth.

Hopping up the last two stairs, she perches her helmet on her hip and pouts.

"No, don't give me that face. You are historically *always* late," I laugh.

Her pout turns into a scowl before her eyes light and she smirks, snapping her fingers and pointing at me. "Technically this time I'm early since we don't need to leave for another ten minutes."

"Not how that works when you were told a diff—"

"Nope! I'm early and you won't take this from me," she strides past me and into the house. One foot over the threshold, she turns back with furrowed eyebrows and pinches my side, "Oh my god, you were standing out here like you were all pissed off that I was late. You're such a little faker!"

I squeal and swat her hand away, "Let's go or we really will be late."

She stomps away, mumbling something about 'stupid early race times' before meeting me at the base of the porch stairs with her bag.

We climb into my car and Cassie plucks the aux cord from the center console. Her phone connects and we quickly find out that I forgot to turn the volume down after last night's drive.

"Hunter drops to his knees in front of me, running his hands up the back of my thighs. He lifts one and drapes it over his shoulder, punching the hem of her jersey farther up my—"

"Ah!"

"Shit. Fuck," Cassie fumbles with her phone and the audiobook cuts off abruptly. Clearing her throat, she slowly turns, "That's my bad."

She switches over to Spotify and queues up a playlist. We blast the music on the highway and belt out every tune like we're performing on stage. Can either of us carry a tune? Not a single one. Do we give a shit? You guessed it, not a single one.

By the time we're pulling off onto the exit, our voices are

hoarse, my cheeks hurt from smiling, and tears flow out of my eyes from laughing at her absurd car dancing.

The back gates to the track creak open for us to pull through and I lean forward, eyes growing wide as I take in the sea of cars.

Cassie whistles and whispers under her breath, "Jesus."

I hum my agreement and pull into the first available spot I find, not wanting to waste time searching since, as I predicted, some slight Atlanta traffic ended up making us a teeny tiny bit late. Turning off the ignition, I unbuckle and shift in my seat to face Cassie. She mirrors my position and rolls out her shoulders.

"I really don't have time to do this right now," I groan.

"Too bad, this one's going to be good."

"But—"

"Nope, we are *so* doing this. It's our thing and it's happening."

"Correction, it's *your* thing. Me? I'm not into the words of affirmation, I'm more of an act of service girl."

"Well, watch me service your ego right now," she smiles.

"I don't want you *servicing* any part of me," I laugh.

"You'd be lucky to be on the receiving end of my 'servicing', thank you very much."

"I'm two seconds from bolting, so if you're going to do it, then do it."

"Okay. Okay," she waves a hand through the air, "Blake Cordelia Stone—"

"Oh, full name."

"You have more natural talent in your pinky than any of

Within two of those five, I slip through the inside and clench second, pushing my car harder until I've got the leader in my sights.

I know it's not an official race with the season still weeks away, but I'm determined to make an impression.

I belong here.

I'm here to drive.

I'm here to win.

I knew pursuing this dream of becoming a race car driver would be difficult. That it was predominantly run by men. That it took practically a lifetime to work your way up and to refine your skills.

But I was going to do it. Ignorant words from angry fans, close minded owners, and sexist competitors be damned.

One early Sunday morning and a grainy view of the race was all it took. By the end of it, my cereal had grown soggy, my eyes were dry from not blinking, and my fingers tingled from the static of being pushed against the screen.

I knew right then that there wouldn't be anything else for me.

I've been doing this for eight years, which isn't nearly as long as others have, but we Stone girls are late bloomers, remember? Sleepless nights, early mornings, double shifts to pay for everything. And now, I've become this person who breathes, eats, and sleeps this sport.

You know those girls who make a show, or book, or song their personality? Well that's me... just with racing instead.

I blink as JR radios on the next straight and put more pressure on the current leader, creeping farther into his space. We approach the last turn and I position myself between his back tire and the inside. He swings wide to avoid making contact between our cars and I take the opening.

I slam on the accelerator and turn tight into the corner, gritting my teeth at the pull in my wheel. I hold strong all the way through and pull out just ahead of him in the straight.

We enter the long stretch, flying towards the checkered flag. A loud pop fills the air and I see smoke bellow out from behind me. *Oh, shit!*

"Blake—"

I block out JR and push the car to its limits. With my foot to the ground, a death grip on the wheel, and each of our teams lining the fence of the pit lanes, we cross the line with a checkered flag waving high above us.

CHAPTER 3

BLAKE

CHAMPAGNE AND SWEAT trickle down my face and into my mouth as celebrations rain down all around me. Cheers mingle with laughter and I squeal when someone pours what's left of their bottle down the back of my race suit. That's going to take some aggressive scrubbing later.

I attempt to wipe my face clear of the bubbles, but only make it worse since every inch of me is covered. This shit is like sand, gets everywhere you don't want it.

A recognizable chuckle sounds from my right, "Here."

I feel him take my hand and wait for the fluttering of butterflies or racing goosebumps to appear. They don't. Am I shocked? Nope. Does he look like I just kicked his puppy when I pull away? Unfortunately.

We dated for a while, but for a person who's supposed to always support, be happy for, and love me... That lasted right up until I consistently stood above him on the podiums.

As Cassie likes to say, 'nobody needs that negativity in their life.'

"Congrats Blake, you were great out there today."

"Thanks Freddy, you too." I smile and take the hand towel, wiping away the excess champagne running down from my soaked hair.

He shuffles from foot to foot and clears his throat, "Listen—"

"Blake," Cassie calls from the side of the stage, waving her hands and jumping around like a lunatic. I huff a laugh and shake my head before turning back to Freddy.

"If I don't go over there, she just going to—"

"Yeah, I understand. Congrats, again," he nods with stiff shoulders and saddened eyes.

"You too. See you out there next time, yeah?"

"Yeah," he sighs.

I step back and grab my first place trophy before jogging over to my now shimmying best friend. She squeals my name as I get closer and I smile, laughing.

When I'm within two feet, she throws herself at me, wrapping her arms tight around my neck and suffocating me with her wild auburn curls.

"Don't get too excited, it's just a practice race," I huff.

"Don't do that. Don't try to downplay your successes, no matter how official they may be," she points a finger at my face.

"Okay. Okay," I put my hands up in defense.

"Now let's try that again." She steps back and shakes out

her arms, jumping and rolling her neck. She blows a raspberry and smiles, "Ready?"

"As I'll ever be with anything when it comes to you," I laugh.

I cringe as her shriek pierces the air before she jumps around me. "You won, you won, you won! My best friend is such a badass!"

My eyes widen and I throw my hand over her mouth as a nervous laugh bursts from behind my smile, "Oh my God, stop that!"

"Too much?" she mumbles through my hand.

"You?" I pull her into a hug and whisper into her ear, "Never."

"Sarcasm noted, but ignored."

We pull away and link arms, skipping down the stairs of the stage and towards the team garage. People wave and congratulate me along the way and Cassie cackles at my every returned 'you too'.

"They aren't the ones who raced Blake," she laughs.

"I'm just keeping them on their toes," I shrug.

"Sure you are," she bumps her shoulder with mine.

"Well maybe they did good work today or had good news with something else or I don't know," I whine.

Cassie throws her head back and laughs at the sky. "You are such an introvert, it's truly comical watching you interact with others—ouch!" She rubs her side where I pinched her and scowls at me.

"Would you look at that, your new habit is contagious," I feign surprise.

"Oh, whatever," she grumbles.

"It's not fun being on the receiving end, is it?" I mock, throwing my arms around her and placing a big ole kiss on her cheek.

"Ugh, you're so annoying sometimes." She shoves my head away.

More cheers and congratulations ring out as we approach the garage and I plaster on my best extrovert mask. One thing I didn't anticipate with racing? The attention.

It's not that I don't necessarily like it. I'm just... awkward. I never know the right things to say, and when I do, it's not what comes out of my mouth.

Don't even get me started on when a camera is involved. Insert meme of Will Farrell in *Talladega Nights*, where he doesn't know what to do with his hands.

I've been getting better, I only stumble over my words every other interview now. I think I threw up a thumbs up the first time someone congratulated me after a race. I don't even remember, obviously my subconscious decided to spare me the embarrassment and block it from my memory.

"There she is," a voice bellows from right outside the garage bay.

"Here I am," I mutter under my breath and Cassie laughs.

"I'm so proud of you," Den squeezes between us and throws an arm around our shoulders.

"Couldn't have done it without you or the crew."

"Well, you practically did."

I wave him off as he eyes who I'm assuming is the

the arrogant douche waffles out there have. Possibly all of them combined."

"That's a bit of an exaggeration."

"You have lived and breathed this sport for the past eight years. Yes, that isn't as long as the rest of them, but honestly? It just goes to show how good you really are."

"Okay, I like that part."

"Someday, someone important is going to see all you have to offer and come chase you down, begging you to drive for their team."

"One can wish."

"You, my talented best friend, are meant for greatness. I see it, your mama sees it, the people here see it, and one day everyone else in the world will see it too."

She raises her eyebrows and smiles wide.

I nod my head and golf clap, "Wow, that was some of your best work."

"I know right?"

"I feel ready to kick some ass now."

"Yes." She pumps her fist in the air. "Words for the win!"

I shake my head and smack my hands on my thighs. "Okay, we gotta go."

"Hey." She grabs my forearm before I can reach for the door handle. "You got this, you know that right?"

I smile and lean across the center console, pulling her into a tight hug. "Thank you, Cassie. I know I poke fun at your little speeches, but I wouldn't be able to do this without you."

"That's why I'm the president of your fan club."

"I don't have one of those," I laugh.

"You do. It's small—"

"Meaning it's you, Den, and Mama."

"But I can feel it in my bones, you'll have to fend off the fans with a stick here soon because there will be so many of them."

"Okay, you goofball. Let's go," I laugh.

We climb out of the car and I lean into the back to grab my gear bag. With it thrown over my shoulder, Cassie and I take off towards the paddocks at a jog.

We round the last corner as I balance my bag while simultaneously sliding the zipper of my jacket down. It slips from my shoulder and I fumble to catch it, tripping over my own feet. Cassie giggles under her heavy breathing as we round the last corner.

"Umph."

Bag clattering to the ground, my arms flail and Cassie squeaks as she collides with my back. A large hand lashes out and grabs my arm before I topple over my best friend and scattered belongings. Once my feet are firmly back where they belong—underneath me—the hand releases me.

"I'm so sorry, I blew around that corner like the devil himself was nipping at my heels and wasn't watching where I was going. Are you okay?"

The person—excuse me—*man* I just barreled into bends and retrieves my bag from the ground before straightening to his full six something height.

The looming figure is dressed in all black with a hat pulled low over his head. I reach out to take my bag and notice he's wearing a singular leather glove. When he extends his arm towards me a little farther, his sleeve rides up, revealing a thick scarred tattooed wrist.

I divert my eyes from it and breathe out a thanks as I clutch my bag to my chest. When I go to look up at his face and apologize again, he's already stepping around us. A quiet grumbled 'excuse me' follows his retreating form.

"Well that seemed more intense than it should have been," Cassie laughs nervously.

"Yeah," I mumble.

Right before he's enveloped into the sea of cars, I yell out one more apology and start walking. "Come on, maybe we can slip in without Den noticing."

Cassie barks out a hysterical laugh and shakes her head. "Ah, you young naive soul."

I shake my head, knowing she's right. Nothing gets by that man.

Checking over my shoulder one last time, I grab her hand and pull. "Yeah. Yeah. Knees to chest Burrows, I've got a race to win."

"Hell yeah you do," she cheers behind me and we laugh all the way to the garage.

CHAPTER 2

BLAKE

"How nice of you two to join us!" *Ah, crap.*

"I guess we can strike international spies off our potential careers list?" Cassie whispers.

I nod my head, pinching my lips tight. Turning slowly, she stands slightly behind me, using me to shield her from— yep, disappointed Dad face.

"Hey," I plaster on my brightest smile and chirpiest voice.

"Don't even try it," he crosses his arms.

"This isn't our fault," Cassie chirps.

"Oh? Then whose is it?" Den tilts his head, leaning a hip against the open garage bay entrance. Cassie and I glance at each other and I widen my eyes at her.

Say something! I internally scream at her.

No, you say something! She stares back.

"We... were out for a walk," I say slowly, "And we got cornered by some crazed fans!"

Her eyes shine with disbelief and I can hear her mental

I close my eyes and take in a centering breath, letting the vibrations of the monster under my control roll over me. *You got this. It's just you and the car.* Blowing it out, I slowly open my eyes and nod that I'm ready.

I accelerate out of the garage, down the pit lane, and around the track with the other drivers in our reconnaissance laps before lining up on the starting grid.

Turning off my car, I climb out and hand off my gear to a crew member before making my way towards the grouping of drivers. We complete our pre-race interviews and stand together for the opening ceremonies before we move back to our cars.

The crew member from earlier hands me back over all my gear and I suit up before securing myself back in the cockpit. Crews disperse around us, exiting the grid as we get set for our formation lap. I'm pulling through the first turn when my radio crackles to life.

"Comms check, Blake."

"Check."

"Do you feel it?"

I smile. "Oh I feel it."

"What do you feel?"

"I feel the need," I sing.

"'The need', she says!"

"The need for speed!"

"That's our girl." JR dives into the rundown on who's where on the starting grid and relaying on what and where we need to focus. I'm nodding along as we go through our formation lap and I pull back into the pole position I secured in yesterday's qualifying.

Five red lights above us illuminate in a steady succession. The sound of readying engines fills the air and grows louder with each light. By the time the last one shines the still air suffocates with their roaring.

I take a deep soothing breath and hold it, blocking out everything around me. The noises fade until the beat of my heart is all I can hear, the wheel tight under my palms is all I feel, and the starting line is all that I see.

I keep holding it until the lights go out and my foot hits the floorboard.

Everything floods in as we start off hard and fast, shooting down the straight. I work to gain as much distance between me and the pack as possible, taking turns at higher speeds, pushing through straights, and finding my groove as the laps pass.

Things are going in my favor, but after I pull into the pit for a tire change closer to the end of the race, things start to go sideways. One of the crew members fumbles a tire, costing us valuable seconds and the guy manning the jack drops my car before they get the wheel on.

Pit stops are crucial in a race and can sometimes make or break the win. Seconds here could cost you minutes out there. It's where I find myself after this disaster of a stop.

When I get back out, I have to push harder to regain the ground I lost. Working my way through the pack, I pick each driver off one by one as I situate myself back in the top three within the last five laps of the race.

offending crew member. Cassie backhands his stomach and he grunts, "Stop staring at him like that. I'm pretty sure he needs to go change his pants now. You're the boss. Lift 'em up, not send them six feet under."

I point at her and raise my eyebrows up at him, "Your spawn is right. We're all a part—"

"Set those murderous eyes on the haters and trolls instead, no one will miss them."

"Cassie!"

"That's my girl!"

Den and I yell at the same time before I squint up at him. He shrugs his shoulders and beams down at his daughter like the proud dad he is.

"You've raised a bloodthirsty animal," I whisper.

He barks out a laugh because it's true. Cassie may look as sweet as pie at first glance, but really she's a motorcycle riding, physical sports loving, will be the last thing you see if you hurt her loved ones kind of girl.

She may say that I'm the badass, but in reality? If there was a zombie apocalypse, I would be picked last for the team... and she's the one choosing the team.

"Do you really expect me to not defend my best friend?" She pops a dramatic hand on her jutted out hip and I roll my eyes.

"I don't even care about what they say—"

"That is a blatant lie," she cuts me off.

"Oh and you so happen to know what my brain thinks more than I do?"

"If you 'didn't even care' about what they were saying,

then why was the only time I got to hang out with you over winter break was if I dragged my ass all the way to the practice track at your ridiculous hours?"

I bristle at her argument and shrug, "Uh, I don't know? Maybe I wanted to get better for myself? Just because the season is on break, doesn't mean I am."

"And you're telling me that the way all these people," she gestures around us, "may see or think of you has nothing with wanting to be your best? Wanting to prove yourself?"

I open my mouth to reply but it snaps shut when nothing but air escapes. She cocks her head and juts out her chin waiting for my answering rebuttal. Only, I don't have one. As much as it pains me to admit it, she's right.

I do care.

I care a lot.

But I've spent years compartmentalizing those feelings, putting duct tape over their mouths and shoving them into the deepest, darkest corners of my mind.

And that's where they stay until I need the fuel for one last rep, to roll my ass out of bed for that 4a.m. run, or to get back up if a race doesn't go my way.

Does it get to me sometimes? Yes. Of course. I'm a living, breathing human after all. I have feelings and just like everyone else, I have a breaking point. I just choose to wallow in a sauna after a hard workout than I do in a gallon of Ben & Jerry's.

It may not be healthy, but who's going to tell my therapist? Me? Ha! I don't even have one of those.

"Fine. Yes, I may care a teensy tiny bit." I hold up my

hand with my thumb and pointer finger millimeters apart before dropping it and sighing. "How can I not when they all keep saying how I don't belong here?"

Den steps closer and drops a tattooed hand on my shoulder, squeezing slightly. "Blake, you know that's not true."

"I know," I shallowly nod, looking down at my shoes and scuffing my toe along the loose pavement.

"Hey." He pulls me into his warm embrace. I wrap my hands around his waist and settle into the comfort of his large frame. "You're proving all of them wrong. In fact, you just did," he pulls away and I tilt my face up to his. "This is just the beginning, Blake."

I smile tightly and nod, "Just the beginning."

"Okay, I've got some meetings to get through before I can get out of here. You girls text or call me when you check into your hotel and for the love of all that is my sanity, promise me you won't do anything that leads to involving the police in any way," he pleads.

"You borrow a dirt bike once—"

"Stole. You stole that dirt bike."

"I brought it back. By definition that is borrowing," she points up at him.

"It was the sheriff's son's bike."

"Well he was a dick and for being the sheriff's son, he didn't know jack about securing his belongings. The idiot left the keys in the ignition."

"At his house!" Den's eyes blow wide and he throws his arms up.

"Pfft! Details," she waves him off.

Den stares at his daughter in horror and she flashes him a cheeky smile. I step between them and pat his chest. "Don't worry, it's a night full of trashy TV, junk food, and face masks for us. There's nothing nefarious for her to get into."

He drops his head back and groans at the sky. "She'll find a way."

Cassie gasps. "I'm not that bad."

"Aw Cas, we know. You just have a wild streak, that's all." I step up next to her and pat back her hair when she leans her head on my shoulder.

"I'm a good noodle," she whispers.

"One might say you're goodles," I murmur.

"Okay you two, get a move on." Den leans in and kisses the top of each of our heads. "Good job. Love you. Be safe."

Cassie pops up and smiles up at him, "Thank you. Love you too. No promises. Okay bye!" She grabs my hand and pulls me away with her.

"Cassiopeia Marie Burrows," Den yells after us, but she ignores him and we stumble closer to the bustling garage, giggling.

We're just about to step through the threshold when a deep voice sounds from the shadows at our right. "That was quite the race you had out there, Blake Stone."

Full name from strangers in dark corners, that's not creepy at fucking all.

Cassie shrugs her shoulders and I sigh, plastering on a smile that I hope doesn't reek of exhaustion and turn towards the voice. I've seen plenty of horror movies where the heroine walks off into the shadows, but I'm not dumb so I stay right where I am.

The silhouette of a tall man steps forward and the breath rushes out of me when he lifts his head. Even with the shadow blocking his eyes, I'd recognise him anywhere. He lifts a leather covered hand to adjust his black baseball cap and Cassie gasps next to me.

Well damn. Universe, we need to have a little talk.

CHAPTER 4

BLAKE

OKAY, what was in that champagne? Because I have to be drunk. Can you hallucinate when you're drunk? Was I drugged? What is happening?

"I—" my eyes flash from the man in front of me to Cassie.

"He's—" I face the man again, eyebrows furrowing as I blow out a quick shaky breath.

"You're—" This isn't real.

There's absolutely no way this man is standing in front of me right now. If this is some kind of trick or mistake then the universe has a seriously messed up sense of humor.

The seconds seem to drag on as we stand there. He watches me. I watch him. Cassie nervously looks between the two of us. Apparently it's too much for her to handle because she clears her throat two seconds later.

"Dear god woman," she groans as she steps forward. "You obviously already know who this wordsmith is, but I'm Cassie. And you are?"

My eyes widen when it hits me. Holy shit Batman! The guy I rammed into when we first came in before the race is—

"Nikolai Morozov," he steps forward and engulfs her small hand with his large, ungloved one. She sucks in a breath at the contact before drawing her hand back, face blooming into a shade rivaling her hair.

"He's the Team Principal for the newest team on the Formula 1 circuit, Nightingale Racing," I mumble to no one in particular. *Yeah, because he doesn't know his own job title, Blake.*

"Oh wow! That's good—no—great news, excellent even! Congrats! Yay!" She pumps her arms in a cheer and I stifle a laugh.

"You good?" I nudge her arm.

"I don't know." Her voice cracks from the high pitch as she buries her face in her hands.

Nikolai clears his throat. "Thank you," his jaw ticks, "Cassie."

She nods, a muffled 'welcome' coming from behind the safety of her hands.

His eyes linger on my now clammed up best friend a second longer before pinning me with his dark amber eyes. "Blake, it truly was a great run you had out there. A lot of drivers, ones that have won championships, would have had trouble coming back from that pitstop. What you accomplished tonight? I haven't seen driving like that from racers who've been doing this for well over a decade, let alone eight years."

I revel in his praise because, holy crap, *the* Nikolai

Morozov, two time world champion, is complimenting my driving. Excuse me while I go scream this from the nearest rooftop.

"Oh. Well, thank you. Coming from you that means a lot."

"I'm impressed. I don't get impressed often. You've got a bright future with a talent like yours."

Cassie bumps my shoulder and I turn to see her smirking at me with her signature 'I told you so' look.

"That future is actually why I'm here tonight."

Her taunting stops dead along with my heart at Nikolai's words. I slowly turn to face him and school my features, trying not to let my hope show. "I don't understand."

"Could we go somewhere maybe a little more," he glances around us, "private?"

When I don't make a move, Cassie huffs and grabs my arm, "Come on."

She drags me into the back side of the garage with a quiet Nikolai following behind us. "This is about as private as you'll get without going into the drivers rooms and those rooms are claustrophobic inducing with just two of us, let alone three."

He looks around and nods at her, "Thank you."

She blushes and shrugs with a small tick in the corner of her lips.

Nikolai clears his throat and locks eyes with me. "I'm going to get straight to the point if that's okay with you?"

I share a cautious look with Cassie and she shrugs her shoulders before I turn back to Nikolai with a nod.

"I need a driver."

My brows furrow. "Okay?"

"I need a driver, but I don't want just any driver. Nightingale Racing is the new kid on the block and not a lot of people are expecting much from us."

"That's hard to believe when you have a four-time world champion as one of your drivers," I point out. *Oh, that sounded so confident. Mental high five!*

"A four-time world champion who hasn't seen a competitive track in over a year. People are seeing it as a risky move to sign him without knowing how he'll measure up to not only his own record, but to the other drivers."

"I'd argue that his 'record' should be reason enough to sign him. The man came in first at one of the hardest tracks all the while sporting a broken wrist. He's probably one of the best racers to ever step foot on the grid."

Nikolai chuckles, "I'll have to tell him you said that."

My eyes blow wide and I raise my hands up. "Please don't."

"Okay, I won't. That one doesn't need anymore boosts to his ego anyway."

Cassie snickers under her breath next to me and I glance at her with daggers in my eyes.

"If only they knew that wasn't the risky move we were planning to take." His words drag my attention back to him and I school my features.

"And what move is that?" I ask cautiously.

Nikolai watches me and my hands begin to sweat under his hard gaze. I have a death grip on my emotions, trying to hold back the stampede of hope and excitement. Until he says the words, I won't be even dancing with the idea of my dream possibly coming true. *Yep, that's me, cool as a cucumber.*

"This industry is full of men who think they're entitled to everything and think they can do whatever they want just because they can distinguish which is the gas and which is the brake. I don't want that bullshit on my team. I need someone who will be in this for the racing and block all the rest of that shit out. Someone who's a part of this not to chase the money or fame, but for the rush of when you slide into that driver's seat."

"Understandable," Cassie murmurs.

"When I told that same thing to the team's new owner, he whole-heartedly agreed with it all. We spent weeks going over the current roster of prospective drivers to see if any of them would measure up."

"I'm guessing none of them did." I connect the dots. "Because if they did, you wouldn't be standing here right now."

He shakes his head, "We need a driver that no one will see coming. We need someone who loves this sport with everything they have and will listen, who will learn, and who will rock this industry to its core. And I think that driver is you."

"Me?"

"You."

"Why?" I laugh in shock.

"Because of what you were able to do out there today.

Because this," he gestures to the garage around us, "means everything to you. This isn't about the money or the fame for you, it's about the love of the sport. This is about passion and you have it in truck loads."

"Passion doesn't always make the best driver."

"No, but it makes for someone who is willing to work themselves until they become just that and you, Blake, are very well on your way to becoming one of the best. I saw it in the first video of you I came across and I saw it out there today. You are what I've been looking for."

Holy. Shitballs.

"Me?" I squeak.

"You."

"Ohmygod," Cassie rushes out breathlessly.

"I've set up a small mock race at our training facility in London for you to show the final decision makers what you're made of. The drivers you'd be up against are seasoned, but I have faith that you'll be able to keep up."

"Uh huh," I agree, dazed in the overwhelming sense of disbelief.

"This is your shot Blake. What do you say?"

———

A couple of days later, I follow behind Nikolai as we walk out of the airport in London, Cassie's arm linked through mine. Mama was on call and the two of them decided the velcro girl that my best friend is would go with me so I wouldn't do this alone.

We pile into Nikolai's car and drive the couple hours outside of the city to where the tryouts are being held. He shows us to our room in a small inn just five minutes down the road and tells us a car will be there in the morning to bring us to the track.

I spend the rest of the night studying the track from Google Maps images Cassie was able to dig up while she helps me go over possible plans of attack until I look over to see her battling to keep her eyes open. I laugh and call it a night for both of us.

Listening to her soft snores, I try to catch as much sleep as I can myself, but I'm still up before my alarm the next morning. I sit with my back against the headboard as adrenaline pumps through my body as my mind whirs with the building anticipation for today.

Cassie rolls over, brushing her wild curls out of her eyes and looks up at me with a sleepy smile, "Hey chick. Today's the day."

I nod, humming.

"You're going to kill it, Blake."

"I know."

"Do you?" She shifts until she's sitting up until she's facing me fully with her legs tucked underneath her. "Because I'm getting a vibe from you that says you're full of shit."

"Cassie!"

"What? All I'm saying is this," she circles her finger around my face, "isn't the face of someone clear of shit."

I shove her shoulder and she falls back laughing as my

own chuckle breaks through. I can always count on this girl to break me out of my spirals. When the thoughts become too much or threaten to take me down a darkened path, she slams the door shut, hammering in nails with booming rounds of laughter.

I don't know what I would do without her.

"I may be a teensy bit nervous."

"Oh, she's a teensy bit nervous," she mocks.

"I'll be okay when I get to the track."

"I know you will." She claps her hands and jumps off the bed. "Come on then. Let's get a move on, girlfriend. In case you forgot, my best friend has some very rich men to impress today."

I screw up my face. "You make it sound like I'm doing something a lot less innocent and a lot more—"

"Yeah, I heard it the moment I said it," she waves me off and dives into our suitcase.

A moment later, my usual race day outfit hits me in the face.

"Now get your speedy ass up and. Let's. Go!"

Laughing, I do as she says and get my ass out of bed. Thirty minutes later, I'm sliding in behind her for the five minute drive to Nightingale Racing's track facility.

We pull up and Nikolai stands in his black jeans, Nightingale long sleeve, black hat, sunglasses, and his black leather glove adjoining his left hand. The car slows as we approach and I peel my eyes from the window to see Cassie smiling at me with shining eyes.

"Don't," I warn.

"I'm not doing anything."

"If you cry, then I'm going to cry and what kind of first impression will I make if my eyes are all red rimmed and puffy?"

"Fine. Fine. Fine," she hastily wipes her eyes and blows out a breath, "I'm just so freaking proud of you."

"I haven't done anything yet, Cas. Save that pride for after the contract is signed."

She squeals and points at me, "Now that's the spirit."

"What?"

"You didn't say *if* the contract is signed. You said after the contract is signed. That right there sister is called confidence. You're confident you'll be signing on with the team."

"I'm hopeful."

"Confident."

I glance out of the window at the training facility and take a deep breath.

"Confident," I whisper.

My heart stutters as my eyes dance over the clean architecture and the Nightingale Racing logo. Eight years of giving everything I have to this sport and this is my shot. I take a steadying breath and nod, slipping into the warmth of adrenaline, determination, and concentration.

Nikolai starts for our car when it pulls up to the curb and I look back at Cassie. She smiles and tilts her head, "You ready?"

"More than."

CHAPTER 5

RYDER

"READY FOR THIS?" Tyson asks, sliding on his headset. He's been my race engineer since I started racing Formula 1. I'd say at one point we could be considered close friends. Then everything went to shite and just like everyone else, I closed him out.

I spent the last year in self-induced solitude. Besides those who were there to warm my bed, I saw exactly two people.

My trainer.

My doctor.

They were the only ones allowed near me because I needed them if I had any shot at coming back. I did the rehab they laid out for me and the training to build back my muscle memory. I gave everything I had left in me.

As the season got closer and rosters finalized, I pushed harder. The fear and anger of this possibly being the end drove me to a breaking point.

I let the darkness consume me and gave into the spiraling thoughts. My worst fears were coming to fruition and all I could think about was how I wasn't enough.

Then my phone rang.

"You're a good man, King. You've got your father's talents and your mother's drive. It was a bad time and the prick used it to get to you. You've worked your ass off this past year and as far as I'm concerned you've earned this spot."

"Thank you for this sir."

"Let's see if you're still thanking me after you hear about an idea we've been discussing."

Nikolai was right, those grateful feelings died the moment he told me they planned on bringing an amateur driver in for the team's second car.

"Let's just get this over with," I breathe.

I push off the wall and stride towards my waiting car. Four other drivers follow me out of the garage, their voices bouncing off our concrete surroundings.

"Holy hell, we've got a short stack on our hands boys," a German accent rings out above the rest, catching my attention. I follow his line of sight and see Nikolai leading a much shorter figure towards the starting grid.

"Can the kid even reach the pedals?" he chuckles and the other guys join in.

"I heard he was actually pretty close to taking pole position."

The four of them freeze and stare at me with wide eyes, no doubt waiting for my reaction. I glare at each of them as they turn to Tyson with varying degrees of confusion while disbelief floods my system.

"What?" I growl.

"They wanted to see what he could do, coming from behind all of you," he gestures to the group, "the difference between your time and his was a tenth of a second."

Tyson tips his head towards the prospect, "Short stack there has got some serious speed." He shrugs before walking away, fucking whistling.

We watch him go in silence, each of us reeling. The group of drivers turn around and avoid eye contact as they move around me, towards their waiting cars.

When the last of their footsteps fade, I tilt my head back, close my eyes, and take a steadying breath. After I gain control of my runaway thoughts, I straighten and roll my neck to rid myself of the building tension in my shoulders.

I turn to face where the cars are lined up in time to see the newcomer climbing into his car. I catch Nikolai's eye and he nods before leaning down through the driver's halo and speaking to the driver. A moment later he straightens and meets me halfway towards my car.

"You good?"

I hum in answer and slip in my earphones.

"Listen. If you need more time—"

"I don't need any more fucking time," I snap.

Nikolai watches me with hardened features and I blow out a breath.

"Sorry," I sigh and shake my head.

"Alright." He studies me with slightly drawn in eyebrows

before nodding and clapping a hand on my shoulder. "If you need anything Ryder—"

"I know."

"Okay then. Let's get this started."

With that he walks off, talking into his headset. I watch his retreating form a moment longer before clearing my throat and continuing on to my starting position.

This season is going to be different.

It has to be.

Callum and Nikolai made it clear that they won't entertain any bullshit talk behind people's backs or two-faced assholes waiting to sabotage you. We go into this season as one or we won't be going at all.

There's plenty of drivers for them to choose from, but their first call was me. And I won't be giving them any reason to regret that decision. If I have to play nice, I'll do it. If I have to act like I care, I'll put on an Oscar-worthy performance. As long as I get to slide into my car every week.

I slip my gear on and hop over my car's halo, latching myself into my seat as Tyson's voice crackles over the radio to run through the final pre-race checks.

When I'm settled and the safety straps are in place, I'm handed my gloves and slip them on. I take the wheel and hit the ignition, bringing the beast to life. My body vibrates as the engine roars behind me and I smirk. *I'll never get tired of this.*

After a formation lap, we line back up at the starting grid and I do one last check of my system and mirrors. "Take care of yourself out there and don't go too hard, mate. The team still needs you in one piece and all that," Tyson calls and the air around me goes still as a flash of blood soaked fingers crosses my mind.

"Understood," I grunt in response, turning my head slightly to scan the pit wall.

I lock on Nikolai standing just behind the fence with his arms crossed and signature scowl. Callum approaches from behind him and claps him on the back.

Their focus shifts to me and Nikolai gives a tight nod before his attention drifts down the line of cars. He watches for a second longer before both men are striding out of view and behind the pit wall.

Shifting back to look down the track ahead of me, my jaw ticks as images of my dad standing above me, my mum crying out for me to walk away, and the sound of my skull crushing reverberates through my head.

My hands flex on the wheel and I squeeze my eyes shut, shaking my head as if that would rid me of my never ending nightmare.

A roaring engine chases out the screams of sirens and my eyes fly open, focusing on the lights hanging above us as they flicker to life, one after the other, in a steady succession. I take an anchoring breath with each one and the horrors in my mind slowly fade.

One. Deep breath in and hold.

Two. Hear the engines roar.

Three. Feel the vibrations of the car.

Four. Visualize the track.

Five. Release.

Lights out.

We soar down the straight and it's a battle through the first turn. Settling into our positions, I work to get as much distance between me and the others as possible.

The race consists of forty laps on our practice track with eighteen turns throughout and I hold first in a firm fist through the first twenty of them.

After a pit stop during lap twenty eight, I pull back out on the track and Tyson informs me that one of the drivers has spun out and retired. The prospect, who Tyson informs me is Blake Stone, has moved up to fourth and is quickly gaining on his next targets.

I enter the straight and chance a glance in my mirror in time to see Stone make his move. The back side of his car glides across the pavement in a controlled drift as he overtakes one of the cars, sliding right in behind second.

"Uh, what the hell was that?" Tyson breaks through the radio with a chuckle in his voice.

I shift down, approaching the next turn and ignore his question.

"Fuck that looked cool. Why don't you do shit like that?"

Is he being serious right now?

"What the hell are you going on about?"

"The drift. Why don't you do cool shit like that?"

"I could do it. I choose not to because that shite isn't beneficial. It slows you down."

"Prove it."

"I don't have to prove it," I growl, frustration mounting.

"Because you can't do it."

"Can you shut the hell up and let me concentrate?"

We're rounding into another lap when I see Stone slip by the other driver on the inside of turn one. Fucking sloppy on the other guy's part for leaving such a big opening for him.

I shift and slam on the accelerator, pushing my car to its limits. Just as I think I'm breaking away, Stone throws me for a loop and matches my pace. In no time, he is breathing down my neck and we move through the circuit in perfect sync.

I'm trying a hell of a lot harder than I thought I would have to, but instead of mounting frustration and irritation, it's almost exhilarating. Bottling up that feeling, I say fuck it and test the car's limits.

I take corners tighter and at higher speeds. I push all out on the straights. When he makes a move to get around me, I match his movements. We enter into a sort of dance. I push and he pulls, and when I swerve he follows my lead.

On the last lap, Stone is practically kissing my back tire and as he moves through a turn, he swings wide. The flash of red paint glints in my mirror as he pushes into the open road next to me. We move through the sequences of turns side by side, alternating who leads who.

For a moment, I get lost in the challenge. I huff as a smirk overtakes my face and a lightness fills my chest. *God, I've missed this.*

Approaching the last turn, I see Stone set up and make a split second decision. Fuck it.

Down shifting, I match his speed and the motion shifts weight to the front of the car. I twist my wheel and lift off the throttle when my backside slides sideways before applying more to balance. We slide through the final turn in a coordinated drift, side by side.

Tysons cheers ring throughout my radio followed by a bellowed 'show off' as we accelerate through the rest of the turn and straighten out for the final stretch. We cross the checkered flag with milliseconds between our times and one thought plays on repeat in my head. *Maybe this idea wasn't so idiotic after all.*

CHAPTER 6

RYDER

I'm up and out of my car before the last driver has pulled into the pit lanes. A crew member appears at my side and takes my gear, handing me a Nightingale Racing hat and my sunglasses.

Glancing over my shoulder, I watch as each of the other drivers climb out. One of them shucks his helmet off and walks over to Stone with a wide smile.

"Hey man, that was—"

He stops abruptly and out of my periphery, I see the others stop and stare with varying emotions on their faces.

Shock.

Annoyance.

Disbelief.

Anger.

The blond German from earlier scoffs and mutters a curse in his native tongue before barreling past Blake and into the garage. His buddies follow with much less heat and quietly give their congratulations. I don't move as they all disappear.

A door slams somewhere behind me and Blake startles, swinging around to face me. The beat of approaching footsteps rings in my ears and the next breath stalls in my chest when bright blue eyes fly up to mine.

Oh, fucking hell.

Standing at somewhere around five foot two, with her helmet on, she would barely meet my collar bone. Thick chestnut brown hair is thrown into some kind of braid on either side of her head and ends just above her quickly rising chest. Shorter wisps slick with sweat clinging to her forehead as a drop rolls down her temple.

My eyes track down over pink cheeks and a soft jaw. Her racing pulse thrums underneath the skin of her slender neck. Her tongue swipes out to wet her parted lips and she takes a shaky breath.

A copper taste fills my mouth as I bite the inside of my cheek to distract from the idea of how she would taste. *What the fuck is wrong with me?*

Blake dips her head towards the ground and I instinctively move forward, causing her head to shoot back up. I stop mid step as I drown in her ocean blue eyes. A slim silver ring lines her pupil, expanding into icy depths that swirl and dance with light gray, almost white, streaks.

A throat clears and her eyes shift over my shoulder. I turn and see Nikolai standing with his arms crossed, "Let's go upstairs and have a chat, yeah?"

Blake nods, but makes no move to follow. She watches his

retreating back, sucking in a shaky breath. Her lips move as she quietly hypes herself up and I find myself curious about why she's so nervous.

Granted, an hour ago, I would have bet my entire net worth on this not working out. There was no way this person had the capabilities to compete at this level. I went into this knowing it would be a mistake and I thought there was nothing that could change my mind.

But then I saw her drive.

Her eyes shift over to me and I see her cheeks blush before she flashes me a small smile, squares her shoulders, and follows Nikolai through the garage.

I'm entranced as she hands her gear to one of the crew members, a shy smile on her lips. He congratulates her and walks away, but instead of continuing farther into the space, she looks back at me over her shoulder.

I get wrapped up in her orbit and without conscious thought, I take a step. Then another. I follow behind her through the bustling garage and towards the stairs leading up to the offices.

Nikolai meets us at the front desk and leads us to one of the smaller meeting rooms. Blake's head doesn't drop the entire time. She wears a mask of pure confidence so well.

Almost as well as me.

But I see through it. I see her darkness and how it mirrors mine in its own way. I see the underlying fear and anxiety that what she's shown them won't be enough.

It's in the way her knuckles turn white with the death grip on her hat. How her lip flames red from the constant kneading of it between her teeth. I see the vulnerability flash in her eyes every time she flicks them in my direction and the nerves bursting out through her thumb tapping against her thigh as we settle into our seats.

The chair's armrest crack under my brutal grip as I watch her spiral and I shove away the urge to soothe her worries.

There's something about her that tames my own demons, quieting them so that I can breathe without the weight of everything crushing my chest. But it also cracks open the window for her darkness to creep in and tangle with mine.

I can't let that happen, won't let that happen. I worked my arse off to get this one good thing back, to race again. I won't let this unfounded infatuation with some pretty girl tempt fate. I won't let my guard down and lean into the false hope of everything good, just to have to go through the pain of losing it all over again.

Peeling my eyes off her, I turn to Nikolai. He watches her as she settles into her seat and takes in the room around her. He leans forward, garnering her attention, and taps a knuckle to the table, "How do you think you did out there, Blake?"

"I could have been better," she answers immediately.

Pushing aside the jolt her breathy voice sends through my body, I turn to her with a frown. That... is not what I expected her response to be.

"Why do you say that?"

"I wasted too much time in the beginning by playing it safe and took too long working my way through the pack. I could have pulled behind first place sooner, giving me a better shot at ending the race ahead. Corners weren't as tight as I would have liked, but I'm still getting used to the power of the car."

"How would you go about those improvements?"

"I'd increase my training in the weight room. I'm not used to that car's pull, but with a little extra muscle I could hold strong at the speeds I'd want to take. These guys have had years to memorize and get comfortable with the different circuits, so I'd up my simulation times and train on the different tracks. It'll also give me close enough practice to the real thing without risking damage to the real cars."

He nods along with her and then looks at me. "Ryder?"

I glance at him and he nods his head towards Blake. I clear my throat and meet her flustered eyes. "I'd work on your overtaking. The drift was successful since it caught the others by surprise, but it cost you valuable seconds. You don't need any fancy moves like that out on the track and there's a chance that the next time you try it, it won't go in your favor."

Blake looks down to the table as her head bobs, murmuring an agreement.

"Overall you did great work out there today and not just in the mock race. You've passed each test with flying colors. You have the makings of a good driver for any of the teams," Nikolai pulls her attention.

"Thank you," she says quietly.

The door opens and Callum plows into the room with an apologetic smile on his face. "Forgive me, I'm still getting used to these hallways."

His eyes slide from one of us to the next as he walks

farther into the room, but he stumbles as his eyes settle on Blake. Something passes in them but he blinks and it's gone.

Clearing his throat, he thrusts a hand in her direction. "Callum Brennan, team owner. You must be Blake, our newest recruit."

She tentatively takes his hand and smiles up at him. "I am," she clears her throat, "I just wanted to say thank you for this opportunity. I know that this whole thing is a risk for the team, but I want you to know that if you sign me, I'll give it my all."

Callum sits and leans his forearms over the table. "I have no doubt about your abilities, Blake. I saw firsthand today why Nikolai has been so adamant about bringing you on."

He leans back and blows out a breath. "But I'm not going to lie, this isn't going to be easy. A lot of people will think what we're trying to do here is exciting, but just as many people—if not more—will think we're completely out of our minds. Are you prepared for all that?"

"Yes sir. I've been dealing with things like that since I first sat in a race car."

"Good, that's good. You might have thought you had it rough in the little small town circuit you were in, but this is a whole other monster. We'll work this into training over the next couple weeks before the preseason announcement and meeting of the teams."

Nikolai pulls some papers out and hands them to Callum, who flips through them with a nod before sliding them in front of Blake. "Welcome to the team, Ms. Stone. I can't wait to see all the things you accomplish in your time here."

With shaky fingers, Blake takes the offered pen and signs on the dotted line. Ten minutes later I'm following her and Nikolai as we head back out into the garage.

I'm slipping my sunglasses on when a flash of red blurs and practically tackles Blake in front of me. The short curvy woman wraps herself around Blake, shaking her from side to side.

"I knew you could do it! I'm so freaking proud of you, chick!"

Blake's shoulders shake and seconds later, her laugh fills the air, the sound knocking me square in the chest.

"You know what I'm going to say," her friend says as she releases her from the tight embrace. She wipes at the tears escaping from her eyes and smiles.

"Go ahead," Blake laughs and I douse water on the fire it lights in my veins. *Fucking knock it off, King.*

"I told you so," her friend chants, hopping up and down until her eyes drift over Blake's shoulder and lock on me. Her eyes blow wide and her jaw drops as the little dance ceases.

Blake follows her line of sight and her face transforms with panic. She whips around to face her friend and whispers something under her breath.

The girl nods, not taking her eyes off me and Blake steps to the side, "I don't think I actually introduced myself earlier. I'm Blake and this is my best friend Cassie."

Her voice shakes slightly and my ego preens with the idea

that I make her nervous, but Mum raised a gentleman, so I slip on a smirk and reach out, "Nice to meet you."

"Uh huh," Cassie's replies as her eyes trace over my face. "So, you're Blake's teammate."

I raise an eyebrow, "That I am."

"Cool," she smiles with a spark of mischief in her eye.

I share a look of confusion with Nikolai and he shrugs, turning back to the girls. "Pre-season testing is happening in just under three weeks, so I'm going to need you back here in a couple days to start training. Also, you cannot tell anyone about this outside the few people we discussed earlier."

Blake nods but Cassie jerks back in confusion. "Wait, you aren't going to announce her signing?"

Nikolai shakes his head. "No. We're keeping everything quiet for now, something about building anticipation."

"Or in case you change your mind," Blake mumbles next to me and it's so quiet that she probably doesn't think anyone heard her.

I look down and as if sensing my eyes, hers shoot up. Her lips twitch and cheeks flush before she gives me a small shy smile and turns back to Nikolai.

They go on to discuss the plan on getting her back here and she doesn't look in my direction again until she's saying goodbye.

It isn't until her tail lights fade over the horizon that I'm finally able to look away.

That night, instead of the angry green eyes of my father, I see shimmering crystal blues. Instead of my mothers cries, I hear quiet laughter. Instead of the sickening crack of my skull

I imagine the feel of soft fingers threading through my hair. For the first time in a year, I don't wake up to a racing heart of fear and agony, drenched in sweat.

I stare up at my ceiling in disbelief. *Don't do it.*

The darkness creeps up in the back of my mind and I growl as it spreads, infecting the momentary relief. *Don't do it.*

Rolling over, I pick up my phone and navigate to the text thread with Nikolai.

NIKOLAI MOROZOV:

What do you think?

My thumbs hover over the keypad as I stare at his last text. A war breaks out within my mind but a trickle of laughter and a flash of blue eyes silences the warnings. It's in that relieving quiet that I find purchase to type out my reply and toss my phone aside.

RYDER KING:

Set it up.

CHAPTER 7

BLAKE

"There's no way in hell I'm packing that," I laugh.

"Why not?" Cassie pokes her head out from behind the poster.

I roll my eyes and turn back to my suitcase. I'm folding my last pair of pants when she thrusts the shiny paper into my face. "But it's funny," she pouts.

"Funny for who?"

"Me. Obviously."

"You're ridiculous. Now, are you going to actually help me pack or continue to snoop?"

"Yeah, yeah, pass me that stack," she holds out her arms, wiggling her fingers.

I hand over the pile of clothes and she strips them off the hangers before folding them. We spend the next hour jamming out to our playlist as we double team the rest of my packing. She belts out the last notes of Taylor Swift's

"Karma" and sits on top of the last suitcase as I wrangle the zipper closed.

There.

Done.

My two large suitcases are stuffed to the max and I had to intervene only twice when she tried to sneak certain items into my bags.

"Girls, dinner!"

"Last one there has to complete a dare of the victor's choosing?"

"What are you? Twelve?" I laugh.

We stare at each other and Cassie narrows her eyes, widening her stance. She whistles the wild west standoff theme and I mirror her. She raises an eyebrow and I wiggle my fingers.

"Girls," Mama calls and we snap into action.

Cassie lets out a battle cry as she jumps over the piles of clothes that were on the chopping block and I dart for the door. I have one foot over the threshold when she hops on my back. We tumble into the hallway and the spider monkey that she is clings to me every step of the way down stairs.

We fall into the living room in a tangle of limbs and Mama huffs a laugh, shaking her head. Cassie rolls, taking me with her over the back of the couch and pins me to the cushions.

"God, I forgot how freakishly strong you are," I grunt when she pins my arms.

She smiles wickedly and boops the tip of my nose. "And don't you forget it."

She hustles off of me, hops over the armrest, and sprints into the kitchen. When I can breathe again, I roll off the couch in defeat and drag myself into the small area pouting. Cassie imitates a cheering crowd as she swings her arms around in victory.

"What was it this time?" Mama asks as she hands me the bowl of broccoli salad.

"A dare of her choosing," I mumble.

"Oh, that's a good one."

"For her," I whine and slump down in my chair, scowling at Cassie who's bouncing in her seat, plating up her food with a smile.

"So, what are you going to have her do?"

"Oh, I'm holding on to this bad boy. Going to use this new found power when the time is right," Cassie teases, taking a bite of her garlic bread.

"Evil," I hiss, scooping a serving the size of my head onto my plate.

It's been a weekend full of my favorite dishes. There's been enchiladas. French toast breakfast bars. Ice cream sundaes every night. A fifty wing contest at our favorite sports bar, which we absolutely crushed.

Tonight, it's my number one favorite, lasagna and Mama's ooey gooey cheesy garlic bread. To make it a little more balanced, she throws in a broccoli salad that I take exactly three bites of before enjoying my carbs. I'm drooling just thinking about it.

"Everything packed and ready?" Mama asks.

I hum around my fork.

"And you have a ride to pick you up at the airport when you get there?"

"Yes," I swallow. "Nikolai said Ryder should be there before my plane touches down." Here's hoping that came out smooth because I'm a jumble of nerves on the inside, but I refuse to let either of these chatty Cathy's know that.

"Oh, Ryder's picking you up is he?" Cassie hums.

"Who's Ryder again?" Mama asks.

"He's my new teammate," I answer simply.

"You know who he is," Cassie winks at her across the table. When Mama stares back at her in confusion, she sighs.

"Wait here." She shovels a forkful into her mouth before dashing up the stairs.

"Cassie! Come on," I yell after her.

"Am I missing something?"

"You're just witnessing the start of my rendition on how to get away with murder!" My voice rises to a yell towards the end so that my former best friend can hear her fate.

She calls my bluff as she comes barreling down the stairs, phone in hand and a beaming smile breaking across her face. Blowing me a kiss, she stands behind Mama's chair and tilts the phone screen for her.

"What am I looking at here?"

"All of it."

"I'm not following."

"The walls," Cassie urges.

Mama leans in and, lord help me, she's zooming.

"Is this Blake's room?"

"Mhm," Cassie dances.

"And this is Ryder?" Mama asks, pointing to the screen with raised eyebrows.

"Maybe," I mumble as Cassie sings, "Oh, that's him."

"And you're going to be living with him?" Mama glances at me.

"I'm not living with him, just staying with him. He offered for me to stay with him for training and then we'll be in the same suites throughout the season. Different rooms though. A lot of teams do it, it's no big deal," I ramble.

"Do a lot of teams also have one driver crushing on the other?" Cassie bats her lashes.

"I don't have a crush on him," I defend.

They stare at me with matching unimpressed faces and I huff, "I had a crush on him when I was like sixteen. There's a difference. That was then. This is now, and twenty year old Blake does not have a crush on him."

"Sure about that?" Cassie raises an eyebrow.

"Mhm," I take a big bite.

"You're such a little liar! If you don't have a crush on him, then what were all those flirty smiles you were sending his way?"

"There were flirty smiles?" Mama perks up.

"No, she obviously needs to get her eyes checked because they were just smiles and in case you didn't notice, he wasn't one to return the gesture."

"Yeah, he's totally got that whole broody damaged boy

like it's candy," Den mutters, wrapping his arms around her shoulders.

I skip over to their little moment and raise up onto my tip toes, placing a quick kiss to Den's cheek. "You're a doll."

"Don't poke the bear when I just successfully tamed him," she whispers.

I back away with hands raised and smile at the father daughter duo. "Love you two! I'll be right back, Denny boy."

"I'm serious Blake! Don't let it happen again!"

"Wouldn't dream of it," I yell back over my shoulder with a beaming smile. Before I round the corner to the back of the garage, I catch his not so subtle eye roll and head shake as he walks with her to the pit wall.

Denver Burrows may look terrifying, standing at six foot five with tattoos covering mountains of muscle, but to me and Cassie he's a giant teddy bear.

The Burrows duo moved to town when we were in first grade, and after finding out that we shared a birthday, an instant life long friendship was born.

At one point we tried to 'parent trap' her dad with Mama, but it turned out that they were better off as friends. Matchmakers? Also scratched off the careers list.

I smile and enter my designated changing room. Locking the door behind me, I hurriedly strip out of my street clothes and rip open my gear bag.

I pull out my suit and slip this body part through that hole, zip here, velcro there, and shimmy the material until everything is where it's supposed to be. When I have my laces tied and tucked, I grab my helmet and remaining gear.

Bursting through the door, I race down the hallway and slip in my earphones. I drag my balaclava over my head before my helmet and secure it with the strap under my chin as I enter the garage.

Team members run around performing final checks and the pre-race buzz floats through the air. The building anticipation is addicting and I take a deep breath, feeling it all as I walk around my waiting car.

An open-wheel, open-cockpit, single seat monster with two wings—one in the front and one in the back—that aide the engine can achieve speeds up to 180 miles per hour.

I run my hand over the halo, a bar that surrounds the cockpit where my head will be, before launching myself up and over it into my seat.

I secure my belt straps across my shoulders and chest, nearly jumping out of my skin when Cassie pops her head over the halo. I huff a laugh as her shoulders shake, a smile breaking across her freckled face.

She reaches out and takes hold of the straps around my shoulders and gives them a sturdy tug. "She ain't goin' nowhere," she shouts over the noise of the garage.

I shake my head at her ridiculous superstition and take my gloves from her, sliding my hands into the worn fabric. I retrieve my steering wheel from the hood, clipping it into place.

Shooting a look at my race engineer, JR, I give a thumbs up and the team jumps into action around us. The car is lowered to the ground, tire warmers come off, and the engine roars to life beneath my touch.

groan of 'and that's what you come up with?' followed by 'amatuer.'

"Yes," she steps in, "They were nuts! Thrusting shirts, hats, pictures, even skin at us for Blake to sign. Don't worry, we stayed away from the blue sharpies."

"Uh huh," Den huffs, unimpressed.

"Yep. I remember you saying something about them being able to use my signature like a stamp if I use the blue pens. Do I understand how it works? Nope. But what you say goes!"

"If what I say goes, then why weren't you here twenty minutes ago when you were supposed to be?" He raises a skeptical eyebrow.

I purse my lips then wince when my side is pinched. "Ouch! Where the hell did this habit of yours come from because I think you should return it and get your money back." I rub over the tender point just under my ribs.

"We almost had him and then you had to go and over detail things," she grumbles.

"Oh and listing off items for me to sign—to include skin—wasn't too much detail?"

"I was talking fast, trying to confuse him."

"You failed, on both accounts. I am neither confused nor 'gotten'," Den breaks our glaring contest.

"I'm just going to go back and change into my gear now," I start inching away.

"Hold it."

"But—"

"You can't do this Blake. You've got to get here when the

schedule says to be here," he lowers his voice and concern lingers on the edge.

"I know," I sigh.

"Don't be upset with her, it was my fault. You know she would have been here first thing this morning if it weren't for me." Cassie steps in front of me. "I'm really sorry. First I was late, but not late, getting to her house. Then we hit some traffic and instead of letting her get out of the car right away, I had to go and do this whole speech—"

"Stroking your ego?" He leans around her and tilts his head at me.

"Can you both not say it like that?" I plead, remembering now where she gets her choice vocabulary.

"In the end, if it wasn't for me, she would have been here on time. So I take full responsibility and will reiterate how truly sorry I am." She sprinkles on a sweet twisting of her shoulders as she widens her eyes and slightly pouts.

"The puppy dog eyes stopped working when you were twelve," he deadpans then sighs, "But, if you promise not to do it again—"

"Yes," she cheers.

"And you make sure to cushion some time in there for these 'speeches' then I'll give you this one," he raises a finger and points at me with stern features, "But just this one. Don't be late again."

"Thank you. Thank you. Thank you." She wraps her arms around his waist.

"You two are why I've started eating heartburn medicine

thing going on." Cassie leans over Mama's chair. "It's kinda hot."

"I had a thing for bad boys too back in the day," Mama sighs.

"No. Stop that. And Ryder isn't a bad boy, he's just been through a lot."

"See, she's already defending his honor," Cassie points at me.

"No, I'm not."

"You kind of are, honey."

"Would you stop taking her side?"

"Okay, okay. Cassie, stop pointing out things Blake is obviously trying to ignore."

"I don't like either of you," I mumble.

They laugh as Cassie plops back down in her seat to finish eating. I push around what is left of my salad and attempt to hide my blazing cheeks.

Two days ago, Nikolai FaceTimed to go over the finalized schedule with me and Mama. We worked out dates where she could possibly come to see me race as well as my availability during our few breaks where I could come home.

We also discussed where I would be staying during training and the season. It took more effort than I'd like to admit to school my expression when he proposed staying with Ryder for training and sharing a suite throughout the season.

I glance at Cassie's phone and the image that's still displayed there. It's zoomed in on a poster I have hanging above my dresser with a younger Ryder yelling as he stands on top of his car. His hands are raised and the words 'world champion' loom behind him.

It's one of many posters I have of him on my bedroom walls, but it's not like I wallpapered my room with his face. There's others up there. I put all of my greatest inspirations up on those four walls, like a real life Pinterest board.

I know she's poking fun and I bet the universe is laughing right alongside her, but as intriguing of a picture she paints about a big romance is, it just won't happen.

We're teammates. That's. It.

This is a chance at my dream and I can't let something as juvenile as a crush with no real merit jeopardize everything I've worked my ass off to achieve.

I mean, everyone has celebrity crushes. Mama drools every time Henry Cavill is on screen and I once saw Cassie literally cry when she saw Harry Styles in concert. I haven't done either of those things. So I should be good, right?

I look at the image one last time before the screen goes black. Glancing up at Cassie, she smiles knowingly at me and I roll my eyes. "Shut up," I grumble as I rip off a piece of bread and shove it in my mouth.

After dinner, Cassie and I tag team the dishes while Mama sets up a movie. Me and her had our night alone last night, but tonight she wanted the three of us girls to have one more living room camp out before I flew the nest.

We plop down with popcorn and Cassie rips open a bag of M&M's, pouring the entire king size serving into the bowl. Munching on the sweet and salty concoction, we laugh and talk and watch movie after movie until Mama has long passed out and we can't keep our eyes open.

Snuggling in next to Cassie, we face each other and share sleepy smiles.

"I'm so proud of you, you know that?" she whispers followed by a yawn.

"I don't think I ever thanked you for going with me, but thank you."

"Pft. I wouldn't have missed it for the world. I just wish I could go with you now. I've never missed a race."

"I know. I wish you could come too, but then who would be here to mold the young minds of our future?"

Cassie rolls her eyes but her smile blooms across her face. She hasn't changed her answer to the 'what do you want to be when you grow up' question since we were first asked in sixth grade. After one last year, Cassie will graduate and go on to be one of the best elementary school teachers.

I'm only a little biased.

With a job lined up at the local school, her future is practically set. The reality is that she can't live out her dream while still being able to travel the globe with me to each race, no matter how much either of us wants it.

"I'm going to miss you," I whisper.

"I'm going to miss you too. Now get some rest, you've got a big day tomorrow."

Try as I might, I don't sleep a wink. My mind runs rampant with thoughts of the season, the schedules, the expectations, and a certain tall dark and handsome teammate until the sunrise filters through the curtains.

Cassie leaves after lunch while Mama and I load my bags into her car. The hour drive to the airport in Atlanta is filled with laughter, music, and memories, giving me the boost of energy I desperately needed after a night without sleep.

"You sure you have everything?" Mama asks, pulling out the first bag in the departures dropoff section.

"Yes, Mama."

"Well, if you get there and remember something, I can always send it to you."

She places my second large suitcase down on the curb with a huff and straightens. Her hazel eyes dance across my face, eyes watering.

"Mama." I rush into her open arms.

"I'm so proud of you baby girl." She pulls away and frames my face in her hands. "I'll be watching every week, already have my alarms set and everything."

Her thumbs brush my cheeks and she smiles. "I know you've worked incredibly hard for this, but promise me you won't forget to also have fun. Live in the moment and just be."

"I promise."

"And don't get swept up in all the bullshit or let them try to change you because you, my darling, are a wonderful girl and are going to do amazing things for this industry. I love you."

"I love you too," I sniff, crushing her to me in another desperate hug.

"Okay, okay. You've got to go. Never know how crazy security will be and you still have to check in your bags."

She helps me shuffle my bags around so that I can comfortably handle all of them by myself before sending me through the automatic doors. With one last look over my shoulder, I head into the bustling airport and take the first step in closing the distance between me and my dream.

CHAPTER 8

BLAKE

"Fuck," *his growl vibrates through his chest into mine.*

I gasp when his fingers slip beneath my underwear and trace over my throbbing clit. Clutching onto his arms, I instinctively roll my hips into his hand.

"That's it, love. Ride my fingers," he nips at my neck, "Take what you need. Use me. Don't stop until you drench my hand."

I moan, tipping my head back. His lips trail down my neck and across my chest as his fingers slide against me. An animalistic sound barrels out of me when his mouth closes around my nipple. He hums against my skin, "Mm, my girl likes a little bit of pain."

I think I nod my head but all thoughts evaporate in a blaze of smoke as my body ignites. I call out his name when the first waves of my orgasm slam into me, fingers digging into his shoulders to keep from falling.

Coming down from my high, I blink open my eyes and tip

my head down. Emerald eyes shine up at me in bewilderment as his lips part on heavy breaths.

"You're beautiful."

I jostle awake when the airplane hits a pocket of turbulence. Wiping the drool off the corner of my mouth, I straighten in my seat and glance out the window.

The captain comes over the intercom to notify passengers and crew members of our final descent into London.

The plane touches down twenty or so minutes later and I breathe a sigh of relief. One thing I've learned recently? I'm not big on flying. That revelation is perfect seeing as my job is now to travel around the world on a smaller plane than the one I'm now impatiently waiting to escape.

I follow the river of people out and down towards the baggage claims where I spend the next thirty minutes shuffling from spot to spot for a clear view.

My first bag comes out quickly and a nice gentleman next to me helps unload it from the belt. With a polite thank you, I slip my backpack off and fumble with it to stay on the handle.

Bag after bag comes out and people trickle out of the area until I'm one of the last passengers left standing. Finally my second suitcase makes an appearance and I jump into action. Gripping tight on the handle, I heave it over the side and nearly crush my toes.

I blow out a few stray hairs that fall into my face and straighten, rolling it towards my other bag. Slipping my backpack back on, I try to set up my hold on both bags so I can roll them without taking anyone out at the ankles.

I step through the automatic doors of the arrivals sector and straight into a real life rendition of *Sixteen Candles*. A bus pulls away from the curb to reveal Ryder leaning against his blacked out Range Rover on the other side of the pick up lane.

As if sensing my arrival, he looks up from his phone. My lips part on a shaky exhale and my mind races to think of anything other than the not so innocent dream I had earlier.

He pushes off the car and strides over to where I stand frozen, his long legs eating up the distance in half the steps it would have taken me.

"Sorry, one bag came out right away, but the other decided to take its sweet time," I blurt out when he's closer.

"Just the two?"

"Hm? Oh, yes." I shuffle the bags around me and he reaches for both of them. "Oh, I can—"

My protest falls on deaf ears as he takes both from my hands and rolls them over to his car. I scramble to follow him and slip my backpack off. He easily lifts both bags into the back of the car and shuts the hatch.

Coming up to my side, he stops short and his eyebrows disappear behind his sunglasses in a frown. "What are you doing?"

"What do you mean?" I peer around my immediate area, trying to pinpoint what he sees is wrong. I take a step back when he reaches by me to open it and I peer inside. *Oh, you idiot.*

76

I smile sheepishly at him. "My bad, forgot about that one."

I quickly move into the passenger seat on the other side of the car and turn to see him watching me with the driver's door hanging open, making no move to get in. His jaw ticks and his chest rises with a deep inhale before he finally climbs behind the wheel.

He pulls away and twenty minutes later, I watch the scenery outside my window transform from a concrete jungle to beautiful rolling hills. I lean my forehead against the glass and take in every little town we pass through and listen to the quiet sounds of the road.

My eyes cross with exhaustion, falling victim to jetlag and I lose the battle. One second I'm watching fields pass by, the next I'm dreaming of green eyes and the feel of coarse hair rubbing against my skin.

———

"Blake."

"Mmm." I snuggle farther into my blanket.

"Wake up."

I crack my eyes and glare at the blurry figure next to me. "We're here," his deep voice covers me like a sweater fresh out of the dryer, heating me from head to toe.

I yawn, sitting up away from the window and pulling down the blanket covering me. Only it isn't that at all, but a large black hoodie. One that does not belong to me.

"You were shivering. I didn't have anything else."

I lift my eyes, praying on all that is holy that he doesn't notice my flushed cheeks. "Thank you," I murmur and he nods.

"How long was I asleep?"

"Just over an hour. You looked pretty knackered, so I gave you the drive to sleep. But you should try and stay awake now to get ahead of the jetlag."

"I look what?" I ask, brows furrowing.

The corner of his mouth twitches slightly. "Knackered. You look tired."

My mouth parts in an 'o' followed immediately by a jaw breaking yawn. My eyes slide forward and I suck in a quick breath, shooting up in my seat. "This is your house?"

"Not what you expected?"

I turn to him and shake my head. "Honestly, not at all."

"And what did you expect?"

"I don't know. Maybe like a penthouse in the most expensive building in the city. Everything would be gray monotone with lots of metal and marble. Lights would turn on as you walk into the room. Doors wouldn't have handles. Floors would be heated. Oh! And there's an underground parking garage where you keep all of your fancy sports cars."

"So I'm Batman?" he deadpans and I huff a sheepish laugh, tilting my face down to hide my flaming cheeks.

"This place obviously isn't a big expensive building and it's far from being in the city. It's more of an earth tone palette with more wood than metal. There are light switches. The door handles are original crystal. The floors are unfortunately not heated but there are plenty of rugs to keep your feet warm. And the garage is around back holding my 'fancy sports cars.'"

He rolls his head against the headrest in my direction and his eyes flash with vulnerability. "I grew up here."

"Oh." I nibble on my lip and smile softly. "Well, it's beautiful."

I startle as a clap of thunder shakes the air and place a hand over my racing heart. "Oh my god, that scared the crap out of me."

Ryder leans forward and takes in the quickly darkening sky. "We should get a move on."

Humming my agreement, I twist and throw open the door. The moment my feet hit the ground, the sky opens up. I squeal at the first sting of the cold water and reach back into the car for the black jacket. Throwing it around my shoulders, I prop up the hood and take off toward the back of the car.

The cobblestones are slick with water and as I'm rounding the trunk, my shoe slips. I throw my arms out as a squeak leaves me followed by a grunt when my hip meets the cold and unforgiving ground.

"Shit." A door slams followed by heavy, quick footsteps.

"Are you alright?" Ryder's warm timbre is laced with worry and I open my eyes to see him leaning over me. His hair, jet black with rain, hangs heavy around his forehead. Strands curl into his furrowed eyebrows and his eyes rake over me.

"I'm okay," I groan and sit up. "Just mortified."

"Come on humpty dumpty, up you go." His hands wrap

around my forearms and when he helps me stand, the proximity sets my senses ablaze.

I take a breath and immediately regret it when his warm amber oak scent envelopes me. The muscles in his arms flex under my touch and my fingers tingle as they soak up his heat.

I flick my eyes up to his face and he watches me, gaze trained on my mouth. Releasing my lip, he snaps out of his haze and meets my eyes. Steam rises around us as the cold rain meets our heated skin and I lick my suddenly dry lips.

"Thank you," I murmur and step away from the temptation of his touch.

He watches me, his clothes melding to his large, honed form. His abs flex with every breath beneath his black T-shirt, powerful legs flex under the thick fabric of his black jeans. The man is a literal wet dream right now and I twist around, giving him my back before I can take in any other large attributes of his.

Opening the hatch, I reach in and grab hold of one of my suitcases, but Ryder slips it from my hand and I startle, looking back over my shoulder at him.

"I got it." He moves to pull out the other suitcase and I shut the hatch door before following him into the cottage.

We enter the small front hallway and he sets down my bags.

"Let me go grab some towels so we can wipe everything off and then I can show you around." He's already halfway up the stairs before I can answer.

My eyes take in the frames hanging on the walls. I step

closer to one where a young Ryder smiles bright with each arm wrapped around his parents' necks.

I'm taken aback at how much he resembles his father. They're practically carbon copies of the other down to the little dimple in their right check. His eyes though? Those beautiful, deep emerald greens come from his mama.

Heavy footsteps sound behind me and I look over my shoulder. He has a slim chain adorned with two silver rings dangling against his chest. His very naked chest. I nearly choke on my own saliva when he comes into view with a dry T-shirt hanging over his shoulder as he runs a towel through his hair.

"You okay?"

"Yep," I croak and take the offered towel, wiping down myself and my bags. Haven't even unpacked yet and I've already made a fool of myself at least three times. *Go, me.*

"I'll show you to your room and then you can have first dibs on the shower in mine since the hall bath is still in a state of chaos from remodeling."

Wait, I'm going to be sharing a bathroom with him? Where he showers? Naked? No. Absolutely Not. No w—

"Mhm," my voice cracks with the pitch.

Jesus take the wheel because I apparently can't be trusted.

CHAPTER 9

RYDER

I FUCKED UP.

There's a chance that I may have been hasty when I hit send on that text, fueled by the afterglow of a night where my demons didn't come out to play. All I could think, feel, and see was her and the magnitude our minimal interaction had on my unconscious mind.

I was foolish to think this fervour need to be around her wouldn't intensify with every passing moment because when she's around, the war inside my head ceases, the water in my lungs drain, and the darkness clouding my heart doesn't seem as treacherous.

She's been here for less than twenty-four hours—blew the hour time cap I usually allow anyone right out of the water—and instead of boiling over with the need to push her out of my space, I'm searching small ways to draw her farther in. *What the hell am I doing?*

It's unbelievable. Staggering. Intoxicating. Terrifying.

But I can't seem to stop searching for her when I turn the corner, or listening for her laugh as she talks on the phone, or find any reason to venture upstairs just so I can possibly bump into her in the hallway.

Ever since she finished showering, she's hidden herself away in her room, only coming out when dinner was delivered. We ate in silence and she was already halfway up the stairs—calling out 'good night'—before she could swallow her last bite.

The girl couldn't get away from me fast enough and I haven't seen her since. The only sign of life being the quiet shuffling as she moved around in her room.

It was a night of little to no sleep and the minutes I did have were filled with crushing metal and pleading green eyes.

I can't do it.

I can't take another night of this, especially so close to the season. And if Blake is the answer to my salvation from these hauntings then I need to let myself get closer to her. However daunting that thought may be.

It's why I jumped at the chance to drive her to the market when she nervously asked after taking in the state of my pantry. List in hand, she struts around, placing item after item in the shopping trolley while I follow her around like a puppy.

Every so often she shows me something and I give wordless nods or shakes of my head, not trusting that I wouldn't say something to fuck it up.

We're checking out when a couple of lads stop by and give their good wishes for the upcoming season. Blake takes their phones when I agree to pictures and pulls a black pen out of her purse when I offer them autographs.

I glance at her when she smothers a laugh as the last man asks me to sign a free spot within his sleeve tattoo, saying he's going to be setting up an appointment at a shop right after.

"You're going to pay for that later," I lean down and grumble in her ear as the small group leaves us to check out.

She sucks in a quick breath, looking up at me with wide eyes and I realize that that is the first thing I've said to her since. "I'll get the trolley."

Clearing my throat, I lean away from her, pay the cashier, and high tail it out to the Rover with her silently trailing behind me. She stays that way through the ten minute drive back home and as we unload the groceries.

I'm about to head up to my room and take this as a loss when her soft, timid voice stops me in my tracks, "Um, Ryder?"

"Yeah?" I turn and lean against the doorway.

"Could I maybe cook something for you tonight? As kind of a thank you for letting me stay with you?"

"Yeah, if you want to."

"Really?" her face brightens.

"Of course."

She socks me right in the chest when she beams at my approval, and it makes me want to give her a reason to keep looking at me like that. With a nod, I back out of the kitchen and head towards the stairs, my lips tipping up at the sounds of her moving around the kitchen.

A few hours later, I follow the sounds of sizzling and slide into a chair at the island. Blake turns around and startles when she sees me there, clutching the cutting board in her hands to her chest. "Oh," she laughs nervously, "you scared me."

I look down at the vegetables she has spread out over the counter. "Smells good." *Jesus. Let's try more than five words next time shall we?*

"Thank you," she blushes, chopping up a bell pepper.

I watch her work, racking my brain at what to say. Blake gets all the vegetables chopped and slides over to the stove, scraping them into the sizzling pan of chicken.

"So," she drawls, stepping over to the sink. "Do you really think that guy is going to get a tattoo of your signature on his arm?"

I lean my forearms on the cool marble countertop and shrug, "Probably."

"That's nuts," she shakes her head, "I couldn't imagine someone wanting to have my signature on their body permanently like that."

"Your day will come and I'll be there handing them the marker."

She giggles and the sound gives me the fuel I need to keep this going. Clearing my throat, I lean back and fold my hands behind my head, "Honestly, it wasn't the first time and it probably won't be the last."

"Seriously? That's happened before?"

I nod, "I used to keep track of the different things people would ask me to sign, but it all got to be too much and now I just roll with it."

"What's th—sorry, do you have a stand mixer?" She bends over to open another cabinet and I slip off the stool, beelining it for the walk-in pantry so my eyes don't have a shot in hell of locking on her ass.

She follows me and watches from the doorway as I reach up and pull it from the top shelf. It's an older model and I cough a little when it brings dust along with it.

"Yeah, I would never have seen that up there."

"Let me clean it for you real quick, it hasn't left that spot in god knows how long."

After a quick scrub, I place the dried standmixer off to the side for her to use. Instead of taking my seat at the island, I lean back against the counter in a corner that's out of the way.

"What were you going to ask?"

"Hm?" She looks over her shoulder as she stirs. "Oh, right. What's the weirdest thing someone has ever had you to sign?" She pops the lid on the pan and turns the heat down before twirling to face me.

An idea pops into my head, a way to make sure she has to speak to me every single day and I suppress the smile that threatens to break over my face.

"Why don't you guess?"

"What? Like a game?"

I nod, "Yeah. Why not."

Blake's smile grows. "Okay, but what do I get when I guess it correctly?"

"Whatever you want," I reply without thinking. *Did my voice drop just now?*

"Whatever I want?"

I nod.

"Okay. Let's see," she taps her chin, "I'm going to go big with my first one. A baby. That's pretty freaking weird. And honestly probably isn't healthy."

I huff a suppressed laugh and shake my head, "No. That one I refuse to do."

She hums, "Okay. What about underwear," she points at me, "but not women's?"

"That, unfortunately, I have done, but I wouldn't say it's the weirdest."

"Okay, okay, okay," she mumbles and nods.

"You get one more."

"One more what?"

"One more guess, I'm capping you at three a day."

"Three a day?" she pouts. "These terms suck and I don't remember agreeing to them."

I outright laugh at her faux pouting, but it dies off quickly when I see her features slacken. "What's wrong?" I grip the counter until the bones in my hands crack to keep from walking over to her.

"Nothing," she smiles softly. "You've got a nice laugh."

She takes the pan off the stove after checking the chicken is cooked through. "What are you making, anyway?" I ask stepping up next to her when she dumps the mixture into the stand mixer bowl.

"Enchilada pie."

"And what the hell is enchilada pie?"

"You'll see," she yells over the sounds of a whirring machine.

When it's shredded to her liking, I step in with a cloth and carry the now immensely hot bowl over to where she has a baking dish, tortillas, enchilada sauce she made earlier, and some shredded cheese out on the island.

"I guess tonight it's more of an enchilada lasagna since I couldn't find a circular dish, but it's all the same."

"I'm even more confused now because pie and lasagna are absolutely not the same."

She snickers, "You've got a point. It's something my mama made when I was a kid. Essentially, it's everything that goes in enchiladas, but it's layered like a lasagna."

Spooning some sauce on the bottom of the pan, Blake instructs me to lay out the precut tortillas so every inch of the bottom is covered. She follows it up with more sauce, a layer of the chicken and vegetable filling, cheese, and then another layer of tortillas.

We repeat the process until we run out of filling and when it's ready to go Blake glides her hands over the dish. "Ta-da! Enchilada pie."

I open the oven for her to slide the dish in. We clean up the kitchen and she sets a timer for when the food needs to come out of the oven. Settling down on the couch, she sits on one side with her feet tucked under her while I lean back into the corner of the other.

"Do you like cooking?" I find myself asking.

"Yeah. I guess," she shrugs. "Mama made it a point to teach me so that when I got old enough, she would have peace of mind knowing I could feed myself if she wasn't there."

"What do you mean?"

She readjusts, bringing her legs up to rest her chin on her bent knees. "Mama's a nurse, so her schedule didn't tend to be family friendly. She wanted me to at least know the basics so I wouldn't fall back on eating cereal for every meal."

I nod in understanding. "It's a good skill to have."

"Do you cook at all?"

I scoff. "You saw the state of my pantry and fridge, you tell me."

"Good point," she smiles.

"Mum was the cook, not me."

Where the hell did that come from?

"When I moved into the city, she used to make all these different meals and bring them to me, knowing I didn't have the time or patience to learn."

Okay, I guess I'm doing this.

Bracing for the look of pity, I glance at Blake but see genuine care shining in her eyes instead. "She sounds like an amazing person."

I nod, clenching my jaw. "She was."

The timer goes off and she smiles reassuringly before standing. She goes to step away but stops abruptly, a moment later she's twisting around the back of the couch and wrapping her arms around my shoulders.

"Thank you for sharing that with me."

My body locks up at her comforting embrace and my breath stalls in my chest when she gives me one last squeeze before straightening and dashing into the kitchen. I listen to the sounds of her moving around in the kitchen as I try to regain my mental footing.

Since Mum's passing, I haven't talked about her with anyone. Hell, I rarely let myself think about her when I'm not at the whims of my nightmares.

But talking about her with Blake, while still holding a bit of pain, was a lot easier than I ever thought it would be. I think it's me who should be thanking her.

I walk into the kitchen and lean against the doorway, watching her plate us each up a serving before opening a few drawers until she locates the forks.

"Need any help?" She jumps at the sound of my voice.

"Um, can you get drinks? I'll have some water, please."

I meet her at the counter with our glasses. "Sitting room okay?"

"Mhm," she smiles up at me.

I settle into the couch and am lifting the first forkful to my mouth when a feminine moan has me fumbling not to wear the food on my plate. I slowly turn to see her head tipped back and watch the column of her neck as she swallows.

She peeks open an eye and her face flushes. "Oh my god, I'm so sorry," she laughs nervously and uses her fork to point at her plate. "This is probably some of my best work."

Raising an eyebrow, I scoop up a mountain of a bite and shovel it into my mouth as Blake watches. "Oh, holy hell," I mumble as the flavors explode on my tastebuds.

Swallowing, I shake my head in amazement at the

surprising girl on the other side of the couch. "Blake, this has to be the best thing I've eaten in I don't even know how long."

"Really?"

"Really." *Lord help me.*

She beams, dancing in her seat. "Score."

Ten minutes later, Blake slides her empty plate onto the coffee table with a sigh. "Clean plate club," she pumps her fist in the air and I shake my head as I reach for the remote.

We spend the next few hours not even watching the screen. She uses her last guess on a tube of toothpaste and even though I've signed some after doing a commercial once, it isn't the weirdest.

She relaxes with every passing moment, and as we talk I get glances of the bubbly girl I imagine her to be when I hear her talking on the phone.

At around eight she's snuggled under a blanket at an angle so she can face me with her head tilted back on the couch, but not long after, her eyes close and soft snores filter through her parted lips.

Not wanting to disturb her, I grab our dishes and head into the kitchen. With the leftovers put away and the counters all cleaned up, I walk back into the sitting room and pause.

Even sleeping, she's a vision. Her hair has a slight wave to it and the chocolate strands drape over the couch. She clutches the blanket to her shallow rising chest and her cheeks are flush with the warmth.

Feeling like enough of a creeper while watching her

sleep, I step into the room and lightly shake her shoulder. "Blake."

"Hm?"

"Let's get to bed, yeah?" *Separate. Separate beds.*

She blinks open her eyes and drags herself towards the stairs.

"Thank you again for dinner."

"I'm glad you liked it," she yawns.

"I haven't had a home cooked meal in what feels like forever. Hell, I don't think I've eaten with a friend in longer than that." *Did I just call her my friend?*

She stops abruptly on the way up the stairs and turns back to me.

"Did you just call me your friend?" *Can she read minds?*

"Well, no—"

"No?" Hurt flashes in her eyes and I scramble to wipe that look from existence.

"I mean, unless you want to be?"

"Really?"

I nod and her smile grows. "Okay. I'll be your friend. I'll be the best friend slash teammate you've ever had." She spins and hops up the stairs.

I shake my head with a smirk and follow her up to the small landing, "Blake Stone, you're really something you know that?"

She smiles, "So are you, Ryder King."

CHAPTER 10

BLAKE

"A can of soup."

"I've signed a can of beans but—"

"What kind?"

"Is knowing what kind really pertinent?"

"Absolutely," I mumble.

Leather squeaks on my right and my hair sways when Ryder huffs a laugh, "Are you keeping a list?"

I hold my phone to my chest and lean against the door. "Maybe." I click the screen off and straighten when he shifts back out of my space.

"I don't want to waste a guess on something I've already said before. Also, if I have an idea and you're not around, I don't want to forget it."

"Okay," he chuckles.

"This is serious business, King."

"Whatever you say, Stone."

I smile down at my phone and move 'can of soup' to the 'has signed' column.

"What else is on the list?"

I peer over at him, "I'm not telling you."

He chuckles under his breath, shaking his head. His eyes go back to the road, but the smirk doesn't drop. I smile to myself and look out my window.

The first time his lips tipped up, I did a double take. From the moment we met, I could sense the dark cloud of anguish enveloping him. I've seen variants of that kind of darkness in people, but I've never met someone who has experienced as much loss as he has.

He was happy and carefree once, the pictures I saw lining the walls of his childhood home proved that much. But somewhere along the way that all changed.

The blissful smile that brought out the dimple he inherited from his father has disappeared under a mask of indifference. The peace in his emerald eyes has been taken prisoner by the ghosts haunting his mind. The once full of life man has sealed himself behind impenetrable armor of numbness, where he's just surviving.

I couldn't stand back and watch this man, who has done more for me than he will ever possibly know, slowly fade away from existence. I don't think I'd survive that kind of loss, especially now.

It was weird at first, I was my usual awkward self but on steroids because the small crush I'd spent all week denying? Well, it was apparently not all that small. It didn't help that as he opened up with every passing minute, I found less and less reason to ignore those feelings.

But after a stern talking to in the mirror, I boarded up the innocent butterflies taking over my stomach whenever he was in the room and shoved them deep—deep—down.

Then the man had to go and say I'm his friend. And I had to go and say I'd be the best friend he's ever had. What the hell was I thinking?

I twist back to look at Ryder as he pulls up to our teams' training facility. His eyes harden and I watch as his mask slips into place. My smile dims as I take in the sharp and modern building looming through the windshield. What if I'm not good enough?

"You wouldn't be here if they didn't think you were."

My eyes shoot to Ryder and my eyebrows furrow, "What?"

"Why do you think you aren't good enough?"

"I didn't realize I said that out loud," I mutter, fidgeting with the hem of my sweater.

"Do you think you can't do this? Because it might be a little late for you to come to that conclusion now," his voice stiffens, agitation flaring behind his eyes.

"I know I can do this, that's not what scares me—"

"You shouldn't be scared. Period." His jaw clenches and he shifts in his seat until he faces me fully. "You can't do what we do with fear of what can happen. That kind of thinking can and will get you killed."

"I know that," I cut him off as frustration mounts.

"Do you? Because—"

"Ryder, I know! I know that this can be a brutal sport and I'm not scared of driving or of what can happen when I'm out on the track."

"Then what—"

"I'm afraid of letting everyone down," I yell over him.

He sits with his back against the door and his eyes soften.

Lowering my voice, I meet his eyes, "I know how risky of a move signing me is. Ignoring the fact that I'm lacking certain parts of most racers, I haven't been through any formal training. I didn't attend the academy or start with karting when I was five. I have no experience outside of my small little circuits back home."

I shake my head and drop my eyes to my hands. "I can guess that the expectations for my performance are low, but that doesn't mean I'm not going to give this everything I have because this is my dream. What scares me is that what if everything I have, still isn't good enough. Then I won't have only failed at the one thing I've spent years working towards, but I would fail everyone who got me here. Nikolai, Callum, Mama, Cassie, Denver."

I raise my eyes to his, "You." I swallow. "I can't not be good enough. I can't fail."

His jaw ticks, understanding flashing in his eyes as they flicker between mine. He leans forward and takes both of my hands in one of his. I suck in a quiet breath at the warmth spreading up my arms from the connection.

"I'll be right there if you need me. We're a team, remember?" His eyes dance between mine, "We do this together."

"We do this together," I whisper back.

He nods and with a squeeze of my hands, climbs out of the car. I glance out at the building and take one last deep breath before hopping out and meeting him on the sidewalk.

When we enter, a group of people quietly talking with one another crowd the large open area. My introverted instincts kick in and I step closer to Ryder. He stands tall behind me, close enough that with every breath I feel the brush of his chest against my hoodie. His scent wraps around me and I take a deep breath, letting the smell of warm leather calm my nerves.

Nikolai looks up from his phone at the side of the group and pushes off the wall. His slight Russian accent echoes throughout the space, "Good, you made it."

"Worried I would have changed my mind?" I joke with a nervous laugh.

"Not at all. Get settled in okay?"

"Yep."

Nikolai nods to the group, "Let's get you introduced to some of the staff that will be helping out over the next two weeks with training."

We walk over to the group of seven people and go around so that they can each introduce themselves with what part of training they'll be in charge of. When we get to a shorter woman with piercing blue eyes and graying hair, she steps forward and pulls me in for a crushing hug.

I squeak in surprise, awestruck with the amount of strength she camouflages under a seemingly frail frame. A moment later, the woman pulls back and beams, "Hi honey, I'm Maeve. The team's primary physio."

"Nice to meet you. I'm really looking forward to all of this."

"I bet," she smiles genuinely as her eyes jump to the quiet man behind me. "Ryder King," she sighs and walks around me, stopping right in front of him. "Welcome back, my boy."

I watch their interaction and the comfortable, almost familial way she speaks with him. His mask slips as he stares down at her, but only for a millisecond before he secures it back in place. With a tight nod he looks away. "Good to be back."

Maeve, unaffected by his coldness, turns and claps her hands. "Okay, now that sharing time is over, let's give you a quick tour of the facilities and then we can get to it. Sound good?"

"Sounds great," I smile.

For the next hour I actively work to keep my jaw off the ground as we walk around the state of the art facilities. It's all so new and shiny. I'm afraid to touch anything in fear of leaving fingerprints on any of the many stainless steel surfaces.

After the tour, we have a moment to change into our training clothes before meeting Maeve and Nikolai outside the testing facility.

Not wanting to be late, I rush through the doors while zipping up my athletic long sleeve. Apparently I haven't learned my lesson about multitasking on the move because the next thing I know, I land flat on my ass after bouncing off a hard body.

"Ow," I wince.

"Shit, are you okay?" Ryder squats down, hands reaching out to help.

"Yeah, just call me a quarter because I bounced right off you," I laugh, embarrassed. Is it too much to ask that I go one day without falling on my ass around him?

He chuckles under his breath. "You sure you didn't hit your head on the way down? You're not making too much sense there."

"What? You've never heard the saying 'that's so tight I could bounce a quarter off it'?"

"So you think I'm tight?" He smirks, taking my hand in his and pulling me up.

I flush and tuck an errant lock of hair behind my ear, "No. Yes. Um, we should get going. Don't want to be late!" I call over my shoulder as I start speed walking towards the stairs.

He jogs up to my side, "So eager to get to the torture."

"Oh come on. It can't be that bad," I roll my eyes.

He barks out a dark chuckle, "You don't know Maeve."

I look over my shoulder at him as we step onto the landing. "She seems nice, what are you talking about?"

"She may seem sweet with her hugs and gentle demeanor, but when you're in her gym—" he smirks, "you know what? You'll see." He pats my arm and jogs off.

"What do you mean?" I ask with wide eyes. "Ryder!

What's going to happen?" I call after him as he swaggers through the double doors into the gym.

I look around nervously before settling back on the doors. Shaking my arms out by my sides, I mutter to myself, "It can't be that bad right?"

The doors open and Maeve peeks her head around the frosted glass. "Oh! There you are sweetheart. You coming?"

"Yep," I chirp, hoping she doesn't pick up on the slight waver in my voice.

Maeve smiles and nods before slipping back into the room. Ryder must be yanking my chain, because that lady does not come off as having a tormentor bone in her body. Plus, she told us that today would be about figuring out where we are now so that we can build out the plan of attack for the next two weeks.

We'll be finding our strengths. Easy.

Blowing out a breath, I straighten my shoulders. "It's like syllabus day back in school. Easy peasy." With newfound confidence, I walk into the gym with my head held high and ready to take on whatever Maeve has to throw at me.

Four hours later I'm lying in a pool of my own sweat, desperately trying to use the cool tiles to chill my overheating body when Maeve turns off the music and calls out, "That was good! We'll call it there. The team should have your ice baths ready for you downstairs."

She gathers up her bag and hops over me, walking towards the gyms doors. "It's a good start. I'll have a schedule up on the boards for you to review when you get here tomorrow. Goodnight and welcome to the team, Blake!"

I wheeze out a thanks and close my eyes, trying to get my racing heart to chill the fuck out. I'm tracing the stars dancing behind my lids when I feel a drip on my head seconds before a cloth smothers me.

I pull the rag off my face and open my eyes to see Ryder standing above me, shirtless and glistening in sweat. The rings on his chest reflect the light and I blink when another drop hits me in the forehead. "Ew," I screw up my face and wipe away where his sweat landed on me. I glare up at him. "Shut. Up."

"Don't say I didn't warn you," he chuckles.

"I'm good," I huff, still trying to catch my breath after that ten mile weighted bike ride. "Peachy even. I could have kept going, but I didn't want to embarrass your old ass," I smile and laugh, but wince at the first contraction of my abs.

"For your information, I'm twenty-eight. I'd hardly say that's old, but tell me, which of us is still standing and which is struggling for breath on the floor?" He tilts his head and raises an eyebrow.

I sigh and throw my arms to the side. "I can't move," I whine.

Ryder bends down, pulling my aching arms until I'm standing on legs made of jell-o. "Come on, you just have the ice bath left, then you can shower and we can finally go home."

"Okay," I groan, "Let's do this."

He smirks, throwing his towel in my face, "Come on, Stone! First one there gets to choose what we watch tonight."

He's already jogging towards the doors and I call out to

him, "You cheated!" His booming laugh fills the quiet room and I smile, taking off after him.

Blake's Guesses Today

~~Can of soup~~

~~Towel after they've used it~~

~~A sculpture they've made of him~~

CHAPTER 11

RYDER

I GROAN as her fingers massage from my temples to the base of my skull.

"People are going to get the wrong idea if you keep making sounds like that."

I crack open an eye and attempt to scowl up at Maeve. "Don't be ridiculous."

She huffs a laugh and shakes her head. "Okay, champ. Sit up."

I pull myself into a sitting position on top of the table as she walks around, picking up her tablet. "How are you feeling?"

"Good." *Fuck, too quick.*

Maeve drops her tablet to the counter and crosses her arms, her blue eyes seeing through my bullshit. "When?"

My knuckles turn white with my unforgiving grip on the table. "This morning."

"Ryder," she sighs. "Why didn't you tell me? We would

have gone easier today—"

"I don't have time to take it easy, Maeve. The season starts in less than two weeks," I snap as rage and fear wrap their fingers around my throat.

"Which is exactly why you need to slow down," she yells back and huffs an irritated breath. "You're going to seriously hurt yourself otherwise. And this time, there's no telling if you'll be able to come back from it."

Her voice hitches towards the end and I drop my eyes before I can see the pity in hers. "You need to listen to what the doctors told you, Ryder. You have to pull back when you feel even the smallest inclination that another flare up is coming."

"I know."

"Do you? Because you pushed yourself harder today than I have seen you do all week. That," she points in the direction of the door, "wasn't you easing up."

I lift my eyes, "I know what's at risk."

"Then why—"

"Because I can't lose this, Maeve," I break. "I've already lost everything else."

She stares back at me, jaw working. Sniffing, she steps closer and speaks in a low voice, "You have endured immense loss in the past two years and I am so sorry for that."

She bends until she catches my eyes. "But that loss was the only one out of your control. Everything else, you were the one to push away."

My jaw ticks at her words but I don't back down from her sharp stare. "I'm fine."

Maeve huffs and shakes her head, tossing her arms out and clapping them on her thighs. "Fine," she breathes. "But if you won't listen to me, then I'll find someone who won't be so easy to turn away."

She dismisses me with a toss of her hand before showing me her back and clicking around on the computer. I stand and stride for the door with the words I couldn't seem to say. *Yeah, Good luck with that.*

———

The minutes between spikes of pain have dwindled to seconds by the time we get home and I escape to my darkened room with the excuse of exhaustion. I don't know how much time has passed when a soft knock rattles through my brain.

"Ryder?" Blakes soft voice glides through the thick wooden door.

"Fuck," I whisper through clenched teeth, too low for her to hear but it sends a pulsing wave of wreckage through my head. *I can't do this right now.*

"Are you okay?" Her voice strains with concern. "I, um, Maeve called me to check in on you? She said you weren't answering any of her calls or texts." *Fucking Maeve.*

Taking several breaths, I clench my jaw and throw my blankets off. Blindly staggering towards the direction of the door, I stumble over my discarded shoes and reach out to catch myself on the bureau. I grunt as the room spins and my stomach threatens to revolt.

"Ryder?" Her voice rises in panic. "I heard a thud, are you okay?"

I want to answer her, but it's taking everything in me to keep upright right now. A wave of blinding pressure rolls over me and I break out in a sweat.

I hear a muttered curse before she speaks through the door, "I'm coming in."

The door clicks open and she sucks in a breath. "Ryder," she whispers and a moment later I feel a small cold hand on my tense back.

"How can I help?" She keeps her voice low and when I twist to look at her my body sways and her eyes widen as she jumps forward, bracing her hands on my sides.

"Bathroom," I grit out.

I feel her head nod against my side as she drapes my arm over her shoulders. She matches my slow pace, guiding me into the ensuite bathroom. The moment I see the toilet, I throw myself onto the unforgiving tiles and heave whatever's left in my stomach.

The faucet turns on and the sound of splashing water mingles with my heavy breaths. Soft footfalls come closer and she kneels next to me.

I lay my head against my arm on the edge of the toilet and blow out a shaky breath. Her fingers delicately brush my hair back before she dabs a cool cloth across my damp forehead.

"You're okay," she whispers over and over. Her hand lightly rubs over my exposed back as she sits with me on the cool tiles.

After another fifteen minutes, and when I'm sure there's

nothing else left for me to purge, she drags me off the floor and back into the bedroom.

Blake spins me slowly until I'm facing her, and with her hands on my sides, she backs me up one step at a time until my legs hit the bed. With my arms over her shoulders, she slowly lowers me until I'm sitting on the bed.

"Do you have anything you can take?" She keeps her voice low and comforting as her hands continue to brush my sweat slicked hair. *God that feels nice.*

I should tell her to leave. I never let anyone see me this way. I don't like to be seen as weak, helpless, useless. *She can't see me like this.*

"You," grunt, "don't—"

"Stop." She places her soft hand on my shoulder. "I'm not leaving you when you're obviously in tremendous pain. So tell me where the meds are or I'll go searching on my own."

If I wasn't in agony right now, I probably would have smiled at the sternness in her voice. Instead I nod weakly, pain striking through my skull at the movement.

"Bedside table," I breathe, not having the energy to fight her.

One hand leaves me to reach for the pill bottle while the other holds me sitting upright. She faces back a second later with two pills and a small glass of water. I take the offered meds and water, only drinking enough to get them down.

"Okay. Let's lay you down, but first," she takes the glass from my shaky hand and slides my chain from around my neck before laying it on the nightstand, "Don't want that to choke you while you sleep."

She pulls back the covers and I hold onto her as she lowers me to the bed. Setting the heavy duvet up my chest, she runs a hand over my head. "I'm going to be right back, okay?"

She doesn't wait for my reply before dashing out of the room. I lay in the darkness, listening to the sounds of her moving throughout the house. My eyes grow heavy and I lose the battle of keeping them open.

When I open my eyes next, I don't know how long I've been asleep, but I watch as Blake quietly moves around my room. Her hair is in a messy bun on top of her head and a vintage band tee swallows her whole, the biker shorts she has on barely peeking out underneath the hem.

She goes around tossing my discarded clothes into a basket at her side. I watch as she bends and gets on her knees, crawling alongside the edge of my bed. She reaches down and grumbles something too low for me to make out before sighing in victory.

"Gotcha," she whispers, falling back on her heels with one of my socks in her hands. She holds it up high and her nose scrunches. "At least it's not all crunchy," she shivers and tosses it into the basket.

"What are you doing?" My throat feels like someone took sandpaper to it, my voice coming out rough. Blake twists around and falls on her ass with a suppressed scream.

"Oh my god, I thought you were asleep," she whispers with a hand pressed to her chest.

I close my eyes tight as the pressure mounts behind them. There's a shuffle and a dull thump before something cold presses against my forehead. I crack open an eye and see her concerned blues trailing over my face.

"Maeve told me that cold compresses could help," her voice is low and smooth.

"It does," I breathe as she shifts the pack to the side of my face.

"Do you think you can eat something? I made a protein smoothie so that it wouldn't be too hard on your stomach."

"Yeah."

"Okay."

Pulling away, she turns and I watch her reach into a small cool box. She retrieves a shaker bottle and opens the top before sliding in a bendy straw. With a giddy smile on her face, she shimmies over to the side of the bed and lifts the straw to my mouth.

I open immediately, holding back a moan when the flavors burst on my tongue. How the hell did she make a protein smoothie taste like a damn dessert?

I get through half of the bottle before calling it quits and she stores it back in her little mobile fridge. She turns back to me with another round of meds and water, leading me to believe I was out for a few hours.

My brows furrow at the realization, "What time is it?"

Blake pulls her knees up to her chest and tucks a wayward curl behind her ear. "Around midnight I think."

"You should sleep."

"I'm okay."

"You don't need—"

"Yes, I do."

"Blake."

"We're a team, remember? We do this together," she smiles.

When I said those words to her last week, I didn't think about how much I truly meant them at the time. The last five days have flown by with her by my side and through it all, with every passing minute, she's inserting herself farther under my skin.

And with the more I learn about her, the less I find myself wanting to keep her at a distance.

I know that her favorite color is green. She always craves any form of carbs but pasta is her go to. If there's ever a chance to dress up, she'll jump at it despite her love for ripped jeans and vintage band T-shirts.

She always ends the night reading whatever book Cassie sends her that week, but hides it away whenever I try to get a peak. The other night she came down the stairs wearing this green cream or something mask, pointing a finger and warning me not to say a single thing.

It was my turn to choose the movie that night and I had the title slide of Jim Carrey's *The Mask* pulled up, ready to go when she brought our nightly hot chocolates into the sitting room. She took one look at the screen and laughed so hard that tears streaked through her mask.

Without warning, this sweet blue eyed woman kneeling next to my bed, on the floor of my freshly cleaned room, hand feeding me, and enduring a sleepless night to help me is quickly becoming a part of my life that I don't want to push away. Possibly ever.

"We do this together," I whisper.

Blake leans forward and holds the cold pack to my head again, trailing it over my temple. Her other hand reaches up, brushing my damp hair back out of my face.

I hum and lean into her touch. "That feels good."

Her lips twitch and she tilts her head. "Mama would play with my hair when I would get these tension headaches after a full day of training. It was like magic, no headache stood a chance." She smiles, trailing a finger over my hairline with a question in gaze.

"What?"

Her eyes flicker between mine. "I could maybe do that for you? I know it may not help but," she shakes her head, "never mind."

I reach out and take her hand in mine when she pulls back, "Blake."

Her eyes meet mine and I ignore the shooting pain in the back of my skull when I nod. She huffs out a relieved breath and smiles.

With a lot of effort on her end, we shift around on the bed so that she's sitting up against the headboard—thankfully staying above the covers—while she lays my head on her lap.

She runs her fingers through my hair, nails lightly scraping against my scalp and I heave a sigh into the pillow. I close my eyes and get lost in the feeling of her.

It's only seconds later that I fall under another round of sleep to the feel of her tracing the scar intersecting my left eyebrow and her soft whispers of magic.

CHAPTER 12

RYDER

THE MORNING SUN doesn't burn quite as bad when I blink open my eyes. I roll my head and sigh when the throbbing doesn't manifest. Usually these migraines last through the next day, but not this one. And I think I have a certain brunette to thank for it.

She spent all night keeping me pumped full of pain meds, electrolytes, and protein shakes. I woke up twice more after I fell asleep to the *magic* of her fingers.

Once to use the bathroom, where she teased me about needing a shower after sweating all night. She was just outside the door the entire time in case I needed her and I stood there trying not to think about her proximity to my naked body.

The second time didn't last more than a few minutes, but I spent them watching her as she slept next to me. Her lips were slightly parted on soft snores and her hair was a wild mess, falling out of her bun around us.

I look around for the woman herself, but find the room empty. Rolling out of bed, I go into the bathroom and decide to take another shower before getting ready for the day. Slipping on some sweat pants and a jumper, I open my bedroom door to the sound of faint music.

Following the beat down stairs, my nose twitches at the smell of sizzling bacon and a smirk pulls at the edges of my lips as I lean against the door of the kitchen. Blake stands with her back to me, hips and head swaying to the music.

She turns around using a piece of bacon as a microphone before taking a bite and the corner of my lips tip up at the vision she is, even first thing in the morning. *God, she's beautiful.*

Her eyes raise and she jumps, dropping her sudo-mic on the floor. Laughing, she shakes her head and points between me and the floor bacon, "I'm taking one of your pieces for that."

"That's fair."

"How are you?"

"Better. Thank you," I clear my throat, "for everything last night."

"I'm just happy you're feeling better."

"I am."

"Good." She smiles before blowing out a breath. "I hope you're hungry, because I made enough to feed an army."

We sit at the island and work our way through the mountain of pancakes, an entire pig's worth of bacon, and a seemingly never ending bowl of scrambled eggs. I'm lifting the last piece of toast to my mouth when I catch her watching me.

I raise an eyebrow at her, "What?"

"I'm just impressed with how much you can eat," she laughs.

"I'm a growing boy and a professional athlete."

"And you haven't eaten anything solid since yesterday."

"There's that too." I polish off the last of the toast and stand, taking our empty plates to the sink. Rolling my shoulders, I tilt my head side to side and massage my stiff neck.

"Hey," Blake puts down the pans on the counter and places a hand on my arm, eyes watching me with concern, "Are you okay?"

I take the pan and plates, turn on the faucet and grab the sponge, "I'm fine, it's just residual tension. It'll pass."

She twists her lips to the side and watches my face before gasping, "I'll be right back."

"Okay." I watch her bound out of the room.

I listen to her barrel up the stairs and her groans every step of the way, no doubt feeling the effects of our leg workouts from yesterday. She shuffles around for a few moments before I hear the creaks of her steps on the stairs, and one loud thud when she reaches the bottom.

"Stupid rug," she growls before yelling out, "I'm okay!"

I'm shaking my head as she blows into the kitchen with a smile on her face.

"Uh, what's that?"

"This," she holds up the tiny glass container, "is Tiger Balm."

"Tiger what?" I place the last dish on the rack and turn to her, leaning against the counter.

"How do you not know what this is? You're a 'professional athlete', remember?" she teases. "I use it for neck and shoulder aches, it's amazing."

Coming up to my side, she uncaps the tiny jar and lifts it, "Plus, it smells all cozy."

I cautiously lean in and inhale, my nose tingles at the strong earthy menthol scent.

"Well?" Her eyes flicker between mine, awaiting my answer, but the words escape me as I take in her flushed cheeks and light dusting of freckles. I no longer smell the spicy aroma of the balm, but soft honey vanilla. My senses fill with her and I fight to keep my eyes from dropping to her lips.

"Good," I grit out and clear my throat. "It smells good."

She smiles and pops the lid back on the jar. We work in tandem, putting away any leftovers, wiping down the counters, and stowing dishes after she towel dries them. After everything is spotless and put away, she guides me to sit on the couch before coming up behind me.

I hear the clink of the jar lid a moment before feeling her fingers on me. Her hand slides around as her thumb strokes from my hairline to the base of my neck. I let out a groan and she huffs a laugh through her nose. *Holy Mother that feels fantastic.*

"How long have you had these migraines?"

"Since the accident a season and a half ago." I roll my head to the side.

She hums. "I don't understand how he still gets to drive."

"I'm gathering you know what happened."

"Only what they showed on TV, but they cut out before you—"

"Hit the ground," I finish for her and shrug. "It is what it is. I technically made the first move, so they deemed it as self defense in his case."

"It's bullshit is what it is," her voice hardens.

"Getting defensive are we?"

"No. Yes. Shut up." She pushes my head playfully to the other side before continuing.

"Like I said, it is what it is. The migraines were worse—"

"Worse?" Her fingers stop and I look up to see her eyes shining with concern.

"They're better now. I get them maybe once or twice a month, but before I'd have them constantly, almost every other day. It's why I wasn't allowed to come back for the season."

"I'm so sorry you had to go through that, Ryder."

"It's okay."

"It's not."

I lean back fully and stare up into her bright eyes. A lock of her hair falls out of the messy bun it was thrown up into this morning and without thinking, my hand raises. I twirl the piece around my finger and whisper, "No, it's really not. But I'm still here and I'm getting stronger."

"You're still here," she smiles.

Her eyes briefly drop to my lips and I take the opportunity to do the same. "What are your plans for today?" I ask, eyes locked on her tongue as it peeks out to wet her bottom lip.

"I don't know. I was keeping it pretty open in case you needed me."

I'm beginning to think I'll always need you and that scares the shit out of me.

"Let's go for a spin then, yeah?"

"Where?"

Anywhere you want. Anywhere there are crowds because if I stay in this house alone with you for another moment longer, I might fall to my knees and make an utter arsehole out of myself.

"Did you get to see any of the city the last time you were here?"

She shakes her head.

"Then I'll take you there. We can go see the sights."

"Can we get some fish and chips?" she asks in a horrible British accent and I chuckle.

"Yeah, we can get you your fish and chips."

"Okay," she whispers.

Twenty minutes later, I'm standing at the bottom of the stairs, lacing up my trainers when I hear the distinct sounds of her coming down the stairs.

I glance up and clench my jaw before it can drop to the ground, thanking the universe that I'm already sitting because otherwise I would have been knocked clear on my arse.

Black distressed jeans hug Blake's toned legs and sit high on her slender waist. She sports a black long sleeve with a cropped vintage Type O-Negative T-shirt tucked into the front of her pants. Her hair lays around her in waves, tamed by a black beanie hat.

"Is this okay?"

"You're perfect." My eyes widen and I rush out, "It's perfect."

We grab our coats and I double check that everything is off except the few lights we leave on, not knowing how long we'll be out.

The drive to the city is about an hour and she starts to fidget with excitement as we get closer. She watches everything pass by with wide eyes and I fight to keep my own on the bloody road and off of her.

"Oh my god, it's Big Ben," she squeals, looking over her shoulder with a beaming smile.

"What would you like to see first?" I ask as I pull into the first available spot I see.

Blake hums and taps her chin. "Everything?"

A laugh bursts out of me and I shake my head.

"I don't know, I can't choose," she laughs. "You choose for me."

"Blake—"

"Please! I know whatever you show me will be amazing and whatever we don't get to see today, we'll just have to come back."

I sigh and she leans against the center console. "Please." She sticks her bottom lip out in a pout and I break.

"Fine," I grumble but I can't help the tick in my lips at her victory dance.

I take her through The Mall and St. James Park, leading up to Buckingham Palace. She takes pictures all along the way and timing must be on our side since she's able to snag a video of the changing of the guard.

I dare her to try and get the men to break their stoic state and she walks off with all the confidence in the world. Approaching them I see her shoulders tighten before she quickly apologizes and scurries back over to my side. I throw my head back and laugh as she drags me away with a tight grip on my hand.

We stroll through Covent Garden Market where she gets her fish and chips. I inhale my food, as usual, and attempt to steal a chip, but she nips at my fingers with a growl. When I fake a pout, she rolls her eyes before her entire face lights up.

Five minutes later, I'm wiping my face off as she giggles at the video she took of her failing to toss a sauce covered chip into my mouth.

After we leave the market, we board a double decker bus to the other side of the city where I take her to Westminster Bridge and to get a closer look at Big Ben.

"Come here." She pulls my arm and I bend down next to her so we have the massive clock tower in frame as she snaps a couple more selfies of us there and at the bridge before I pull her towards our last stop.

The London Eye.

We enter our pod, other families and tourists milling about the area and she pulls me over to an open spot by the waterside window. I stand behind her, shielding her from the crowd behind us and we watch in silence as the pod rises to the top.

"It's so beautiful," she whispers, placing a hand on the glass.

I slip out my phone and take a couple pictures of the moment.

"Yeah," I agree. *You are.*

She turns to look at me over her shoulder and I don't move to put away my phone. I capture one last picture of her smiling before slipping it away and stepping closer.

Blake turns and taps a woman standing next to us. A second later, she's handing over her phone and stepping to my side. "Come on. One last picture."

I wrap my arm around her shoulders without complaint. She looks up at me and laughs. "Smile, Ry." *Please, Ry.* Mum's voice filters through the fog and I look down at Blake.

"You two make a darling couple," the woman holding her phone comments.

I don't correct her.

I don't look away from Blake.

She doesn't look away from me.

A phone clicks and when the woman hands over Blake's phone, she pulls away and thanks her with a smile. We go back to looking out the window as the wheel spins around. It isn't until the ride back to the house that I realize she didn't correct the woman either.

Blake's Guesses Today

~~Receipt from sex shop~~

~~Postcard from London~~

~~Leftovers container~~

INSTAGRAM POST

Carousel of images:

1. Ryder's head tipped back as he's pulled away by a small unidentifiable woman.

2. Ryder holds the door to Covent Garden Market open as a woman walks under his arm into the building.

3. Ryder and a woman exiting The London Eye, heads drawn down.

Caption: Formula One's Prince seen for the first time in a year catching the London sights with a woman. We've got questions Mr. King.
Where have you been? What happened between you and your teammate last season? Are you ready for this year? And I think the one now on all our minds, who's the girl?

Comments:

@betweenthestreets: I think I just heard the cry of women around the world.

@doaburnout: Maybe now his driving won't be so shite.

@ryderkingfanpage: Noooooo!

@thejacecollins: You have some explaining to do, mate.

@fortheloveofracing: Can't wait for the upcoming season!

CHAPTER 13

BLAKE

You know how sometimes when you're driving somewhere, but when you pull up, you don't remember how you got there at all?

Well, that's how this last week has gone for me, because it feels like one moment I was walking into the second half of training, then I blinked and now I'm sitting in the passenger seat as Ryder drives us home from our last session.

We shuffle into the house in silence, both exhausted from the last push Maeve gave us before sending us on our stumbling way.

Okay, I stumbled on legs that looked like they belonged to a newborn deer.

Ryder on the other hand strode out of the training facility like the goddamn terminator. I mean, he has to be a machine to not feel the aftereffects of today's workout, right?

"You can have the first shower," he nods towards the stairs, but I don't move.

"What's wrong?" He comes to stand at my side while I stare at the steps.

"I don't think I can do it."

"Do what?"

I whine and flail my hand forward. He follows my motion and chuckles.

"Come on, pipsqueak, hop on," he bends down in front of me.

"You are not carrying me," I laugh.

"Why not?" He stands and faces me.

"Because... because, what if you drop me?"

"I won't drop you."

"Ryder."

"Blake."

"Don't be ridiculous."

"We'd be up there by now if you would have just climbed on."

I huff and cross my arms, glaring up at him. "I can do it myself, I was just being dramatic."

"You? No way." I roll my eyes as he moves to the side and throws his arm out towards the stairs. "By all means, after you."

I step up to the bottom of the stairs and a squeak leaves me when I try to lift my leg before I drop it like the dead weight it is. I groan and look over my shoulder at my smug teammate.

With a smirk on his stupid handsome face, he pushes off the wall and bends in front of me. I stare at his strong back for a moment, hesitating.

Our touches thus far have been innocent. Yes, I'm counting the ones where I spent all night brushing my fingers through his silky hair last week and he wasn't even awake for those. *Wow, that sounded a lot more creepy than it actually was.*

I'd be a fool to completely ignore the way electricity shot through my veins at every touch, though. It's dangerous, this pull I have towards him. There's a lot on the line, for both of us.

He's been through more than I could ever begin to imagine and has worked his ass off to get back here. Racing is all he has and it's all he wants, I've heard him say so himself while I waited outside the physicians room last week.

I won't be another pot hole in his road to redemption. I want to help him get to where he deserves, not slow him down. So I'll continue to bottle up these growing feelings and stow them in concrete boxes before tossing them into the deepest depths of my mind.

I steel myself and take one last breath before stepping forward and wrapping my arms around his shoulders. He reaches back and grips me behind my thighs, holding tight as he goes to stand.

I squeal when he jumps to get a better hold and clutch tight around his neck. He laughs, wrapping my legs around his waist and I giggle as he starts to trot up the stairs.

"Giddy up!" I laugh.

Ryder's back vibrates and I bite my lip to hold in a groan at the feel of it against my chest. We reach the landing and he slowly slides me down his back.

My breath stutters with every brush of him and completely stalls in my chest when he turns around, eyes dark and lips parted. His heated eyes trace over my flush face.

Swallowing, I meet his emerald eyes. "Thank you for the ride," I joke.

"Anytime," his voice is low, gravely.

"I'm just going to—" I throw a thumb over my shoulder.

"Yeah. Yeah," he nods.

I turn and walk into my room, gathering up a change of clothes and lock myself in his bathroom. The entire time I shower, I can't stop thinking about the look in his eyes.

I must have been seeing things. I had to have imagined it. There's no way he looks at me the same way I try not to look at him.

After getting out of the shower, I glance at the time and text Cassie. Hopefully with her unlimited romance novel brain, she'll have the answers I need.

BLAKE:

Ryder just carried me up the stairs and when he put me down, I swear there was a second where he was going to kiss me.

CASSIE:

Okay, hi. Um. What?

BLAKE:

We just got home from training and for the life of me, I couldn't get my legs to cooperate.

So...

He offered to give me a piggyback ride up the stairs. When we got to the top, he slid me down his body slower than needed and when he turned around, I swear it looked like he might kiss me.

CASSIE:

Okay.

We aren't going to freak out, yet.

What did you do?

BLAKE:

I got the hell out of there is what I did!

What the hell else would I have done?

CASSIE:

You'd climb that man like the tree he is, is what you'd do!

BLAKE:

Cassie...

CASSIE:

You're telling me that you don't want to do dirty dirty things to that man?

BLAKE:

Why are you the way you are?

CASSIE:

Answer the question.

BLAKE:

I mean, of course I would like to... do things with him...

But I can't.

We're teammates and I don't even know if he feels the same way.

I could have misread that entire thing.

CASSIE:

You're teammates, not siblings. You can do whatever you want and I have a feeling homeboy wouldn't turn you down.

BLAKE:

What the hell are you talking about?

CASSIE:

I saw the way he watched you at the tryout.

BLAKE:

???

CASSIE:

He looked at you like he wanted to eat you whole.

BLAKE:

You are of no help.

CASSIE:

Wait!

Fine. I'll be serious.

BLAKE:

Thank you.

CASSIE:

So let me get this straight. You've had a crush on this man ever since you were twelve.

BLAKE:

You didn't need to go back that far, but sure.

CASSIE:

You're currently living with said crush and have even developed a sort of friendship with him. Would it be so wrong if this friendship developed into something more?

BLAKE:

Cassie, I don't know.

CASSIE:

I've seen the posts about you two.
Everyone else might not know it's you, but I do.

BLAKE:

They were just photos, Cas. He was showing me the city.

CASSIE:

Photos where for the first time in years, he looks undeniably happy, Blake.

BLAKE:

What does that have to do with me?

CASSIE:

Look, I'm just stating what I see and if you're worried that these feelings might be one sided, don't be.

Something's telling me that he's crushing on you just as hard.

Trust Me.

BLAKE:

Maybe.

Shaking my head, I finish getting dressed and open the bathroom door only to freeze. Ryder stands at his dresser, shirtless with his shorts slung low on his hips. His back

130

muscles ripple as he pulls open drawers and I swallow with a suddenly dry throat.

I drop my phone and he turns at the sound as I scramble to get out of his way. "All yours," I yell over my shoulder and escape into the safety of the hallway, far away from my half naked—soon to be fully naked—teammate.

I distract myself with cooking and by the time I'm plating the chicken fettuccine alfredo, he's setting up our movie for the night.

We eat in a comfortable silence and he helps me clean up before we settle in the living room. He turns on a video game while I try to finish the last of me and Cassie's romance book of the week. I read the same paragraph three times before I decide to call it quits as Ryder curses when he crashes.

"You're telling me you can drive that circuit with your eyes closed in real life, but you have yet to finish it in this game higher than P8?"

"Okay hot shot, let's see if you do any better," he tosses me the controller.

"Prepare to be amazed," I sing.

I finish the race in P2 and glance over at him. His arms are folded over his chest and he stares at the screen like it personally offended him.

"You know what, let me try again. I think I can get first this time."

"Fuck no." He reaches for the controller, but I move back to hold it out of his reach.

"Blake, give it to me," he growls.

"I don't think I should."

"And why do you think that?"

"Because I have a feeling you won't let me ever play again if I do?"

"I absolutely won't let you if you don't give me the controller."

I take a moment to weigh my options, but he sees it as his opening. I squeak as his body tackles mine and scramble to keep the controller away.

We're a tangle of limbs as he stretches over me. "Ry!" I squeal when he holds on to my side with one hand and the other wraps around the wrist holding the controller.

He freezes, abandoning his pursuit and stares down at me.

"What?" I try to catch my breath.

"No one calls me that." His voice is low and I fight the shiver threatening to roll through my body in response. His eyes shine, dancing between mine. "My mum was the only one to ever—"

"Oh. I'm so sorry. I won't—"

"No," he says quickly, swallowing. "I like it when you do."

"Oh," I breathe.

The hand around my wrist tightens when I shift. I gasp when I feel the friction of his thigh between my legs and without thinking, I move again. My cheeks heat when a moan slips out before I can stop it.

Ryder's chest rumbles with a growl and he drops his hips, pressing his thigh harder against me. My free hand shoots out and clenches onto his arm.

"Fuck," he grits out through clenched teeth as his hand moves up from my hip to wrap lightly around my neck, tilting my head up. "What are you doing to me?" *What am I doing to him? What the frickity frick is he doing to me?!*

My mind dives off the deep end, tumbling down into a black hole of lust and need. I don't do this. I don't get attached to people I know aren't capable of giving me the same.

But I can't seem to stop when it comes to Ryder. Because when it comes to him, I'm scared to think that I'd give him just about anything he would ask for.

His chest brushes against mine with every breath and I feel my nipples grow tight at the contact as he pushes me farther into the cushions.

"Ry," I arch into him.

"Tell me to stop," he leans down, lips brushing against my jaw.

"I," breathe, "I—" he cuts me off with a slight roll of his hips. *Oh, god.*

"Please," I whimper.

Ryder smirks, "I've got to say, I like it when you're all confident and handing me my arse, but," he leans down until his lips brush my ear, "I think I love hearing you beg even more."

I moan as he nips my neck.

"This is a bad idea."

"Maybe."

"We shouldn't be doing this," he hisses.

"Probably not."

He pulls back, pinning me with heated eyes and I try not to squirm under his stare.

My hair is a mess and my sweatshirt has ridden up from the tussle. His eyes flick between mine before dropping to my lips. His jaw ticks and I watch the battle rage in his eyes. I open my mouth to apologize and tell him it's okay, but he cuts me off.

"Fuck it." He slams his lips to mine.

All the carefully stowed and bottled up feelings from every interaction over the past two weeks shatter at once and drown out any argument I had to walk away.

Sparks ignite over my entire body as he presses in and if it weren't for the weight of him on top of me, I'm pretty sure I would have floated up to the heavens.

His lips are soft but demanding, consuming and taking everything I'm willing to give him. I widen my legs and he shifts himself until his hips fit with mine. We both moan the moment he brushes across me and become frantic, dry humping like a couple of teenagers.

"Fuck. I can feel you through my shorts."

"Uh huh," I whine. *Good lord, could I be any more needy?*

His hand snakes down my chest and under my shirt. I hiss when his palm covers my bare breast and he pinches my nipple. He moves steadily on top of me, pressing me further and further into the couch.

I run my hand down his sculpted back, around his waist, and over his perfect ass. He leans into my touch as I pull him in and moan into his mouth at the pressure.

"What are you doing to me?" he asks breathlessly as we race to euphoria.

Pleasure builds at my core until I'm on the cusp of detonating.

"I'm—" I gasp as he pinches my nipple and grinds into me harder than before.

Boom.

My eyes roll and I scream out his name as my body racks with release, giving myself over to wave after wave of pleasure.

I'm catching my breath when I blink open my eyes and find him watching me. His eyes trace over my face and I watch fire rage through the cracks of wanting. He blinks and without a word, throws himself off of me.

I listen as he races up the stairs and flinch when his door slams shut. My hand slackens and the controller clatters to the ground, filling the still room with the sound. I stare at the broken controller as the fear that all we've built has shattered right along with it.

CHAPTER 14
RYDER

I'm. Fucked.

CHAPTER 15

BLAKE

Do you know how hard it is to avoid someone when you live with them, work with them, and rely on them for transportation? It's nearly impossible.

I don't know if Ryder has been letting me work through my own thoughts or if he too was on a downward spiral of *what the fuck* and wanted his own self isolation to think this through. Either way, I'm thankful for it.

It was forty-eight hours of...

Oh my god!

What the fuck?

What do I do now?

Fix this!

Run away!

Why didn't you stop him, you idiot?

Round and round I went with my emotions about what happened before I realized that the person I should actually talk to about it was the man himself.

Did I do that though? Nope. I'm too scared. I just need a little more time.

Apparently Ryder doesn't though.

"Hey stranger."

I scream, stumbling over my bags as I wheel them to the top of the stairs. Ryder jogs up and grabs onto them so I don't go tumbling down under their weight.

"Yeah, I didn't quite think that one through."

"It's okay," I breathe.

He carries them the rest of the way down the stairs and out to the car. I take one last look around the cottage before meeting him at the door.

"I'm going to miss this place," I sigh.

"Me too."

"Okay! Let's go before I get teary eyed," I say as I slip between him and the door.

We settle in for the hour drive to the airport and I should have known this is when he would plan his attack. Moving vehicle. Locked doors. Nowhere to hide.

"About the other night—"

"We don't have to do this."

"Oh, but we do."

"Why?"

"What do you mean why?"

"I don't know," I cry and bury my face in my hands.

His low voice breaks the building silence a moment later, "I'm sorry I ran off like I did."

"What?" I look up and see his jaw tick, knuckles white on the wheel. "Ryder, it's okay."

"It's not," he whispers. "But—"

"But?" I squeak.

"But, I don't regret it," he says slowly.

"Why do I feel like you don't even believe the words you're saying right now?"

His eyes flash over to mine before looking back at the road. "Because I don't think it should happen again. We both need to focus on racing. It's my first season back and it's your first season, period. Neither of us can afford a distraction."

I open my mouth to say, I don't even know what, but all that comes out is my whispered agreement.

We pull into the private airfield an hour and some change later and Ryder turns off the car before turning to me. "I don't want this to affect us. We had a good thing going and if I'm being honest, you push me to be better, make me want to be, both on and off the track."

"Ryder," I sigh.

"I'm serious, Blake. You're incredible and I really am lucky to have you as a friend."

"Well, I did say I'd be the best teammate slash friend you'd ever have," I smirk.

"Yeah, you did," he whispers and clears his throat, "I'll still be here every step of the way."

"Teammates?"

"Teammates."

"Maybe even friends?" I smile.

He barks a laugh, "Yeah. Maybe even friends."

"You've got yourself a deal, King."

He shakes his head and hops out of the car. I follow

behind him as we load the team's private jet before settling into our seats and I watch as he gets comfortable.

I could see the hesitancy in his eyes when he said there shouldn't be a repeat. Whether he was uneasy about how I would react or if it's what he really wanted, I don't know. But I couldn't blame him for his decision. This whole thing could get messy real fast. For both of us.

So, I agreed. I fortified my heart and threw away the key. Teammates is what he wants, so teammates is what he's going to get.

My lips tick up when his eyes meet mine. *But, maybe even friends.*

———

"Need help picking up your jaw?"

"Let me have my moment." I wave my hand at him and continue to gawk at the buildings around us in the pit lane. "I can't believe this is all really happening."

"Well believe it. Because this is only the beginning." Nikolai walks up to us with a few others trailing behind him.

"Mr. Morozov," I smile.

"I told you to call me Nikolai."

"And I told you I'd work on it. I clearly need more practice."

He chuckles, stepping to the side. "I wanted to introduce you to a couple people. This is Michael, your race engineer." A twenty-something curly haired brunette man steps forward and shakes my hand.

"This is Peter, your press advisor. He'll be with you most of the time and will help you with the press." The second youngish man with red hair and golden eyes steps forward.

"And this," a curvy blonde about two inches taller than me waves with a blinding smile, "is Sydney Collins. She's the head of social media for the team."

Sydney jumps forward with an extended hand. "It is so nice to meet you, Blake. Not going to lie, I didn't know you were a she, so this is all even more exciting. I mean, a female racer? Brilliant, this whole thing is just brilliant."

"I have a meeting to get too, but I believe Sydney has some stuff to run by you." Nikolai promises to check in later while Michael and Peter say they'll be in the garage if I need them.

Sydney turns to Ryder with her arms crossed. "Haven't seen you in over a year and that's how you decide to greet me? With a grunt?"

"Syd—"

"I understand why you did it, but I don't approve of the way you handled everything. Especially where Jace is concerned."

He dips his head and I see the muscles in his back tighten. I know how hard it was for him to push everyone away, but I also know that it was his way of taking back control when everything else was spiraling around him.

He didn't want to push away the only people that he had left, but he will fight all of his battles alone before his hurt can touch the ones he loves. I know he wants to let them back in, but it's going to take some time. And I'll be there every step of the way.

I step forward and her hardened eyes soften when she looks from Ryder to me. "So, Sydney, if you don't mind me asking—"

"Is my brother Jace Collins? And how could I have ended up here when he drives for another team?" she finishes for me and I laugh.

"Yep. That," I chuckle.

"I've always wanted to work in the industry. Growing up around it all, I guess I found a home here. My only stipulation was that it wouldn't be anywhere near my brother. I love the guy, but I served my time when we were kids."

"Was he that bad?"

"Worse."

"Yes."

Ryder and Sydney answer at the same time and I notice her soften towards him. She clears her throat and steps closer to me, "I just want to apologize again for assuming you were a guy."

"Don't even worry about it. Comes with the territory of the name," I wave her off.

"Well, I'm excited for this season. There aren't a lot of women in the industry, let alone drivers. We're going to have so much fun, I just know it," she gushes.

"Fuck," Ryder grumbles rubbing his temples. I instantly go on alert and have to lock my legs so I don't move to him.

"What's got your knickers in a twist now?" Sydney jabs, her tone lighter than before.

"This," he wiggles a finger between us, "is a recipe for trouble."

I share a conspiring look with her. "Good. I love trouble." I tilt my head and I swear his eyes heat. *Oh shit, abort, abort!*

Sydney is oblivious to the thickening air around us and drags me towards our team's clubhouse down the pit lane.

"Okay then, let's get into some trouble then shall we?" Ryder calls out.

Sydney stops and we slowly turn back to face him.

"Don't play with me Ryder," she points at him.

"Will you stop hating me if I go along with any of the social media challenges, interviews, games, or other crazy concoctions you've got running through your head?"

"I never said I hated you, but sure."

"Okay, then set it up."

"All of it?" she squeaks.

"All of it," his eyes slide to mine and he smirks, "I just have one condition."

"Damnit, I knew it was too good to be true," she grumbles.

"Blake has to do every single one with me." *Exsqueeze me?*

"What?" I say at the same time Sydney screams, "Yes!"

Ryder steps closer, "I will do the stupid dances. I will take the ridiculous quizzes. I will sit in a chair and rip off pieces of paper with googled questions about me." He stops by my side and leans in, "As long as this one is right there with me. We do this together, right?"

I look up at him and everything around us fades. I get lost in his gaze and find my body swaying towards his. His eyes dip to my lips and I suck in a breath.

"Oh, yeah. This is going to be so much fun," Sydney squeals and then launches herself at me chanting 'thank you' over and over.

She steps back and aims for Ryder next, but he pushes her away with a hand on her face.

"Don't even think about it."

She swats him away and pouts. "Whatever, I have to go get all of this laid out. This is going to be so good!" She turns to leave but spins back around and hops up, placing a quick kiss to Ryder's cheek. "It's good to have you back, King."

We watch her disappear into the clubhouse and Ryder takes a deep breath before looking down at me. I turn and look over our surroundings and shake my head. *Someone pinch me because I need this not to be a dream.*

"Ow!" I squeal and rub my raw throbbing side.

"What? You said to pinch you."

"I really need to work on keeping these internal thoughts, you know, internal," I mumble.

He chuckles and tosses an arm over my shoulder. "Come on. We've got work to do."

I tip my head back and inhale deep before blowing it out. "Okay. I'm ready."

"Yeah," he smiles and his eyes trace my face, "you are."

Blake's Guesses Today

~~Picture of him inside his house, taken from right outside the window~~ — well this one cost you both your murder documentaries and the rest of today's guesses

CHAPTER 16
RYDER

SHE'S NERVOUS.

She barely talked this morning at breakfast and was quiet throughout the team meeting. Subtle head nods and one word agreements is all she's given any of us today.

Nikolai stands and leans against the table in front of her. "You're going to do great out there, Blake. There's no pressure this weekend. Just go have fun, and show them what you're made of."

"Yes, sir." She nods.

I haven't pushed her for more than she's willing to give, but as we walk towards our rooms to change, I can't take it anymore. I actually miss the incessant babbling.

"Blake."

"Hm?"

"Stop for a sec." I gently pull on her arm.

"What's up?" she asks, looking anywhere but at me.

"Would you look at me?"

"I am," she holds my eyes for a second before moving on.

I sigh and cross my arms, "I didn't like this idea at the beginning. In fact, I thought it was reckless."

Her eyes shoot up to mine with confusion, "Oh wow. Okay." *Bingo.*

She goes to step back but I reach out and grab her arm, "But then you proved me wrong. Just like you're going to go out and prove all of these guys wrong today. You're truly a force to be reckoned with and you, above anyone else—above me—belong here."

"You really think that?"

"I really do."

She smiles up at me and I smirk. "You got this. You're ready."

"Well, I still need to get dressed—"

"You know what I'm talking about."

She huffs and closes her eyes.

"Blake."

"I know. I know," she groans and covers her face with her hands. "I'm just all in my head," she mumbles into them.

"Well don't be."

She pulls away and scowls up at me, "That's easy for you to say. You could do all of this in your sleep."

"You could too—"

"Not like you."

"You don't need to be like me. Just be you."

"Just be me?"

"Yes, just be the incredible, talented, optimistic girl that you are and everything will be alright." My fingers twitch at my sides to pull her into my chest, but I cross my arms again to stop myself.

"You make it sound so easy," she rolls her eyes.

"It is that easy."

Her eyes flicker between mine and she blows out a frustrated breath. "I just need to get out there. Rip the band-aid off. Jump head first into the deep end—"

"Throw yourself to the wolves?"

"Exactly," she laughs.

"Well, whatever it is you do, I'll be right there with you."

She sighs and meets my eyes with a small smile. "Okay," she whispers.

"Good. Now go get changed. I'll meet you out on the track."

She walks over to her door but stops with her hand on the handle. "Thank you, Ryder. I really wouldn't be here without you."

Before I can reply, she's disappearing into her room. She says she wouldn't be here without me. But I couldn't imagine being here now without her.

I stand outside her door a moment longer before moving to my own room and changing into my racing suit. Thirty minutes later, I'm leaning against the side of the building when she walks outside.

My breath stalls in my chest as I take in the way the new team race suit hugs her subtle curves. Her hair is in her signature two thick boxer braids, falling over her shoulders, and black Ray Bans cover her eyes.

I smirk.

Last week we were unloading groceries and she overloaded her arms with bags. "This is a one trip house," she declared as she contorted her body to pick up the last bag.

In her pursuit, her sunglasses fell off and she stumbled, crushing them on her way down with the ten other bags. After helping her back to her feet, I slid mine off my face and onto hers, took the surviving groceries, and silently laughed my way into the house.

She never returned them, just like she never returned my black hoodie. I bought a new pair of each because there was no way I would ask for either of them back. I like the look of her in my clothes too much.

"Nice sunglasses," I say as she walks closer.

"Thanks. They belonged to this famous driver once. I think they'll give me his skills if I wear them long enough," she smiles.

I push off the building and we walk side by side towards the back entry of our team garage. I'm about to step through the threshold when a voice stops me in my tracks. "Would you look at that? You are alive."

Blake looks up at me with furrowed brows and I turn to the man behind us. "Jace—"

"You're an arsehole, you know that?"

I am. Jace is one of my oldest friends and one of the first I pushed away. I had to.

I couldn't dim his light, because Jace Collins has always been the brightest of my friends. He's always there to show you the positives when all you see are the negatives. He's the guy that will come the moment you call, even if it's just in a towel with shampoo dripping down into his eyes because he was in the shower at the time.

He's one of the best, most compassionate, and loving people I know and yet I casted him aside like there isn't a lifetime of memories between us.

He steps closer and lifts his finger, pointing hard at me as anger, pain, and hurt flash in his eyes. "Do you have any idea how out of my mind I've been? Ryder, you just disappeared!"

"I know."

"I don't think you do," he shakes his head.

Time to rip off your own band-aid, King.

"I know I've been an arsehole. I shouldn't have shut you out like that. There was a lot happening all at once and I couldn't take it. I was going down a dark road and there's no way in hell I was going to drag any of you down with me."

He stares at me, "Fuck off. We would have been there no matter what, held the goddamn flashlight so you could find your way back. We were there, but you bloody—" he cuts off with a frustrated growl. "You didn't just shut me out, Ryder. Beckham was crushed when you didn't show up for his birthday."

I sigh and drop my eyes. "I didn't want him to see me like that. I didn't want anyone to see me like that."

A small hand grips my forearm and I look over at Blake's encouraging eyes. Blowing out a breath I meet Jace's gaze. "I'm sorry. I'll say it to Beckham too. But, I am truly sorry. I didn't think I'd ever be able to feel anything other than this emptiness. Didn't think I deserved to," I glance at Blake, "but someone recently showed me I was capable of overcoming that feeling. That I wasn't alone even when I wanted to be."

Blake's eyes shine with pride and I clear my throat, facing Jace. "I know it'll take some time but I'm working on letting people back in. Just have some patience with me, yeah?"

Jace stares me down, but the anger recedes in his eyes. "Ah, fuck," he takes three giant steps and pulls me into a crushing hug, "I'm here, I never went anywhere. I've just been waiting for you to realize that." He pulls away and claps my shoulder, "Welcome home, brother."

"It's good to be back."

"Da!" Jace's face lights up and we turn to see his six year old son, Beckham, sprinting down the lane. He comes to a stuttering stop when his eyes slide to me.

I huff, "Becks."

His face breaks into a beaming smile and he pumps his little arms, running full speed as I squat down. "Uncle Ryder!" he screeches, barrelling into my chest.

I hold him tight before picking him up under his arms and launching him in the air. His carefree giggles crack off another piece of ice surrounding my heart and my lips tip up.

"Jesus, you're getting too big for this," I grunt as I catch him for the third time.

He wraps his arms around me in a tight hug, the cool metal of his bracelet pushing against my heated skin, and I hold him impossibly tighter.

Beckham was the hardest to let go.

I was there the day he was born, the day he took his first steps, taught him his first word, stayed with him and Jace overnight when he was in the hospital, bought him his first kart.

He was my little shadow, my tiniest best friend.

He was too pure and I refused to let my darkness infect him.

But as he squeezes his short arms around my neck, I know there's no way I'll be letting him go like that again.

Beckham pulls away and flexes his arms, "Da says I've got those Collins genius, that's why I'm so big."

"Looks like you've got his brains too," I ruffle his dark brown curls.

"It's genes, spud. G-E-N-E-S," Jace laughs.

Ignoring his father, he looks over my shoulder, "Who's that?" *Oh shit, Blake.*

I turn and see her standing at the threshold of our team garage, watching us with awe flooding her eyes. Jace saddles up to me and bumps my shoulder with his, "Yeah, who's that?"

She shakes herself out of the frozen state and steps forward, "Hi. I'm Blake."

Jace shakes her hand. "Jace Collins."

"I know," she blushes and Jace winks.

"Knock that off," I growl as I backhand his chest.

I know I have no right to feel this jealousy after we agreed to stay only teammates, but that doesn't mean I want her to be hit on by a guy—let alone one of my oldest friends—right in front of me. Or ever.

Jace raises his hands in defense before taking his son from my arms, "And this little monster is Beckham, my son."

"Are you a driver?" Beckham asks, looking over her race suit.

"She's my teammate," I say simply, stepping over to her side.

"No shite," Jace smiles.

"Yes! That's a pound in the swear jar," Beckham cheers.

"Hush, grown ups are talking," Jace puts him on his feet.

Blake laughs, "That was about my reaction when Nikolai approached me."

"Well, it's good to have you. The grid has been far too boring as of late. Now, if you don't mind, I've got to drop this one with the sitter."

"Of course. It was nice meeting you," she tilts her head to Beckham, "both of you."

Jace walks off with his son after clapping me on the back one last time and I turn to see her standing in a daze. "You okay?"

"Hm? Oh, yes. I just realized that I'm going to be meeting a lot of my idols today so I'm mentally locking up my fangirl side until we get back to the hotel."

I smirk. "Did you have to do that with me?"

She blushes and looks away. "Um, no." She moves around me and practically speedwalks into the garage.

My smile grows and I jog after her. "You totally did."

"It amazes me how you're able to fit that big head in your helmet."

We walk onto the starting grid where every team's cars are lined up on either side of the road and my smile drops as I take in the drivers, crew members, and press mulling around.

Flashes of the accident cloud my vision momentarily and I bump into Blake. I didn't even realize she'd stopped walking and was turned, watching me with furrowed eyebrows.

"Hey," she nudges my shoulder, "We do this together."

My lips twitch. "We do this together."

She faces the crowd again and I see her shoulders tighten, "Plus, I called dibs on the nerves today." Everyone watches us as we stand just outside the crowded area. Some lean in to whisper to others while the majority outright gawk.

"Listen, we're just going to go out there and ignore all of that bullshite okay? We're going to go look at our car, do the promotional crap, and then we don't have to worry about anything else but testing."

"Solid plan," she nods.

Raising her chin, she strides confidently through the crowd and I follow behind her like a shadow following the sun, marveling at her strength.

Stopping at the model of what our cars will look like, she whistles, "Damn, she looks—"

"Fitting," I finish for her.

"I was going to say really cool, but sure," she laughs.

The car is all black with harsh lines and red accents. An abstract Nightingale is painted on the nose of the hood with its wings spanning along the front wings of the car.

She's right, it does look fucking cool.

It's almost down right menacing.

It also looks like it could win.

"You know I half didn't believe him, but here you are," a deep and gravel voice drawls.

154

I take a steadying breath as I turn, "Lawson."

"You're back."

I nod.

He nods.

And that's that.

Lawson Moore, man of few words and expert at battling demons. Where I've been trying to survive mine for the past few years, he's been friends with his own practically his entire life. If anyone would understand why I did what I did, it would be him and yet I plan to make it up to him. To Jace. To all of them.

"You must be Blake," he steps forward and takes her hand in his bear paw.

"It's nice to meet you," she smiles.

"If you have any problems with this one," he motions towards me, "let me know."

She laughs, "Eh, he's not that bad."

"Hey arsehole, you said you'd wait for me," Jace punches Lawson's shoulder.

"No, you asked me to wait for you."

"Semantics."

"Important ones."

"Blake! So, what do you think?" Jace ignores him and throws an arm around her shoulders, guiding her back to our car.

"She sure is pretty," Blake nods.

"Picked out a name yet?"

"Name?"

I roll my eyes. "It's this thing he does every season."

"Oh, um," her eyes flash to mine, "what do you think?"

I throw my hands up and shake my head, "Nope. This is all you, pip."

"Okay," she studies the car with a tilt of her head, nibbling on her bottom lip. "Nyx," she smiles. "Nyx the Nightingale."

"Oh, that's a good one. Goddess of the night. Very mysterious."

She laughs and Jace sighs, "Now let's go look at a real race car."

"Oh fuck," I call out as we turn, but stop in my tracks when I see the man standing feet away with an arrogant smirk on his face, "you."

CHAPTER 17

RYDER

I TAKE a menacing step forward but a hand holds me in place. Peeling my eyes off my former teammate, I look down to see Blake watching me carefully.

"He's not worth it," she whispers before shifting to focus on him. "Blake Stone. It's nice to meet you Mr. Beaumont." She steps around me with the amount of grace only she has and gives the undeserving twat her hand.

Ignoring her hand, he continues to stare down at her as if she has no business being here.

"Okay then." She steps back, closer to my side.

His eyes slide down her body and I fist my hands to keep from doing something stupid. Like knocking his fucking lights out, for one.

He sweeps his cold eyes to me and his face breaks into a wolfish smile. "Ryder King. I'll be honest, I've kind of missed you. I've grown quite bored with the," his eyes flick to Jace, "lack of quality competition."

"Fucking prick," Jace grumbles.

"I was hoping this season would be different," his smile drops as he shifts to Blake, "but I'm feeling underwhelmed already."

"I guess we'll see," she tilts her head.

Jean takes one last perusal of her body before spinning and walking away. "I really don't like that guy," she sighs when he's out of earshot.

"Kind of hard to like a viper," Lawson spits.

"I can't wait for you to beat his arse," Jace bumps her shoulder.

A siren goes off and we all cringe, covering our ears. "Shit! Well I guess that's one way to get your attention," Alek, the head PR guy for the league, calls out. "If you are not in a race suit, please find your way off my track!" Once it's only the drivers left standing, he directs us to our first set up.

We fall into place and I lean into Blake, "You ready for this?"

She smiles up at me, "Ready as I'll ever be."

We spend two hours shooting promotional footage, standing by our cars, putting on and taking off our gear, climbing in and out of our cars, and finally we file inside for the intro video that'll play before each race.

It's draining, being poked and prodded until the footage is just right. I check in with Blake every so often, but she flashes me her gorgeous smile and says she's okay every time.

I want to believe her and a part of me does, but I've quickly gathered that she doesn't like to feel like a burden. She'll say she's okay over and over again until she's blue in the face before ever admitting something's wrong. *Sounds familiar.*

They're pushing her hard already, playing up her gender and amateur status. Formula 1 hasn't seen a female driver since before I was born. All eyes are going to be on her and this team this season.

So, if she thinks I'm going to stop checking on her, even when she's adamant that she's okay, then she's sorely mistaken. I told her we were in this together, and I meant it.

After we're freed of the filming crew, each team makes their way to their team's garage. She visibly relaxes and is practically sprinting to the garage.

I take off at a run and she squeaks. She may be fast, but my legs are much longer. I eat up the distance in no time and she yells after me as I pass her.

I'm leaning against the garage bay when she slows to a stop in front of me and bends at the waist, hands on her knees while she catches her breath. "That—" gasp, "is—" heave, "so unfair."

"Nothing I can do about it, pip." She scowls up at me and I smirk.

"Ah, there you two are!" Callum booms across the bustling bay.

Blake steps up beside me with a smile and set shoulders.

"Ready for the fun part?" He rubs his hands together, matching her level of excitement.

"You have no idea," she smiles.

Callum steps towards her and steers her to the right side of the garage with his hands on her shoulders. She glances over her shoulder with wide eyes, pointing at the car. "This—"

"Is all yours."

She smiles, stepping up to the car. Callum makes his way over to me and clears his throat, inclining his head to the other side of the garage, "And this is yours." My eyes roam over the monstrous machine in front of me and I nod.

"She sure is a great looking car." He runs his hand over the paint.

"Ryder," Nikolai calls out.

"Yeah?"

"We'll start with you." He doesn't look up from the clipboard in his hands, brows furrowed in concentration.

I almost forgot that this is a day full of firsts for this team, including his first season as a Team Principal. Hell, I think it's the first time he's been back to a race track since his accident two years ago.

Without another word, he walks over to Blake and movement on the other side of my car catches my eye. Tyson nods towards the driver's seat with a smirk and I slip my gear on before launching myself over the halo, settling into the single seat.

I slip my gloves on as his voice breaks over the radio, "Ryder King."

"Tyson Montgomery."

"You ready for this, mate?"

I sigh and lock my wheel in place. I flex my hands on each side of the controls and roll my shoulders. "Let's do it."

He chuckles before reading off the car's levels and as he continues, I glance to my left.

Blake stands on the other side of her car with Michael. She watches studiously as he shows her all the screens, nodding along. As if sensing my eyes, she peeks over in my direction, but I don't look away. I seem to never be able to look away.

She gives me a thumbs up before returning her attention to Michael. I linger on her a moment longer, then focus forward while I switch the ignition on. Tire warmers come off, and I pull out into the pit lane.

"Okay, Ryder. Let's do a couple slow laps to get some readings and then, if all looks good you can go all out. Sound good?" Tyson's voice floats over the radio.

"Understood."

For the next hour, I pull in and out of the box so tires can change, engineers can test, and information can be gathered. By the time our first session is up, the crew is ready to make any adjustments needed for the next time I take it out.

"Thoughts?" Nikolai asks at the end of my session.

"She feels good. Smooth. A little lag on acceleration and she fights in tight corners but nothing that can't be fixed."

"Good. Good," he nods. "Go get some water and rest time. Blake's up."

I make my way into the garage but pause when I see Blake slip on her helmet. She shakes out her shoulders before climbing into her seat. She locks in her steering wheel and starts the engine. The garage fills with its roars, but she freezes when given the signal to pull out.

The guys look around at each other in confusion and I step over to her car, motioning for a headset. Michael hands them over and I lean down into Blake's line of sight. "Hey, pip."

"Hi," she breathes.

"What's wrong?"

"Nothing."

"Uh-huh. Mind telling me why you're still idling in the garage instead of out there?" I incline my head towards the track.

"It's stupid."

"Nothing you say or do is stupid. A little crazy at times, but never stupid." I'm trying to stop the downward spiral she's on and I'm taking it as a win when I see the fog in her eyes recede.

"Cassie always did this thing before I went out on the track. She would tug on my chest straps and say 'she ain't going nowhere'. I didn't realize that I needed her ridiculous ritual."

I study her for a moment and don't take my eyes off of her as I reach over and lightly tug on her straps. "She ain't going nowhere."

She sucks in a breath and her eyes glitter as she watches me pull back. I pass the headset back over to Michael and step away from her car.

Blake nods and accelerates out of the garage. I step over to her team's screens and watch as she runs through her warm up laps. Once she's given the go ahead to push it, she holds nothing back. Michael turns to hand me another headset with a smile, "You should hear this."

Her screams of joy ring over the radio and I pull one side away with a chuckle. "Is that—"

"The song "Danger Zone" by Kenny Loggins? It sure is." He smiles. "Nikolai gave me a thumb drive with strict instructions that it plays in the background while she drives."

I shake my head, but my lips tick up. "It keeps her zoned in. That playlist has been on a loop during training, I'm pretty sure I could tell you the order from memory."

Blake blazes by us and Michael shakes his head when her time pops up on the screen. "Seems to do the trick."

It does. Nightingale Racing ends preseason testing two days later with the quickest lap recorded in the past five years.

And it wasn't my name next to it.

Blake's Guesses Today

~~Headset~~

~~Microphone~~

~~Flag~~

THE GRID GIRLS

EPISODE 201: LIGHTS OUT AND AWAY WE GO!

(Theme song fades)

Leah: Hello hello! I'm Leah.

Zoe: I'm Zoe.

Tess: And I'm Tess.

Leah: It's the start of a new season.

Tess: For us and our namesake.

Leah: Yes, it is. But just in case you don't know who we are or where you're at... We are The Grid Girls, three Formula 1 obsessed friends who sit around and discuss the races, drivers, and of course, the drama.

Tess: We give you deep dives on everything from the technical aspects of racing—so you can have those awesome new pick up lines—to off track developments. Because I don't care who you are, we all like to gossip.

Zoe: On today's episode, we'll be talking about preseason testing and the upcoming season. For those of you who don't know, preseason testing is where all the teams gather for the first time before a season begins.

Leah: It's where the teams, drivers, and the fans get our first peeks at the cars.

Tess: It's also where a lot of tweaking takes place on the engineering side. For three days, these teams will be running test after test. The goal?

Leah: To get their cars in the best shape possible.

Zoe: Overall, this preseason series looks like it went pretty well for a lot of the teams.

Tess: No more so than the newcomers over at Nightingale Racing.

Zoe: Oh yeah. I mean, they walked out of there with the two quickest laps recorded in years. The top one being two seconds faster than the reigning record.

Leah: Did either of you see that coming, because I didn't.

Tess: I don't think anyone did.

Zoe: To be fair, there were a lot of surprises that came out of that particular garage this weekend.

Tess: I'm sure it's made headlines by now since I saw the Instagram post about it not thirty minutes after the session started, but... If you don't know, Nightingale Racing debuted a new face as their second driver.

(Zoe squeals)

Tess: Blake Stone, a female driver, has entered the race alongside her teammate and four-time world champion, Ryder King.

Leah: I seriously didn't think I would live to see the day.

Zoe: And let me tell you, this girl came in swinging *(brief pause)* HARD.

Tess: You're telling me. The girl blew her own teammate's record out of the water.

Zoe: Did you see the images of him cheering her on from the garage?

Leah: Gah! That was so cute. The one where it's zoomed in on his smirk is my favorite.

Tess: Inside sources said that he was actually a big advocate for her signing. Even offered for her to stay with him during the season.

Leah: Honestly, I think that's a really smart idea.

Tess: Living with Ryder King? Yeah, me too.

(the girls all laugh)

Leah: No you horn dog. I'm talking about teammates living together, especially when one is new.

Zoe: It's definitely a good way to force them into getting to know each other.

Tess: Oh, I do love a good forced proximity.

Zoe: What is going on with you today?

Leah: I think she's overstimulated from the excitement of a new season.

(Tess puts one finger to her nose and points the other at Leah)

Leah: But then again, who isn't? There's so many new things to look forward to this season. New cars, new teams, new drivers.

Tess: I know we still have two months before we lock in our predictions for the championship, but Blake Stone has gotten my attention already. If she was able to get those numbers with the car now, just imagine what she'll be able to do with it modified.

166

Zoe: The other teams need to watch out, Nightingale Racing is coming in hot and don't look to be pulling any punches. They already have The King of the Grid as one of their drivers. This was a solid first look at someone who has the makings of a Queen.

(Tess gasps)

Tess: Oh. My. God. Yes!

(the girls all laugh)

CHAPTER 18

BLAKE

"You're up late."

A scream barrels out of me and I spin away from the window. "Jesus! I need to put a bell on you or something," I breathe, placing a hand over my racing heart.

Ryder chuckles and steps up next to me, "Sorry."

"I don't think you are," I peer at him.

"I'm not."

I shake my head with a smile and look back out the window, taking in the lights of the city below. I breathe in slowly, holding it until my lungs burn before releasing.

Tomorrow.

My first race.

And I'm currently freaking out.

I should be excited that I took P4 in qualifying, but all I can think about is how I'm going to be able to keep it. Tomorrow it's not just me out there, and that's... terrifying.

"Hey," Ryder's smooth, low voice brings me out of my

thoughts and I look over to see him watching me. "What's going on in that head of yours?"

"Too much," I sigh.

He studies me before tilting his head towards the living area of our suite, "Come on, I want to show you something." He walks over to the couch but instead of sitting on it, he settles on the ground. Propping his back against the front cushions, he bends his knees and drapes his arms over them.

"You coming?" *Don't I freaking wish.*

I slowly slink my way over, crawling onto the floor. I aim for the spot next to him, but his arm shoots out, scoops me up by my waist and deposits me between his spread legs.

"Uh, whatcha doin' big guy?" I laugh nervously.

"Big guy?" He chuckles and I twist to meet his raised eyebrow.

"Yep, if I'm pipsqueak, then you're big guy. If you don't like it then too bad, you did this to yourself when you poked fun at my height."

"Fair enough." He spreads out his legs to where there's a slight bend and takes my hands in his, raising them as if we're gripping a steering wheel. "Oh, I almost forgot."

My breath seizes in my chest when he reaches over and tugs on the strings of my hoodie, his knuckles brushing against my thinly covered breast. I can feel my nipple harden under his fingers and clear my throat, locking my body so that I don't chase his touch when he pulls away.

I don't need to look at Ryder to know he's wearing that smug smirk of his, like he knows what he's doing to me.

Pushing against my back, his breath tickles the hairs on my neck as his lips brush my ear. "She ain't going nowhere."

It takes all of my concentration not to shiver at the gravel in his lowered voice, fear of him knowing what he does to me when we'd just agreed to stay only teammates. *Maybe even friends.*

I turn my head and our noses brush. His eyes drop to my lips and I suck in a shaky breath. I watch as the amber around his pupils spreads, burning through the green until an all consuming heat is what's left.

Teammates don't do this to each other.

I don't even think friends get this close.

The kind of closeness where I can see my reflection in his eyes. Feel every breath he takes as the air brushes my lips. Hear the thudding of his racing heart like it's calling out to my own.

No. Friends don't look at friends the way he's looking at me and I don't have it in me to stop him. But apparently he does.

Clearing his throat, Ryder leans back and mutters something to himself as his fingers guide mine to where the ignition button would sit on our steering wheels.

My eyes lock onto his strong hands and the contrast of his tan skin with my paleness. I tamp down my breathing when it threatens to escalate at the feel of his rough palms. *Am I a hand girl now? I think so. Ryder's, specifically.*

I feel his eyes on me and turn my head, meeting his stare. "Close your eyes, Blake."

"So bossy," I whisper but do what I'm told.

I swear I hear him whisper 'good girl' but it's hard to make out my own thoughts with my heart beat raging in my ears. He settles behind me and I pinch my lips together, tamping down the reaction to arch into him when he shifts. *Good god woman, concentrate.*

"One. Deep breath in." His chest presses against my back and I lean into his hold.

"Two. Hear the roaring of the crowd." His breath dances across the shell of my ear.

"Three. Feel the power of your car vibrating around you." His hands flex with mine.

"Four. Visualize the route." I open my eyes and see the open track ahead of us.

"Five. Breathe out." Everything stills.

"Lights out."

I feel his leg flex at the same time mine does and he calls out our positions as we take off down the straight. With his fingers laying atop mine, he downshifts going into the first turn.

Pulling through the second, his fingers move with mine as we shoot through the gears. His arms hug mine, twisting through the chicane and pinning hard to the right for turn eight.

"This is the tricky one," he whispers in my ear as we round into turn ten.

"I got it," I shift so our fingers interlock and take control, tapping the downshift and tilting our arms into the deep angled turn.

"Yeah, you do." He lets me guide us through the rest of

the track and when we pass the starting line, I twist to look at him over my shoulder.

"Again," he says and I nod, moving back into position.

We run through the circuit three more times and even though we both know I have it, he doesn't break our connection. He slowly disentangles his limbs from mine, after the fifth lap, brushing his fingers across my skin as he goes. I blush at the goosebumps he leaves behind.

Swallowing, I turn on my knees and face him. He watches me with warm comforting eyes and my body vibrates with the urge to touch him.

Apparently I haven't mastered that whole mind over body concept because the next thing I know, I'm launching myself at him and throwing my arms around his shoulders.

I greedily take lungfuls of his warm woodsy scent with a hint of leather, and nuzzle into his neck. "Thank you," my lips brush against his neck and I feel him lock up for a second before wrapping his strong arms around me. "How did you know that would shut up all the voices in my head?"

"Because it's the only thing that works for me," he mumbles into my hair.

I pull back and bring my knees to my chest, not wanting to move from the comfort of his closeness yet. Leaning my chin on my knees, I tilt my head with a small smile. "Do you do that before every race?"

"Yeah," he looks down at his hands, "My father used to sit me on his lap and talk me through each track before he left for the races. I picked up the habit when I started karting." He chuckles, "It used to drive Mum nuts. I'd sit in the front seat and do it over and over until we pulled through the gates of the track."

He shakes his head and looks up, meeting my eyes. "As I got older I switched to visualising the night before since my schedule on race day tends to get more and more hectic than the one before. I run through the entire race—"

"Every lap?"

"Every single one. And I run through a couple laps in my dressing room before the race."

"That's amazing, Ryder."

"It's the only time when I'm not racing that I'm able to shut everything out."

I raise my head, eyebrows furrowed, "What do you mean?"

"The thoughts. The fear. The voices in my head telling me I'll never be enough."

"Ry—"

"My father is—was—a legend, my mum in her own way too."

"And that's a lot to live up to," I whisper.

"A crushing amount," he blows out a heavy breath, shoulders sagging.

"Hey," I scooch closer and place my hands on top of his. "Ryder, you're an incredible driver. You've accomplished so much in a short amount of time that most don't in an entire career," I shake my head, "But not only that, you're an amazing person. I have to believe that your parents would be so proud of the man you are, on and off the track."

His jaw ticks, "You don't need to say that—"

"I know, but I want to."

"Blake."

"Ryder," I smile and trace a finger over his knuckles. "Should we finish the last fifty laps? Chase out the rest of those voices?"

His eyes flicker between mine and his lips twitch up at the edges. His eyes don't leave mine as he shakes his head slowly. "I think I'm okay."

I smile. "Yeah?"

"Yeah," he breathes and I see a crack splinter in the walls he hides behind. He looks away, clears his throat and reaches up, kneading the back of his neck.

"Alright, come on," I get up, toss a pillow onto the floor, and sit cross legged behind it on the couch, "You helped me. Now it's my turn."

"I'm—"

"Fine? Well, I'm just going to make extra sure that you are."

"Blake—"

"Here. Now," I point to the pillow.

"Now who's the bossy one?" he teases, crawling over until his back rests against my knees. I lean forward and pat his head lightly, "Good boy."

His head snaps to the side with furrowed brows, "Absolutely not."

I giggle and straighten only to twist my lips at how far away he is. I'm short. I have short limbs and these nubs I call arms will not comfortably reach his head with my legs crossed the way they are.

He twists to look over his shoulder and must come to the same conclusion because before I know it, he grabs my ankles and spreads them until his broad shoulders nestle in the cradle of my thighs. *Why was that hotter than it probably should have been?*

"Better?" His voice vibrates through his back and against the inside of my thighs.

"Mhm," I squeak and raise my hands.

My fingers slide through the silky dark brown curls and I graze my nails over his scalp. A groan bursts from him and he drops his head back. I freeze for a moment at the position, but shake myself out of the haze and run my fingers along his temples.

"Fuck," he breathes.

"Good?"

"Very," he groans.

I continue massaging his scalp, slowly making my way to the base of his neck and across his trapezius muscles.

"Do you think you could put some of that orange cat stuff on the back of my neck?"

I pause, "You mean the Tiger Balm?"

"Yeah. That."

"Sure," I laugh and tap his shoulder, sliding not so gracefully out from behind him.

Digging through my bag back in my room, I take out the jar and walk out into the living room. When I look up, the jar slips from my hand and I scramble to catch it. Preparing myself mentally, I slowly walk towards the couch.

The shirt he had on when I left the room? Yeah, well, it's

gone. And now I have to pinch my lips closed to keep the drool from escaping.

Climbing back onto the couch, I uncap the jar and take a good amount of the minty smelling balm on my fingers before rubbing my hands together to warm it up. I suck in a breath when his hand wraps around my ankle and traces small circles against the bone.

Swallowing, I work to ignore the electricity shooting up my leg from the contact and focus on eliminating the knots in his tense muscles. Ten minutes later, his skin shines with an orange glow and I'm on the edge of euphoria just from his thumb rubbing my ankle.

RUBBING. MY. ANKLE!

"Thank you," he says when I lean back, relaxing into the deep set cushions.

"Mhm," I hum.

"We should probably get to bed, big day tomorrow." He doesn't make a move to get up and I'm one more swipe away from completely embarrassing myself.

"Yep. Yeah. We should do that," I say a little too loudly and catapult myself over the back of the couch. My socks slip on the tile and I catch myself before my chin can slam into the edge.

"Jesus, you okay?" Ryder jumps to his feet but I wave him off.

"I'm fine! I'm fine. Good night and, uh, thank you for," I flail my hands towards the couch, "the visualization and... yeah, good night."

His low chuckle nips at my heels as I high tail it to the

safety of my bedroom. I close the door, lean my back against it, and lock the handle for good measure.

Pushing off the door, I flop onto the bed with a groan. I'm in so much trouble, but at least I'm not freaking out about tomorrow's race anymore, right?

CHAPTER 19

BLAKE

My phone rings, cutting off my staring contest with the morning sunbeams streaming through the cracked curtains. I roll over and smile at the picture of Cassie lighting up the screen.

"Who's ready to rumble," she cheers.

"I think you've got your sports mixed up there," I laugh.

She waves me off. "Semantics. Anywho! Look who I've got."

She pans the phone to her side and a close up of Denver's annoyed face fills the screen. "Can you take it down a few notches, baby girl? The coffee hasn't kicked in yet," he grumbles.

"Rookie, you went to sleep?" I tease.

He takes the phone from her and holds it at a more reasonable distance. She slides up next to him and rests her head on his shoulder.

"I told him not to, but you try keeping his old ass up past eleven," she snickers.

"I am not old. I just work hard and if you haven't noticed, there's been a lot of it since my best driver left me," he side eyes me.

"Sorry, not sorry."

"Me neither," he smiles.

"Mama B wanted to be here but the hospital called her in. I promised to text her updates throughout the race," Cassie shuffles closer to her dad.

"Yeah, she called me earlier to wish me luck."

"She's really proud of you, we all are," he says.

"Wouldn't be here without you," I smile.

"Nah, this is all you Blake."

There's a light knock on my door before Ryder's muffled voice calls, "Blake? You up?"

Cassie leans forward and grabs the phone from her dad. "Is that Ryder? Hi sexy," she yells and I scramble to turn the volume down on my phone.

"Who are you talking about?" Den growls.

"Hush, this has now transitioned into girl talk so I'm going to take this in my room," she waves him off and hops off the couch. Denver calls out to her retreating form, but she ignores him and I shake my head.

She plops down on her bed and I see her legs swing behind her. "So are you going to answer the door, or leave him hanging?" *Oh, shit. Ryder!*

"Y-yes," I yell.

"Smooth," she snickers.

I throw my blankets off and grab my sweatpants off the chair in the corner. I slip them on and warn Cassie to be on her best behavior before unlocking the door.

Taking one last breath, I swing it open and smile up at a disheveled Ryder. His hair sticks up in all directions and the imprint of his pillow still lines the side of his face.

My eyes dip to his bare chest and my lips part as I take in the lean muscle. His sweats sit low on his tapered hips and my mouth waters with the overwhelming urge to lick the 'v' cut into his hips, leading down to a trail of dark hair.

"Good lord," Cassie breathes, snapping me out of my gawking.

My eyes shoot up to his face and that sexy smirk of his. "Morning," I whisper. My nose scrunches and eyes widen before I slam a hand over my mouth.

"You okay?" his eyebrows lift.

"Mhm," I mumble behind my hand, "Morning breath. Could you—"

"Yeah, I'll get the coffee on."

"Perfect," I rush out and take off towards the bathroom.

"Morning Cassie!" he calls after me and she lets out a high pitched squeal.

She has the good sense to wait until I have the door closed and faucet running before opening her mouth, "I wish I had your amount of self restraint."

"Stop," I laugh.

"I'm serious, Blake. How has that not been a thing yet?" I ignore her question and shove my toothbrush in my mouth. "Oh my god," Cassie gasps, "Oh my god!"

I quickly spit and bring the phone close to my face, "Sh!"

"Young lady, have you been keeping some dirty little secrets?"

"No. Yes. Maybe." I put the phone back on the counter and finish brushing my teeth.

"You so freaking have!"

"I'm going to hang up if you don't stop yelling."

"If you hang up right now, I'm going to post the picture of you at our thirteenth birthday party where you dressed up as—"

"Okay! There's no need to be rash here."

Cassie smiles victoriously, "Now. Tell me what I want to hear."

Closing the toilet lid, I drop down and tell her about what happened on the couch. By the end of it, she's vibrating with excitement. That is until I tell her we decided that being just teammates would be the best for both of us.

"What? Oh, boo. No!"

"Cassie—"

"No! You can't sink Brayker before she even gets out into the open waters!"

"Good God, you already gave us a couple's name?"

"Pft," she waves a hand, "I came up with that on day one."

"I'm serious Cassie. Nothing can happen."

"But why?" she groans, throwing herself back dramatically on her bed.

"Because," I laugh, "I need to focus on driving. He needs

to focus on driving. There's a lot on the line and it can all get messy real fast if it doesn't work out."

"But that's if it doesn't work out. Emphasis on the if." She gives me a pointed look.

"I caught that." I smile and shake my head.

"I guess I'll let it go for now, but let me leave you with this. While you were daydreaming about taking a trip down his happy trail, homeboy was playing out his own fantasies."

"What the hell are you talking about?"

She smirks, "You had the phone tilted towards him when you answered the door. While you were mentally undressing him, I was watching him do the same exact thing to you."

I open my mouth but nothing comes out. A knock sounds out the door and she chuckles, "I think it's time for you to go. Love you and good luck today."

"Yeah, I love you too. I'll text you after?"

We hang up and I shut off the faucet. Looking in the mirror, I blow out a breath. "You got this," I whisper. With a nod, I throw open the bathroom door and follow the heavenly smell of coffee into the kitchen.

"Good talk?" Ryder asks, slicing up some fresh fruit.

I grab a piece of watermelon and pop it into my mouth, "Yep! Cassie says hi."

Ryder chuckles, sliding some fruit onto a plate and setting it in front of me. I dig in with a quiet thank you and slide my journal over.

Opening to a new page, I date the top and write about my dream from last night. I don't know what it is, but ever since I was a kid, I have had these vivid dreams almost every single night.

After I shared the first one with Ryder, I found a leather bound notebook on my nightstand the next afternoon. He told me that it might be cool to have a collection of all my dreams so that one day I could look back on them and see if any of them come true.

I hope there isn't a day where I come into contact with a polka dotted shark walking around like it's a dog—thank you NyQuil for that one—but there are a few I wouldn't mind coming to fruition. One in particular coming true, now that I think about it.

"What was this one about?" he asks, sipping his coffee.

"It wasn't too exciting." *Liar.*

"Oh?"

I shrug, "Yeah, we were on a boat."

"We?"

"Mhm. It was the Monaco Grand Prix and we had a boat day with everyone."

"That sounds fun. Did anything else happen?" *Well, later that night, you took me into the bedroom and we let the motion of the sea guide us together. That is, after you consumed me like I was your new favorite dessert.*

"Not really," I squeak and he peers at me like he doesn't believe it.

"Okay then." He checks the clock and downs the rest of his coffee. "Shit, we have to get a move on."

I jump out of my chair, shoving one last piece of watermelon into my mouth. "Meet you back here in five?"

"Let's make it three," he calls out, rushing into his room.

Two minutes and thirty seconds later I stand with a smug smile on my face as he jogs out of his room. He pokes me in my ribs on his way to the door and I squeal, chasing after him.

We hustle to the track and inch our way through social and press obligations before settling into our team meeting.

The time ticks by and before I know it, I'm tucking the last shoelace of my racing boots and straightening the fabric on my frame in the mirror. Blowing out a breath I look around my room when a knock sounds at my door.

"Hey," Michael smiles.

"Hey," I sigh and take in the big black box he's holding.

"Nikolai wanted me to give this to you."

"Oh. Thank you," I reach out and take the box from his arms.

"You've got another thirty minutes before you need to be out there."

"Awesome. Thank you!"

I close the door and set the box on the table. Nibbling my lip, I lift the top and pick up the white card laying on top of black silk fabric.

Let's show them what we're made of.
— NM

I put the card off to the side and gingerly lift the fabric. I huff a laugh as I pull out the helmet, turning it in my hands to marvel at the customized design.

The front has Nightingale wings spanning each side

from the visor and overlays a sleek black geometric pattern that continues around the entirety of the helmet. My driver number is on each side in the team's vibrant red, making it stand out against the dark intricate design. A small American flag emblem rests at the base, just under the right side of my visor, and I run my thumb over it with a smile.

It's perfect.

Sitting my new helmet down carefully, I sit on the small bed and close my eyes. When I can't get my mind to quiet, I blow out a breath and drop my head back to stare at the ceiling.

My lips tick up at an idea and I shift onto the floor, positioning my legs and arms like I'm sitting in my car. Closing my eyes, I imagine the lights, the crowd, the roaring engine.

The second light goes up and large warm hands glide down my arms until they intertwine with mine on the wheel. Ryder's voice rumbles in my ear and we take off.

I open my eyes when I pass the starting line and smile at the wave of calm flushing out any nerves and anxieties. Checking my watch, I get up from the floor and grab my helmet before striding out into the garage.

It's a flurry of movement as the crew works to get us into our cars. I sneak a peek to Ryder's side of the garage and he winks at me before pulling on his own matching helmet.

With a smile, I pull on the rest of my gear and climb into my car, taking one last look at him before we're given the go ahead to exit the garage. We drive an installation lap where afterwards we settle our cars in their designated spots on the starting grid.

Opening ceremonies seem to drag on with it being the first race of the season and my leg bounces with anticipation to get started. Once the last note of what feels like the hundredth anthem is played, I'm practically sprinting to my car.

I'm checking over my stats on the wheel when a shadow falls over me. I look up and jerk my head back as much as the HANS device lets me. "What are you doing?"

Ryder bends down in his full gear and reaches into my cockpit, pulling on my chest straps. "She ain't going nowhere," he bellows over the sound of engines coming alive.

My eyes lock on his and a flood of emotions barrels into my chest. I open my mouth to say something, anything, but the man has left me speechless. On my next blink, he's straightening and taking off towards his car in the P1 spot.

Did he really just run over here to do my stupid superstitious tradition seconds before the race starts? I might need him to come back and pinch me to make sure!

I don't have time to think about it as I watch the first light illuminate above us.

One. Deep breath in.

Two. Roaring engines drown out the cheering crowd.

Three. I flex my fingers on the wheel and revel in the vibrations.

Four. I stare down the long stretch ahead of me.

Five. Everything stills.

Lights out.

CHAPTER 20

RYDER

I've missed this.

God, how I've missed this.

I pull into the designated first place spot and shut off the engine. Climbing out of my seat I throw my hands up as the crew cheers behind the barrier. Jumping over the halo, I jog over and the rowdy Nightingale Racing crew pulls me into their celebrations.

I grit my teeth when hands hit my helmet, and pull away at the first ripple of tension. Taking off my gear, I hand it all over and take the hat handed to me as well as the rest of my personal effects before making my way over to a post race interview.

Afterwards, I'm escorted to the cooldown room. Jace enters a few minutes later with the biggest smile on his flushed face and a miniature version of himself on his shoulders.

"That. Was. Awesome!" Beckham cheers with his fist held high.

I guzzle down some water with a tick in my lips. Jace swings Beckham to the ground and the moment his little feet hit the pavement, he's running into my legs.

"You were the best, Uncle Ryder!"

"Hey, you said I was the best!"

Beckham giggles and I pick him up, sitting him on my hip as he looks at his father. "Yeah, but Uncle Ryder won, so he really is the best."

I bark out a laugh at the same time Jace pinches his son's side, "Then how are we both the best? Huh, you little punk?"

Beckham doubles over laughing into my shoulder, attempting to evade his father, when the door opens. His laughter slows as Jean saunters in with a smug smile on his face.

Without looking in our direction, he walks over to the table, grabs a water, and sits in the designated third place chair. My jaw clenches and I hold Beckham closer, using him as an anchor to keep my mounting frustrations at bay.

"Where's Miss Blake?" Beckham asks, oblivious to the charged silence around him. I turn my head to him, ready to answer but a thick, arrogance filled voice cuts me off.

"Not here," Jean smirks and my body goes rigid.

He's not worth it. Blake's voice echoes through my mind and I fall into the memory of her soft touch. Taking a page out of her 'kill them with kindness' book, I opt to spare the French fuck a trip to the hospital and ignore him instead.

"Why?" Beckham asks, apparently on a completely

different chapter of this whole 'ignore the succubus in the corner' than I am.

"Because she doesn't belong here." His voice drips with disdain.

I feel, more than see, Jace turn to stone next to me. His blue eyes are hard and trained on Jean. Beckham's expression isn't much different from his fathers with furrowed brows and twisted lips.

I give the little man an encouraging smile and drop my voice low, "go to your father real quick okay buddy?" Without protest, Beckham shuffles over to Jace's side as I turn. "I'm not going to defend her to you because Blake can do that herself." *And she'd probably kick my ass if I did anyway.*

"But I'm also not going to stand here and let you continue to think that you are God's gift to racing, because you're not." I shake my head and hold back a snarl, "You drive dirty. Taking unnecessary risks that could," my jaw clenches, "that have gotten people hurt."

Jace steps forward with a hand on my shoulder and whispers, "Remember the cameras." I nod in acknowledgement, not taking my eyes off of my old teammate.

Jean's smile grows and he scoffs, shaking his head. "Still blame me for that, do you?"

"For what? Taking me out for the rest of that season and the next one or the bullshite leading up to it? Take your pick because as far as I'm concerned, you were the catalyst to both."

A knock sounds, cutting through the boiling air. Beckham wiggles from his father's hold and bolts for the door, swinging it open. "Oh, well hello there," a crew member laughs before looking up into the room with cautious eyes, "They're ready for you guys."

I don't back down from Jean's glare as he slides out of his chair and walks towards the door to my left. He pauses at the threshold and leans in, "Next time it won't be for just a season or two. You had your time on the track, King, and you wasted it. You don't belong here anymore and your little girlfriend doesn't either."

He steps close and lowers his voice so that only I can hear, "You talk about me being an unnecessary risk, but it isn't my team that has a little girl playing dress up as one driver and a has-been who's hiding a career ending impairment as the other."

My heart stops.

"You don't know what you're talking about," I grit through clenched teeth.

"Don't I? Because it's like you said, I am the one who caused it after all." Jean gives me one last wolfish smile before turning and striding out the door.

Alarm tickles the back of my neck as I walk out to the winners ceremony a few moments later. I see and hear everything that goes on around me, but it's all fazed out by the anxiety clouding my mind.

Muscle memory takes over as I wave when the announcer says my name, stand tall for the British anthem, and hold my trophy high as the crowd cheers. My free hand raises, pointing a finger to the sky. *This is all for you.*

A voice rings out above the others and I look down into the cluster of Nightingale crew members. The fear holding me by my neck releases and recedes into the dark corners of my mind when our eyes meet.

I take my first full breath as my demons recoil from her bright smile and shining blue eyes. With flushed cheeks from the heat of the race, she cups her hands around her mouth and yells out, clearing away the lingering clouds.

My arm drops until I point right at her. *This is all better because of you.*

Blake's hands drop from around her mouth and she smiles. Biting her lip, she points right back at me before jumping along with the rest of the crew and their cheers.

———

I'm bolting down the stairs the moment we're released from the ceremony. I don't stop moving as I shake hands and offer quick head nods to the people congratulating me on my way towards the team garage.

"There he is!" Callum calls out when the bays come into view.

I walk closer and catch sight of the board displaying my P1 spot and Blake's P6. Hands clap my back as I work through the group until I'm standing next to Nikolai and Callum.

"Before we take the photo, I wanted to say a few words," Callum settles the small crowd.

"I know today was only the first of many races to come," he shakes his head beaming, "but boy what a first day it was." Cheers ring out all around and my eyes track over each face, coming to a stop when I spot those distinct boxer braids.

"Today, this team walks away with not only a first place win," the crew goes nuts and he nods towards Blake, "but a P6 standing in a debut race!" I watch the guys jostle her shoulders and yell out her name.

"I'm damn proud of all of you, not only for the work you've done today, but for all you've put in these past months. Thank you for taking a chance on me and this team," his eyes slide over everyone, briefly pausing on her, "I'm sure there's more to come, but let's go ahead and take this picture so you all can go out and celebrate!"

The group crowds behind the board with me and Blake on either side. I hear a pop seconds before we are doused in champagne and a smirk pulls at my lips when she squeals as she tries—and fails—to shield herself.

When the flows slow, crew members scatter to get their after race duties done before heading home for the night. I take the towel handed to me as someone walks by and wipe my face.

The same person hands one to her and she takes it with a soft thank you before rubbing it over her face and hands. As if sensing my gaze, she looks up and her smile grows.

I take one step then another until she's looking up at me and I can see the faint freckles dotting the bridge of her nose.

She's breathing heavily and her face is flush as she watches me get closer.

"Blake—"

"Hey! Can I get one of just the two of you?" Sydney pops out of absolutely nowhere, cutting me off and causing her to jump.

She laughs, "Yeah, of course. Right, big guy?" She looks up at me with shining eyes and I would like to see anyone say no to her when she looks at them that way. *Because I don't think I ever will.*

Wordlessly, I throw my arm over her shoulders and pull her into my side. Sydney steps back and raises her phone with a victorious smile on her face. When she gets what she wants, she drops her arms and mouths 'thank you' to Blake while flashing her eyes to me before taking off into the garage.

I stand there a little longer, watching the hustle of everyone around us as they tear everything down. She shifts under my arm and my heart stops at the possibility of her wanting to step away.

Instead, my mouth ticks up when she wraps her arm around my waist and steps closer into me. I look down at her as she watches the crew around us. Her hair's drenched with sweat and champagne, faint lines from her helmet still accenting her pink cheeks, and she doesn't have a stitch of makeup on. *She's never looked more beautiful.*

"We did it!" She smiles up at me and squeezes my side. My fingers brush over her sleeve as I drift off into the sea of her gaze and watch as the last of my restraint drown under the waves of her rapture.

The vision of her cheering me on from the crowd at the winners ceremony flashes in my mind and the mounting pressure in my chest releases as I stutter a breath.

In the past year I got used to the silence. The emptiness. I resigned to my fate, that all I had left was racing. I leaned into it because when I was behind the wheel, they were with me and I wouldn't feel so alone.

Those couple hours with the connection that allowed me to feel something other than empty were what kept me going. Racing kept me going and I was okay with it. I didn't have time or want to make any for anything else. I didn't need anything else.

Until her.

This wasn't supposed to happen. Having her here was supposed to deter the wrath of my past. That's it. All I needed was for her to give me enough reprieve from the dark abyss so that I could take my first full breath in over a year.

She wasn't supposed to become the thing I breathed for. The match that lit my world on fire in the best of ways, bringing heat back to my dead cold heart. She wasn't supposed to burrow her way into my soul and make a home out of what was left.

I can still feel the darkness lurking just under my skin and in the recess of my mind, but she decimates every single one of their advances with her sweet smiles, bright eyes, and contagious laugh.

The tranquility I experience behind the wheel doesn't dissipate the moment my boots hit the ground—exchanging a few hours of peace for days of desolation—when she's around. I don't fear the void of time between races when she's there, filling them with her laughter.

I don't feel like I'm barely surviving because just being around her breathes life into me. When I wake up, she's the first thing I think about and want to see. When she isn't around, I'm constantly looking for her. When she's near, I have to physically hold myself back from pulling her into my arms.

And I'm done.

I'm done shutting down every thought I have of us together. Of telling myself that I don't deserve her. I know I don't, but I'm a selfish prick and I'm. Just. Done.

I told her that we couldn't happen, but I also told her that we'll do this together. Only one of those was a lie.

A crew member comes over and picks up the team board, jolting me out of my thoughts. Blake steps out from underneath my arm and I clench my fist so that I don't reach out for her as she walks towards the private rooms, taking my revived beating heart with her.

POST-RACE CONFERENCE TRANSCRIPT
SAUDI ARABIA GRAND PRIX

Nikolai MOROZOV, Ryder KING, Blake STONE

Q: Nikolai, I'd like to start with you. What a great start to the season for Nightingale. Two first place wins so far for King, and another top ten for Stone. Do you feel confident that this trend will continue the farther we get into the season?

Nikolai MOROZOV: I'm confident in both drivers. Ryder has had two good races so far with more than a ten second gap between him and second each time. After the unfortunate accident that took him out two seasons ago, he worked his ass off to get back on the track and that hard work is obviously paying off. Blake is still learning. This is her debut season and the pressure on her shoulders is immense, but she's taking it in stride. While she doesn't have the experience that Ryder brings to the team, she's young, passionate, and determined to get every millisecond she can out of the car. They're both highly-skilled drivers and it's up to us now to give them the car to match those abilities.

Q: So you'd say Blake is settling in well? Are you impressed with her performance thus far this season?

NM: Like I said, Blake is new and it takes time to fully get comfortable within a team as a seasoned driver, let alone one just starting out. We're working with a completely new crew as a fresh team, but she's blending well with them. There are growing pains, but we're all pivoting where we need to in order to make things work. Overall, she's a great addition to the team and the circuit, and we're happy to have her on board. As for her performance, it's only the second race of the season. Give her some time and give us a chance to get her the best possible car and we'll see what she can really do.

Q: Speaking of the car. With the two week break between Jeddah and Australia, are you planning on making any major changes or upgrades?

NM: We have a decent sized upgrade coming for Australia and possibly a little more coming later, around Miami, but it all depends on the drivers and engineers feedback.

Q: Back to the drivers. Are there any noticeable differences in strengths between the two of them?

NM: It's difficult to say with it being this early in the season. Obviously Ryder has an advantage with being here, in this circuit, before. But they're both experienced in their own ways. Blake is adapting quickly. She's learning from Ryder and from each time she gets behind the wheel.

Q: Do you ever miss being the one out there behind the wheel? *(Nikolai remains silent and the floor is motioned to continue with the next question)*

Q: Ryder. Were you happy with how everything went for you with the race today?

Ryder KING: I won, so I'd say yes.

Q: Will we see you on the podium for the next race in Australia?

RK: Possibly.

Q: Tell us, do you see a fifth championship for you this year?

RK: There's still a lot of racing left to do and right now I'm focusing on taking it one race at a time.

Q: And this one coming up is the anniversary of your accident and confrontation with your previous teammate, Jean. How are you feeling?

RK: Like Morozov said, I worked my arse off to get back here. I don't plan on letting the mistakes of the past affect my performance out there on the track.

Q: How are you liking the car so far this season?

RK: I think at the moment, I'm pretty content with the car. There were some balancing issues in practice runs that seemed to be tweaked by the time the lights went out, so for the time being I'm good with the car's performance.

Q: And how about the performance of your teammate Blake?

RK: I think she is doing incredibly well for her debut season. In case any of you have forgotten, in mine I didn't hit top ten until the fifth race. She's done that twice now. Two for two so far this season. And I know with time, tweaking, and practice, she'll stand on the podium one day.

Q: So would you say signing her was a good move on Nikolai's part? That maybe more teams should be looking at this route in the future?

RK: I think signing Blake was risky but it was also the right move.

She brings a lot more to the team than a lot of people expected and I for one can't wait to see where she goes in this industry. As for teams replicating this in the future? That's for them to decide.

Q: Blake, I'd like to move on to you. First off, congratulations on finishing P8.

Blake STONE: Thank you.

Q: How are you settling in with the team?

BS: Yeah, it's been relatively smooth. The team is great and has been very welcoming since day one. Obviously I'm new to the circuit and am still finding my way, but I'm not in it alone. Everyone has kind of stepped up and helped me when I've needed it. I'm very thankful for this opportunity and for everyone here.

Q: How do you see this season going for you? Any podiums?

BS: That's always the goal right? There's a lot of races to go and I'm hopeful, but I guess we will see.

Q: Despite your record times in preseason, we have yet to see you break the top five on race days. Do you think you were properly prepared to race alongside professionals?

RK: To clarify, she *is* one of those 'professionals'.

BS: I don't think you're ever fully prepared for what goes on out there. As you so eloquently pointed out, my times during the race and the ones I had at preseason testing don't match up. You have to keep in mind that during testing, I wasn't having to battle it out with anyone in the straights or avoid colliding with someone in the corners. Just like practice and qualifying, racing is a whole other ball game. I'm still getting my footing, but give me a couple more races to get comfortable with the crowded lanes and I'll be right up there with this guy. *(nods to Ryder)*

Q: You've really shocked the industry so far this season, Blake. It's safe to say there are a lot of eyes on you and your performance. How are you doing with being under all that pressure and criticism?

BS: You can't be a woman in a male dominated sport and not have thick skin. I've heard it my entire career, that I don't belong here. That I'll inevitably fall short. There's a lot of hateful comments out there and things being said, but instead of letting it get to me, I use that as fuel to be better. What's that saying? 'Sticks and stones may break my bones but words will never hurt me.'

Q: One last question for both drivers. It's no secret that Ryder has had a history of bad pairings when it comes to his teammate, but this time around it seems like things are going well. How are you two getting along so far?

BS: I'll be honest, he's a legend and was actually the driver who inspired me to race in the first place. So you could say I was awestruck, intimidated, excited, and nervous all at the same time. He's been really helpful with me finding my footing on the team and has been a big part of why I feel like I'm doing so well with the transition from my old circuit to this one. I'm very thankful for him and the entire Nightingale team.

RK: *(clears throat)* I wouldn't want anyone else to be in that second driver's seat.

CHAPTER 21

RYDER

THE UNIVERSE HAS a horrible sense of humor.

Of course the moment I decide to confront my growing feelings towards Blake, our schedules become a giant clusterfuck of interviews, promotionals, and training. For two weeks, neither of us are left alone except for the few hours of sleep we are granted each night.

For two weeks I bit my tongue, waiting for the right moment where I could finally get her alone. And of course those tended to be moments before a race, but what was I going to do? Tell her that I think I'm falling in love with her, wink and then dip out of there with the promise to catch her after the race?

Maybe—No. I'm going to do this right. I have to do this right.

Because if I lost her—*I can't lose her.*

But I also can't wait any longer. I'm not 100 percent

confident that the words won't just burst out of me the next time she smiles in my direction. Kind of like she is right now.

My mouth fills with the distinct taste of copper as I clamp down on my cheek to keep from yelling out to her over the crowd. With one final wave, me, Jace, and Lawson exit the stage and make our way towards the garages.

"So where are we going tonight?" Jace throws an arm over me and Lawson's shoulders.

"We have an eight o'clock flight in the morning, mate. What makes you think either of us want to go out tonight?" Lawson scowls.

Jace looks at me for help and I shake my head. "I'm with him on this one." *I've got things to do, a girl to see, and feelings to concede to.*

A squeal pierces the air and Sydney barrels into her brother's chest.

"Congratulations!" She steps back and goes to hug Lawson next but veers off at the last second and swings around to me. I give her my best 'absolutely not' glare and she shakes her head, laughing.

Blake catches up behind her and like the magnets we've become, we gravitate towards the other. The moment she's close enough, she launches herself into my arms.

"Congrats, big guy," she whispers.

I sigh at the feel of her and wrap my arms tighter around her waist, "You too, pip."

"Oh so she can do it," Sydney mocks a pout.

"Do what?" Blake looks between us when she steps away and I scrunch my nose at her, shaking my head. Jace trades our shoulders for the girls, "I was just asking these fine gentleman where they would like to go celebrate tonight—"

"Really?" She looks at me with pleading eyes. "Can we?"

"Loner boy said he didn't—"

"Okay," I cut in, ignoring the shocked look on Jace's face and the annoyed scowl on Lawson's. All I see is how she lights up. And for that, I can hold off for a little longer... easy.

———

This is absolutely not easy. Why the fuck did I agree to this again?

I look up from scowling at the concrete and Blake sends me a beaming smile over her shoulder as her and Sydney walk arm in arm into the club. *Oh yeah, that's why.*

A small group of guys passes them on their way in and my hands fist when one of them lingers, eyes roaming over Blake. The girls, oblivious to the wolves circling around them, move around them with a small 'excuse us'.

As I pass the tall blond with his eyes still glued to Blake's ass, I step closer and shove my shoulder into his. His slurred voice calls out as I follow the girls down the darkened hall, "Hey—oh holy shit, I think Ryder King just bumped into me!"

"Smooth," Lawson drawls from behind me and I shrug.

"We're going to go dance," Sydney drags a smiling Blake behind her onto the crowded floor the moment we step into the open space.

"I'll be at the bar," Jace calls over the deafening music.

Lawson nudges my arm and juts his chin towards the back. Nodding, we weave through the packed outskirts and settle into the corner booth with a perfect view of the girls.

A waitress takes our order and Law gets one for Sydney. I order Blake the same thing and a water before picking out a beer for myself.

I usually don't drink during the season, but my jittery nerves and quick temper towards anyone even looking in her direction tell me I'm going to need it tonight.

I glance over to where the girls are and my skin heats with the way her hips move in sync to the beat, but my jaw ticks when I see someone approach her from behind. She quickly turns around, waving him off and—lucky for him—he takes the hint, disappearing into the crowd.

Blowing out a relieved breath that I won't be going to jail tonight for beating the shit out of some prat, I unclench my hand and take a sip of my beer when the waitress drops them off.

"You going to tell her?" Lawson calls out, taking a draw of his beer.

"I don't know what you're talking about." I don't take my eyes off of her when I reply.

There's no way in hell I'm having this conversation with him before I even get the chance to have it with her. If I'm cracking open my chest to anyone for the first time in a long time, it's not going to be to my six foot four moody best friend.

"So you're telling me you aren't wrapped around her dainty little finger?"

I stay silent because the man's right. I am. If I wasn't, I wouldn't be sitting in this booth right now. All because she batted her baby blues up at me.

"That's what I thought." He leans forward and taps his glass on the table. "I just want you to be careful, mate. That," he nods towards Blake, "is a slippery slope and one you won't be able to come back from."

"I know." I down the rest of my beer and slam my glass on the table. He's right. There's no going back for me.

"Do you? Because this could end in disaster for the both of you Ryder. And from where I'm standing, I honestly don't know which of you would come out of that with the bigger wound."

My eyes slide to Lawson, "How about you listen to your own advice, because if anyone is standing on the edge of a disaster here," I glance at Sydney before turning back, "it's you."

With a hard jaw, Lawson shakes his head but his eyes slide to the dance floor and his body locks up. I whip around and follow his line of sight.

Two men approach the girls, circling them. One of them yanks on Sydney's hips while the other pushes his front to Blake's back. Not a second later, we're flying out of the booth and pushing our way through the sea of bodies.

Blake whirls around on the drunk bastard clawing at her and pushes at his chest. Her frantic eyes meet mine over his shoulder and I watch them fill with relief.

Lawson uses his much larger frame to edge the other guy

away from Sydney while I grab hold of the one trying to hump Blake's leg. He swings around and my hand pulses on his shoulder before he's shoving it off. Well, well, well.

"Fuck off, you can have her when I'm done," the blond from earlier slurs.

"Not likely," I growl as Blake moves between us, wrapping her arms around my middle. I lay my arm around her shoulders and she leans into my side.

The blond's buddy comes stumbling over with panicked eyes and pushes at his chest, checking over his shoulder. I glance over Blake's head and hold in a chuckle at the menacing shadow Lawson creates, standing behind a fired up Sydney.

I turn back to tweedle dee and tweedle dumbass with flaming eyes and pull Blake in front of me, shifting my arm so it lays across her chest and neck. Her hands reach up and hold onto my forearm, leaning farther into my body.

"I think it's you who should fuck off right about now," she shouts.

The blond backs away with one last glare in my direction before stumbling with his friend off towards the bar. She relaxes fully when his form disappears and turns in my arms. She smiles up at me and pulls away, taking my hands, "Since you're out here—"

"I don't dance, Blake."

"Please." She steps back into me and sticks out her bottom lip. My mouth instantly waters with the urge to bite it. *Goddamnit, this girl could easily make me do whatever she wanted.*

206

I huff at her pouting and the corner of my lips twitch. Her smile spreads and she thrusts her hands in the air in victory. Holding my hand above her head, she leads me farther into the crowded dance floor.

I glance behind me to see Lawson standing like a sentinel over Sydney as she dances around him. His eyes are locked on her movements and there's the slightest tilt in his lips when she lifts his arm to twirl herself.

I shake my head and turn my attention back to the siren in front of me.

She stops and turns, looking up at me. Still holding onto my hand, she lifts it up and moves to the beat vibrating around us. I don't move. I can't move.

I'm too mesmerized by the carefree smile that wasn't on her face before I joined her on the floor. By the heat searing through my palm with her holding tight. By the sound of her laugh breaking through the music when she opens her eyes to see me standing there like a twat.

Tucking her bottom lip between her teeth, she spins and I gravitate towards her, guiding her until her back meets my front. We stand there, slightly swaying, and she drops her head back against my chest.

Tilting her head, she ensnares me in her glacial eyes as she begins to move her hips. Slowly, she guides my hands to her sides and my fingers flex when she brushes against my quickly hardening cock.

She rolls her hips again and I move with her, chasing that constant connection as music pulses around us. We're as in tune with one another here as we are on the track.

She shifts, I shift.

She rolls, I roll.

She leans farther in, I hold her tighter.

We become one as song after song breaks the air.

She turns and loops her arms around my neck. I lean down until our foreheads touch, groaning when she twists her fingers through the hair at the base of my skull.

"Blake," I breathe and slide my hands up her sides, pulling her impossibly closer. She leans back slightly and I open my eyes. My jaw ticks and my eyes drop to her lips as her tongue peaks out before I slowly draw them back up to her icy depths.

"You can't look at me like that," she pleads.

"Like what?"

"Like we aren't just teammates or even friends."

"Maybe I can't be just teammates with you." I lift my hands and cup her face.

Her eyes flutter at my touch and her fingers drop to my chest, fisting my shirt.

"Maybe I don't want to have to choose between you and racing."

She leans into me, eyes flickering between mine with overflowing affection, and takes a stuttering breath, "Then don't."

She rises up on her toes at the same time I descend and crushes her mouth to mine. I groan at the first taste of her and thread my fingers through her damp hair, pulling until she has to tilt her head back.

Everything fades until all that's left is us and I dive in head first, freefalling into her orbit.

Into the feeling of her and how perfect she seems to fit against me.

Into the taste of her when she opens for me and how I'm already craving more.

Into the sounds she makes that echo through my mind like a favorite playlist on repeat.

She pushes up farther, trying to get closer and I wrap my arms around her, lifting as she wraps her legs around my waist. Our tongues dance and she whimpers when I nip at her bottom lip. *Fuck, I need her to make that sound again.*

A body collides into me hard from behind and I stumble. She breaks away with a gasp and I tighten my arms around her, catching myself before we go down.

"Oi! Get a fucking room," the guy yells before following the giggling drunk girl he's with back into the swaying sea of bodies.

"Sorry," she calls out breathlessly and slides down my body agonizingly slowly. She drops her head to my shoulder with a stifled laugh and I drop my head back, trying and failing to calm my racing heart.

I tilt my head back down when she leans back, watching me with cautious eyes and a small nervous smile. Fueled with the need to ease her mind, I bend down, softly kissing her forehead, her cheeks, her nose, and finally her lips.

"Are you sure?" Her lips brush against mine as she speaks.

I ease back and take her face in my hands, breathing in deep and finding the comfort I need reflecting in her crystal eyes. "I've never been so sure about something in my entire life."

CHAPTER 22

BLAKE

IF SOMEONE TOLD me months ago that I'd soon be living my dream of driving for Formula 1, I would have waved them off. Yet here I am.

If they would have told me that the man who jump started my love for the sport, who was the object of my adolescent affections, and who I idolized for most of my career would be my new teammate, I would have laughed in their face. Yet here he is.

If someone would have told me that I would fall head over heels for the dark, brooding, haunted man he's become and after weeks together he would kiss me like I was the air he desperately needed to breathe, I would have driven you to the nearest hospital to have your head checked. Yet...

"Scale of one to ten."

"Blake," Ryder growls.

"Fine, sad face to smiling face."

He huffs a laugh against my lips and pulls back, leaning

against the elevator wall. He gently cups the sides of my face and strokes his thumb over my cheek. "You're ridiculous."

"I just want to make sure you're really really sure," I drop my eyes and fiddle with his shirt, nervous that I'll show too much under his warm emerald eyes.

Too scared that he'll be able to see just how much I want —have wanted—this since he left me to pick up the pieces of that shattered controller.

When he said that we couldn't happen again, I agreed. I did so for his sake, because I could see the war between what he thought he wanted and what he knew he needed rage on under the thin veil of absolute. I could see it tearing him apart from the way his knuckles turned white on the steering wheel, just so he wouldn't reach out to me.

I took myself out of the equation because I knew he wasn't ready. It takes a lot of work to break down those walls you've built around yourself when you've sealed them with your whole being.

So I waited.

And hoped.

And waited some more.

There may have been a wish on a shooting star that very well may have been a plane now that I think about it.

I stepped back and gave him the space he needed to think about every possible outcome. A man like Ryder doesn't just jump without looking at what's below him. When we did eventually take the leap, I wanted him to be unwavering in what he wanted from me.

Because it's more than just my career at stake. A whole

lot more.

"Blake," he sighs, cut off when the elevator doors open. Taking my hand, he guides me down the hall and into our joint suite.

The door clicks closed behind us as he walks us over to the couch. I go to sit on one of the cushions next to him, but he tugs on my arm and I fall into his chest. Giggling, I brace myself on his shoulders and readjust on his lap so that I'm straddling him.

His hands slide up my thighs bracketing his hips and over my shoulders until he's cupping my face. *Gah, I love when he does that.* I smile softly at the look of adoration reflecting in his eyes as they trace my face.

Mimicking his position, I slide my hands over his shoulders and up the back of his neck until my fingers lace through his hair. He groans at the first scrape of my nails and I huff a laugh, watching his eyes close in bliss.

He takes a deep breath and slowly opens his eyes. His features waver with trepidation and he licks his lips before speaking softly, "What happened on the couch that night freaked me out."

My body tenses and I drop my eyes, trying to hide the immediate hurt of rejection. *Okay, this is not how I thought this was going to go.*

"Not because of you," he rushes out, tilting my chin up. "I was freaked out because I've never felt like that with someone. I've never felt this... this pull to another person before."

Oh.

Jaw ticking, he tucks a piece of my hair, "My entire life, racing has been my sole purpose, my only focus. With both of my parents being involved in the sport, it was all consuming. There was nothing else. I didn't need anything else. I had an incredible father. A loving mum. And a reason to get up every morning."

He clears his throat, "Then I lost everything I'd ever cared about one by one until there was nothing left." He holds me tighter as if touching me is the only thing keeping him together. As if I'm keeping him afloat from the past traumas threatening to take him under their suffocating depths.

"I couldn't bring my parents back or rewind the clock so that I would walk away from Jean's taunting. I felt like everything was spiraling out of my control and I grappled with any way to get that back."

At the mention of Jean, I brush my finger over his scarred eyebrow and down his scruff covered jaw. No one knows what was said between the two of them that day and I'm not going to ask him about it now. Whenever he's ready to tell me, I'll be here to listen.

For now, I'm just going to hold onto everything he's giving to me in this moment. I'm going to show him that I can be his safe space and I don't plan on going anywhere.

He turns his head and gently kisses the inside of my palm before continuing, "There were so many voices coming at me after Mum passed and later on after the incident with Jean. Telling me they were there for me and it would all be okay."

Shaking his head, he drops his eyes down to our laps, "It

became too much and I just wanted it all to stop. Needed it to stop. So I took back the control I'd been desperate to retain and pushed every last one of them away."

His jaw ticks, "Eventually I found solace in the quiet. I adapted to the dark. Succumbed to the terrors and used that fear to push myself until I could get back here. I thought it was what I wanted. What I deserved. All I would ever need."

He raises his eyes, "But then I met you."

I stutter a breath as Ryder thumbs away my rogue tears. "The first beat my heart took in over a year was when you turned around and ensnared me in your arctic eyes. Instead of pushing you away, I wanted you closer. Instead of shutting you out, I brought you to my childhood home. Instead of staying away, I found the smallest of excuses to be around you."

Affection shines in his warm eyes. "You've dismantled every last one of my walls, brick by stubborn brick and then rebuilt them with you on the inside. I don't fear the darkness because you're my guiding light. I don't surrender to my demons because they cower against your strength. I don't feel like this is it."

His hands flex, "Like all I'll ever be is this empty shell of a man. For so long I thought that the loneliness, the quiet, the hurt and pain was all I deserved. Everything good in my life was either ripped away or I was too weak and broken to let what was left stick around."

He sniffs and his voice cracks, "I don't want to be alone anymore, Blake."

I shake my head and shuffle closer on his lap, taking his

face in my hands. "You're not, Ry. I'm right here. Anything you want or need, I am here and I don't plan on going anywhere. You don't need to hold in your pain by yourself anymore. Let me shoulder some of it for you."

I bend forward and lay my forehead against his. "You are not alone. I am right here and I want—have wanted—every part of you. The good. The bad," I pull back and my eyes flicker between his, "The broken."

His chest heaves and I gently lean farther into him. "Give me your pain, Ry. I can take it. I will take it. Because what I can't take is seeing you suffer. So, please. Lean on me," I beg.

"Give me—" I roll my head against his. "Give me everything."

"Blake," he sighs.

"Ryder," I whisper, leaning in and brushing my lips against his.

He pulls back taking a deep breath and stroking his thumb across my cheek and bottom lip, "You keep asking if I'm sure, but what about you? Are you sure you want this, Blake?"

Vulnerability flashes in his eyes and I blink back the rest of my tears threatening to fall.

"I want this," I whisper, threading my fingers through his hair at the back of his head and looking into his deep jade eyes, "I want you."

"Thank Christ," his breath fans across my lips. I huff a laugh and his hands tighten in my hair as he pulls me in, his lips brushing mine as he speaks, "Because I'm pretty sure you've had me since that first day."

CHAPTER 23

RYDER

HER LIPS ARE as soft as I remember.

The noises she makes are still the sweetest melody I've ever heard.

The kiss starts off soft, slow, curious. It's not like our first or second where we were fueled by pent up need and weeks of teasing. We're taking our time, savoring every touch, taste, and sound the other draws out.

A lightning bolt ignites a burning inferno under my skin with every press of her against me. Her fingers dance across the base of my neck and I suppress the shiver as a trail of goose pimples flare in her wake.

My hands map out her body, across the soft curve of her hips and around the perfect roundness of her arse. She rocks her hips and I hiss when she pushes against my straining cock. I tease the seam of her lips with my tongue and she opens immediately.

"Fuck," I growl and nip at her bottom lip when she shifts against me again. Giggling, she leans away and smiles.

"What?"

"You've been waiting to do that."

"I've been waiting to do a lot to you, love. You're going to have to be more specific."

My eyes drop as she leans in, taking my mouth with hers. It's her tongue that seeks entry first this time and I open eagerly, hungry for that next taste of her. I'm pretty sure I'm addicted to this girl. And there's no way in hell I'll be asking for a cure any time soon, if ever.

A moan rumbles out of my chest when her teeth bite into my lip. She pulls slightly before releasing and sits up with a devious smile. I slick my tongue out and the corner of my mouth tips up when I taste copper. *I think my girl likes it a little rough.*

Visions of Blake pinned beneath me that first time flash through my mind. How she leaned into it more than fought it.

With a growl I lace my hand through her hair and pull her back into me. This kiss isn't soft or sweet. Tongues dance, teeth clash, hands roam. It's devouring. It's seeking. It's the release of everything that's built up over these months.

All the soft and innocent touches.

The late night movie marathons and early morning video game showdowns.

How every time I rub my head or neck she watches me.

The laughs and smiles she's gifted me before pulling some out for herself.

Everything has led us here. And there's nowhere else I'd rather be.

I drop my hand from behind her head and trail it down the side of her neck. She rolls her hips and I push up with mine, meeting her movements.

"Ryder," she gasps when my hard length presses against her.

"What do you need, love?" I brush my lips over her jaw and down her neck. Her chest rises and falls on heavy breaths as she arches into my touch. I flex my hips and ground up into her, "Is this what you want?" She nods her head, but that's not enough. "I need to hear you say it."

She tips her chin and soft eyes meet mine. She releases my hair and gently frames my face with her small delicate hands. Leaning forward, she presses a single kiss to my lips before resting her forehead against mine, "I want you."

She squeals and clings to me when I wrap my arms around her and flip us so she's lying beneath me on the deep seated cushions. Propping myself up, I take her in.

Her wavy hair is splayed around her like a dark halo. Creases tickle the edges of her eyes, between her eyebrows, and her nose scrunches as her chest vibrates with laughter.

God, she's beautiful.

She blinks her eyes open and smiles softly. Slowly her hand lifts and she brushes a strand of hair off my forehead. "You are too," she whispers and my eyebrows furrow. "Looks like I'm not the only one who has trouble keeping inside thoughts," she taps the side of my temple, "inside."

I watch as lust washes away any remaining humor in her

depths, one hand splayed across my back and the other encircles my forearm. Without breaking eye contact, I pull away my arm and capture her hand.

Her breathing picks up as I lace our fingers and slowly guide our hands above her head, using my free one to trail over her shoulder and up her neck until I'm cupping her jaw.

I bend and nip at her ear, "Do you remember what it was I said I loved to hear coming out of this pretty mouth of yours?"

"Y-you love... to hear me beg," she breathes.

"So then beg, Blake," I roll my hips into her and she writhes underneath me.

She moans, arching into me, "Please!"

I slam my mouth to hers. She grapples with my shirt and I lean back, releasing my hold on her and rip off the fabric. I smile and hum in approval when her hand stays put above her head.

Bending down, I brush my lips across her shoulders, teasing the edge of her quickly rising chest. "Ry, please," she gasps when I kiss her breast over her top.

With quick fingers, I flick open the button on her jeans and yank them down her hips. After tossing them to the side, I turn back to her with furrowed brows.

"Why are you wearing a bathing suit?"

She bursts out laughing and leans up on her elbows. "It's not a bathing suit. It's a bodysuit. Kind of like a one piece swimsuit but for going out."

"How the hell do I get it off you?"

"Clips."

"Where?"

She nibbles on her bottom lip and without looking away, widens her legs and drops her knees. "Ah," I breathe as my eyes lock on the three snap buttons between her thighs.

"I'm going to be honest though, there's really no sexy way to get out of this thing so maybe I should do it and you could close your eyes?"

"Everything you do is sexy," I murmur as my eyes drag over her body. She flops back down, rolling her eyes. "I'm serious. Even the way you brush your goddamn teeth is sexy to me."

A laugh bursts out of her and she shakes her head, "Well this will definitely be the first then."

"I've got an idea that might help you get out of that pretty head of yours."

"Mhm? What's that?"

I run my hand up her right leg and she sucks in a breath as I crest her knee, descending down her thigh. Her eyes close, her body softens, and her mouth drops open on a sigh when I cup her.

"How about we see what happens first. You getting this bathing suit off—"

"Bodysuit."

"Or I get you off," I break the snaps and her eyes fly open.

She shifts back up onto elbows and I take the opportunity to wrap my arm around her lower back, lifting and scooting her towards the corner of the L-shaped couch of our suite.

"What do I get when I win?"

I slide my lower half to the ground and lift each of her legs over my shoulders, kissing them as I go. I press my mouth against the inside of her thigh, "Whatever you want."

She hums and I lift my head, "Not going to ask what I get if I win?"

She smiles, "If you win then you get whatever you want, King."

I smirk and wink, "Then game on, love." Hooking my arms around her hips, I take the black lace thong between both hands and pull.

"Ryder! That was my nice pair!"

I don't answer. I can't.

I'm too busy getting lost in the beauty that is her. I can say with all the confidence in this universe and the next... Blake is beautiful from the tips of her toes all the way up to the highest strand of hair. Everywhere and everything. She's. Perfect.

"I'll buy you as many pairs as you want," I lean in and press a kiss to her smooth mound.

Her hips flex and I smile against her skin. She squirms and I lock my arm over her stomach to keep her lower body still.

The first swipe of my tongue is teasing.

The second is a little slower as I revel in her pooling need.

By the third, I'm done for.

She arches into me as I run my tongue up and around her clit, gently sucking on the bundle of nerves. She chants my name, her fingers threading through my hair and pulling me to her. My eyes roll and muscles tighten at the taste of her.

Sweet.

Tangy.

A slight hint of honey.

Blake.

"Fuck. You're my new favorite meal, love."

"Uh huh," she breathes. I pull away and look up at her face twisted in ecstasy.

"Better get to work, or are you giving up already?"

She peers down at me, but gasps when I plunge in a finger. Leaning down, I work over her clit as I thrust in and out of her tight pussy, curling slightly to reach that sweet spot.

The sound of shifting fabric spurs me on and I add a finger. She clenches around them and her legs on my shoulders shutter when I suck hard on her clit.

"Fuck! Ry, I'm gonna—"

"Come," I growl against her.

Her hips push up and her moans pierce the air as she detonates.

I watch every second. Afraid to look away. Afraid that this is just a dream.

But it's not. And when she slowly blinks her eyes open before pulling me up by my hair and sealing her mouth over mine, I know that fear has no place when I'm with her.

She hums at the taste of her on my lips. Her nails drag down my neck, across my chest, and down until she's gripping my belt.

"I need you," she breathes against my lips.

I stand, unlatch my belt, and unbuckle my pants.

Hooking my thumbs, I shuck my jeans and briefs down in one go, tossing them to the side.

She doesn't take her eyes off of mine the entire time and her eyes trail down my naked torso. I see her swallow when her eyes land on my cock, hard and aching for her.

I take a step and freeze, "Fuck."

"What?"

"Condom."

Her eyes shoot back up to mine, "You don't have one?"

"Wasn't planning on needing one this season."

"Why not?"

"Because if it wasn't going to be you then it wasn't going to be anyone," I run a frustrated hand through my hair.

"Well... It is me... And..."

"And?"

"I'm on birth control," she whispers.

"Blake—"

"I got tested when we were in training."

"Me too," I take a step towards her.

"Maybe we can—"

"Are you sure?" I kneel.

"Are you?"

"Only if you want," I wrap my hand around her spread thighs.

"I want you," she whispers as she threads her fingers through my hair.

"Okay," I breathe.

"Okay," she closes the distance between us and kisses me.

Her hand brushes down my chest and I grunt at the feel

of her hand wrapping around me. She pumps me and I pull my mouth away, breathing heavy. I look down at her hand stroking my shaft before she lines me up with her entrance.

"I don't know if I can be gentle with you right now," I huff as my body vibrates with need.

She cups my jaw and I raise my eyes to hers, "Then don't." She pulls at the same time as I dive in. Our mouths clash and I swallow her moan when my head slips inside her.

I grab her hips and slam forward until I'm buried to the hilt. My head drops back and a groan barrels out of my chest as she contracts around me.

"Yes," she cries into my chest.

"I'm not going to last long," I grit my teeth, "You feel too fucking good."

Our mouths fuse as her hips roll into my heavy thrusts. The room fills with the sounds of our bodies, her soft moans and my deep groans.

I pull back slightly and watch her tilt her head back in euphoria. Face flush. Hair wild. Lips parted. She's beautiful. She's everything.

She's mine.

I take her jaw and tilt her face back up to mine. "Who's your King?"

"You are," she answers breathlessly.

"Come with your King, love."

She nods and her nails dig into my back, legs tightening around my hips. I bow my head and bite down gently on her shoulder as the pressure in my spine ignites.

Slipping my hand between us, I swirl my thumb around

her clit and feel her head roll on my shoulder. I moan at the first flutters around my shaft.

Her nails score through my skin as I pound into her harder and harder.

Her mouth opens and the feeling of her teeth against my skin set me off.

I come on a roar.

We stay there with me buried inside her and her wrapped around me until our breaths even out and our limbs start to regain their strength.

Sliding my hand under her, I hoist her up and twist before laying us down with her half on top of me. "One of these days I'll get you to a proper bed," I mumble against her lips.

"I don't know. I think couches are kinda our thing now."

She giggles when I huff a laugh and shake my head, "You're kinda my thing now, Blake. I'll go anywhere, be anywhere... do this anywhere you want."

She leans forward and kisses my scarred eyebrow, then my cheeks, nose, and mouth. With her forehead against mine she speaks softly, "You're kinda my thing now too, Ry. Wherever we go, whatever we do. We do it together."

We do this together.

THE GRID GIRLS
EPISODE 213: LET'S GO TO THE BEACH

(Theme song fades)

Leah: Happy Monday! Welcome and thank you for tuning in, I'm Leah.

Zoe: I'm Zoe.

Tess: I'm Tess. And we're The Grid Girls.

Zoe: We're three Formula 1 obsessed best friends who's sleep schedules go out the window during the season.

(Tess laughs)

Tess: A worthy sacrifice.

Leah: We sit around, drink our much needed coffees, and talk about the races, the teams, their drivers, and of course, all the drama on and off the track.

Tess: This week, we are in Miami and let me tell you... I'm super excited for it.

Zoe: Who isn't? It's the first race of the season in the US and there's so much to see. It's like spring break here with the parties and celebrity sightings.

Leah: There is that, but I'm honestly excited to see how a certain American driver performs for her first home race.

Tess: Isn't she from the south east?

Leah: A small suburb just outside of Atlanta, Georgia I believe.

Zoe: If the trend continues, I'd say our girl could possibly place her first podium here.

Tess: Both of the Nightingale drivers could. I don't know what's gotten into them but they have been dominating the past two races. Blake held a strong P4 position in both the Japan and Chinese Grand Prixs. From start to finish.

Leah: And Ryder broke both track records for fastest lap, walking out of the Prixs with two more first place wins.

Tess: Have you seen the team's socials too? They are blowing up!

Leah: I don't think we've ever seen this much of Ryder even before his disappearance from the grid.

Zoe: He looks happy. They both do.

Tess: How could they not be? Blake is living her dream and Ryder is very well on his way to another world championship. I'd be happy too in either of those positions.

Leah: They look like they're getting along well enough too.

(Tess's eyes widen and she nods her head, wiggling her eyebrows)

Tess: I ship them. #Blyder all the way.

(Leah and Zoe laugh)

Tess: I'm working on a better name, I swear.

Zoe: Please do, because that's not it.

Leah: Do we think this is just a teammate slash friend kind of relationship or could it be something more.

Tess: Please, Lord, let it be more.

Zoe: Hear, hear.

Leah: I don't know ladies, I'd be a little hesitant about that one. So much could go wrong if a romantic relationship didn't, well, go right. Like her career could be in jeopardy, as well as her reputation.

Tess: Well so could his, if we're going to talk about it. Both parties have a lot at stake.

Leah: Of course, I wasn't trying to say that she was the only one who would be affected by the outcome. I'm just saying that this is her debut season and she's only been signed for a one time contract with Nightingale. Would starting a relationship with the one and only teammate she has had during her time here be worth the potential consequences? What if they remove her from the team and another one doesn't step up to sign her? What if the team as a whole is caught in the backlash of fans who think she's only here because she was seeing the other driver? What if—

Zoe: You could play the 'what if' game until you're blue in the face, but in the end, that's all between Blake and Ryder. I mean, we're talking about a relationship that probably isn't even happening. There has been no indication of it so far, anyway. And I'm sure if the time ever did come then they would let us know. Or not. I don't know, *that* is their private lives and as far as I'm concerned, if it doesn't affect their performance on the track in a negative way, then who cares?

Tess: Hear, hear.

(All three girls laugh)

Leah: I agree with you, and obviously whatever *is* going on seems to be working because they are running the races. I know Blake hasn't placed on the podium yet this season, but it's going to happen soon. I can taste it!

Zoe: The girl is hungry for a place up there, that's for sure.

Tess: You think this is her week?

Leah: Maybe. This one will definitely have more pressure put on her with it being a US race, so I'd understand if it doesn't really go her way.

Zoe: Yeah, I agree. BUT, I think the fact that this one is close to home will drive her to push harder. I think this week, she'll walk away with at least third.

Tess: At least? You think she could contend with Ryder up on first?

Zoe: We've seen that girl do a lot of things no one thought she would be able to do, so I wouldn't put it past her to do that now.

Leah: Hear, hear.

(Zoe and Tess burst out laughing)

CHAPTER 24

BLAKE

"Last lap. Go get him."

"Understood."

I slam on the accelerator, chasing Ryder down the straight and into the series of eight turns. We glide through nine and into the soft curve of ten, the distance closing between us.

As he slows for the tight series of turns ahead, I hold on a second longer and meet him on the outside. He pulls out ahead by inches, blazing down the long straight and I engage DRS, utilizing the zone to meet his higher speeds.

We're side by side through the last three turns and pass under the waving checkered flag with our team lining the fence on one side, and stands of crazed fans on the other.

I blow out a breath and look over as he matches my speed. His visor is up and his eyes shine bright as he points in my direction. Smiling, I mirror him and stick my right arm out. As we approach the first turn I switch and wave towards the stands.

My radio crackles and a second later Nikolai's booming voice echoes through my ear, "P1! That's P1! You just won your first Formula 1 race!"

I'm laughing in disbelief as we pull into the winners area and I'm directed into position. I shut off the engine and stare at the marker with a big number one on it.

This race has haunted me for the last week. Being the only American driver on the circuit is a big deal, but being the only female driver from here is a whole other monster in itself.

I didn't want to disappoint the fans, the team, my family, or my country. I feared I would crumple under all the pressure... but Ryder wouldn't let me.

All week he handed me coffee between sim races at four in the morning. He created a playlist of every Miami race weekend for us to watch and dissect. Before bed every night he would wrap himself around me and we would visualize the track.

He didn't push me when I closed myself away for hours at a time to work through my thoughts. When I was done, I would open the door and there he was, sitting against the doorframe, waiting to help me through it.

He wouldn't let me break. He knew I could do this.

And I did.

Holy shit. I won!

The deafening cheers flood back in and I disengage my

wheel, setting it on the hood, before pulling myself out of the cockpit and standing on my seat.

Lifting my arms above my head, the crew goes wild and I squeal when strong arms pull me over the halo and into a crushing hug.

"That's my girl!" Ryder sets me down and grabs either side of my helmet, leaning in until his bumps against mine. I reach up and grab the side of his and soak in the pride flooding his eyes.

After a couple seconds, he steps back and gestures towards our crazy crew. "Go get 'em."

I smile and take off towards my garage team, jumping into their waiting arms and laughing as they go nuts with slaps on my shoulders and helmet. Prying myself away from their celebrations, I turn and Ryder throws his arm over my shoulders, guiding me to the cool down room. A room I didn't think I'd be seeing this season in third, let alone first.

———

My eyes burn from the happy tears that haven't stopped rolling. My cheeks ache from the smile that won't wipe off my face. My ears ring as the final notes of the US national anthem fade into the British national anthem.

I glance at Ryder from where he stands on the podium for second place. He meets my eyes and his lips tip up in a smirk. My face flames when he winks and I quickly avert my eyes back to the now cheering crowd as the announcer's voice booms over the speakers.

Right now, in front of the entire world, is not the time to be thinking about how he pulled me back into the cool down room as everyone was leaving and kissed me within an inch of my life. He only pulled away after Jace called out for us to 'hurry the fuck up'. With one last peck and a pat on my butt, he sent me through the doorway and guided me towards the stage.

I watch as the presenter hands Jace his third place trophy and then Ryder his for second. The crowd settles down as he steps back into position and a charge fills the air.

My stomach hollows out, my heart rate increases, and my hands start to shake as the announcer calls out my name. The crowd is deafening as I'm handed my trophy and my knuckles turn white with my harsh grip before I lift it above my head.

I laugh through more tears and step back, setting the surprisingly heavy trophy down.

We pick up our oversized champagne bottles and on the cue, corks explode and the guys don't give me a chance to go for cover. In seconds, I'm dosed from three different sides as my squeals fill the air.

By the time the sprays cease, my soaked hair sticks to my face and my suit drains with more champagne than sweat. A deep chuckle sounds from my left and a hand lands on the back of my head before a cloth wipes down my face.

"There," Ryder murmurs and I look up into his shining green eyes. "Beautiful as ever."

Jace bumps into us and throws his arms over our

shoulders, "We are so celebrating tonight. Hey, when's Ca—oomf." Ryder elbows him and scowls.

With raised hands and an apologetic look, Jace backs away.

"What's that about?" I ask as Ryder guides me back to our podiums.

"No clue," he says, bending down and scooping up both of our trophies.

We walk down the stairs and every time I try to take my trophy from him, he twists out of my reach while his eyes run over the crowded area.

Giving up, I huff, "You're acting suspicious."

"Don't know what you're talking about. Gatorade?" He lifts a bottle in offering and I take it with squinted eyes.

"Good at deflection, you are not. I can sense you're up to something."

"Okay Yoda," he laughs, glancing around.

"Something's going on."

"Nothing is—okay, brace."

"Wha—ah!"

Ryder catches me and the person who has suddenly latched themselves onto my back before we can go down. "My best friend is a straight up badass," an all too familiar voice screeches in my ear.

"Cassie?" I cry and spin around when she releases me. She smiles big and her eyes flick over my shoulder when I feel a warm body at my back.

"Happy birthday, love," Ryder whispers in my ear.

———

"I can't believe you're here," I lean my head on Cassie's shoulder in the middle row of the SUV as Nikolai drives our rowdy group to the night's choice in club.

Yep Mr. All-Business-No-Fun is going out to a club. When I told Cassie he wouldn't she strutted her fiery butt out the door, telling me to 'watch this' and that she'd meet us by the car.

I wished her luck, knowing there was no way she'd get him to come out when we've been trying all season. But I forgot how much she loves to prove me wrong because the next thing I knew, she walked out of the gate with him trailing behind her.

"Daddy's coming out to play," she cheered victoriously.

"For the love of—don't ever call me that again," he grumbled. She winked, passed by our slack jawed group, and climbed into the waiting SUV.

So now I'm about to party with my boss on me and Cassie's birthday.

"I couldn't miss celebrating our 21st," she laughs, "But I couldn't have pulled it off without your man up there." She nods towards Ryder in the passenger seat, "He's a keeper, that one."

"Yeah," I watch him talk with Nikolai in the rearview, "he really is."

Ten minutes later, our group of seven crowds into the front door of a club in South Beach. The two party animals,

Jace and Cassie, lead the charge into the packed area filled with writhing bodies and pulsing music.

The guys peel off to the bar while us ladies hunt down a table. When we spot one in the back, Cassie and Sydney all but sprint to claim it before anyone else.

"I think it's so cool you two share a birthday," Sydney calls out as we slide into the booth.

"Our friendship was meant to be." Cassie smiles, turning to me, "Does she know?"

"Do I know what?"

"About Blake and Ry—ow! I'll take that as a no!" She rubs where I pinched her and scowls at my wide eyes, but a hysterical laugh draws our attention to the blond across from us.

"Oh, I've known for weeks," Sydney waves a hand, "Those two suck at hiding their feelings, especially Ms. Blush-Every-Sing-Time-Ryder-Looks-At-Her. We've all known, even Nikolai."

"What do I know?" he asks as he places a drink in front of Cassie. We shift so the guys can slide into our large round booth, and us girls wind up closed in on either side.

"About your two love birds," Sydney waggles a finger between me and Ryder who sits on the outside edge of the table. He chokes on his drink and Lawson pats him on the back.

"Nothing goes on with my team that I don't know about," Nikolai cocks an eyebrow, taking a sip of his beer. "Plus, I saw it that first day at her tryouts. Boy didn't stand a chance."

I stare at my team principal in shock but his steady eyes

linger on Ryder. A silent conversation passes between them before his eyes slide to mine. "As long as it doesn't interfere with your driving I don't care what goes on. Especially if you two replicate what went on out there today."

"Yes!" Jace booms. "To Blake on her first win of the season!"

Everyone cheers and glasses clink before we each take a sip of our drinks. Ryder watches me over the rim of his and winks when he catches me looking.

The conversation flows from there and three drinks later, Cassie is dragging me and Sydney out of the booth, leaving the boys behind as we weave through the sea of gyrating bodies.

Music vibrates through the floor and into my bones, as I get lost in the beat. Sydney and Cassie sandwich me as we dance, laugh, and sing off key to every song.

Every once in a while we have to fight off wandering hands and unwanted attention, but when a body collides with Cassie, almost taking the three of us out, she turns around ready to give him a piece of her mind.

I can't hear what she says over the pulsing music, but I watch the guy lean into her space and reach around to grab her ass. She slaps the guy and he turns back to her with fury in his eyes.

His mouth moves at lightning speed and my stomach drops along with her shoulders. Her entire body curls in on itself, like she's trying to cover up anything she can.

My eyebrows furrow and I take a step in their direction, but a large hand gently pushes me to the side. Nikolai strides up behind her and glares down at the stocky man yelling in her face.

When he notices Nikolai, his eyes slowly slide up and widen in panic. A second later the man and his buddies scramble to get away, pushing through the crowded floor.

Nikolai walks around her and bends so they're eye to eye. He brushes hair out of her face and I see his mouth move. Her head shakes, nods, and shakes again before his jaw clenches.

In the next breath, he bends and picks her up bridal style, carrying her through the parting crowd and out towards the exit.

The guys meet up with us and we follow them out of the club and into the humid night air. Nikolai stands off to the side from the flow of people walking on the sidewalk with my best friend's face buried in his chest.

I step up next to them and tuck a piece of her wild fiery hair behind her ear. "Cassie?"

"I'm okay, Blake. That guy was just an asshole." She wipes away a tear and my heart clenches. No one should cry on their birthday.

I look up at Nikolai but his hard eyes are on the girl in his arms. Ryder steps up next to me and takes my arm, pulling me to the side. "What happened?"

"I don't know, we were just dancing and then that guy bumped into us and—I don't know." My eyes slide to his. "I need to make this better."

"What can I do?"

"I don't know," I mumble, worrying my bottom lip and

racking my brain for a way to try to salvage tonight as I glance around the busy street.

A sign across the way catches my eye and a smile spreads across my lips as nerves settle into my stomach for what I'm about to put myself through.

I nudge Cassie's arm. "Use your dare."

"What?"

"You still have that dare from the night before I left, remember?"

"Yeah, so?"

"What's the one thing you've been wanting to get with me since we turned eighteen, but I've been too much of a chicken shit to do it?"

She looks at me in confusion, but a second later her eyes light with understanding and her frown turns upside down. *Yes!*

"You wouldn't," she laughs.

"You know I take dares seriously."

"Really?"

"It's two birds, one stone. I get to zero out your dare balance and I'll pay for it as my birthday gift to you since you aren't home to open the one I already sent."

She throws her arms around my shoulders and I hug her tight. "I dare you," she whispers into my hair and I chuckle.

Hand in hand we walk across the street with our confused group trailing behind us. We stop in front of the neon sign and Cassie flashes me a smile.

"I'm down," Lawson walks over to the door and holds it open.

"Why not," Jace laughs.

"I've always wanted one," Sydney shrugs and follows her brother and his friend inside.

"You sure?" Ryder asks, wrapping an arm around me.

"Nope, but anything for Cassie," I wink at her and she squeals before grabbing Nikolai's hand and dragging him into the shop.

Ryder chuckles and walks over to the door, holding it open for me.

"Does it hurt?" I ask him.

"Don't worry, I'll hold your hand."

"That's not as comforting as you think it is right now," I mumble as he laughs and pulls me into the tattoo shop.

CHAPTER 25
RYDER

ARMS WRAP around my waist and hands smooth over my bare chest. "Morning handsome," Blake murmurs into my skin before placing a kiss between my shoulder blades as her fingers brush against the crown tattoo on the left side of my ribs.

When we walked into that tattoo shop two weeks ago, the nerves were rolling off of her. She was going to go through with it for Cassie's sake, but I didn't want her to suffer alone.

I talked one of the artists into moving their setups so I could be right next to her. We got ours at the same time. I laid on my back while she laid on her stomach, our hands clasped between us as the two artists worked.

"This healed up really nicely," she moves around to study it.

"Yeah. Line work tattoos tend to heal a lot faster than fully colored ones." I run my thumb over the sun at the top of her spine. "Still like it?"

"I love it," she smiles, looking over her shoulder at her reflection in the mirror before meeting my eyes. "Still think it's sexy?"

"I think everything about you is sexy." I wrap my arms around her and nuzzle into her neck. "When's Sydney supposed to come pick you up?"

"In about half an hour, which means..." she trails off and reaches for a container I've come to know all too well.

"Blake," I sigh.

"Please," she begs.

"I'm supposed to meet the guys down at the docks in forty minutes."

"It has aloe in it. That's good for sun kissed skin," she points to the ingredients list.

"Then I'll let you slather it on me when I get back."

"I'll make it worth your wild." She waggles her eyebrows.

I cock an eyebrow and grab her hips. She squeals as I place her on the bathroom counter and cage her in with my hands on either side of her.

"Do your worst," I concede.

She smiles and unscrews the top, scooping some of the green paste before placing the container to the side. Facing me, she kisses my nose and lips before smoothing the cool goo over my face, avoiding my stubble.

She leans back and marvels at her work before picking up the container and holding it out for me. I dip my fingers in and take out a small amount. Mimicking her, I kiss the tip of her button nose and lips before smoothing out a layer of the mask across her skin.

She closes her eyes and leans into my touch. "Don't go past my cheeks, please."

Humming in agreement, I continue to work until the entire top half of her face is covered.

She closes the container and sets it aside before leaning in and brushing her lips along the underside of my jaw. I tip my head back as her lips trail down my neck and over my chest.

"Blake," I sigh as my skin heats at her touch, my cock hardening in my boxer briefs.

Her hands run up my abs and she gently pushes at my chest. I step back as she slides off the counter and takes my hand before leading me to the bedroom. She stops in front of the large floor mirror and faces me.

Leaning up on her tiptoes, she laces her fingers through the hair at the back of my head and pulls me down, taking my mouth with hers in a slow kiss. Her tongue meets mine and we moan at the contact.

She pulls away and kisses her way down my neck and chest. Looking up at me, she slides her thumbs into the waistband of my underwear and pulls them over my hips. My hard cock bobs free, already leaking with precum.

My lips part on heated breaths as she slowly lowers to her knees in front of me. She helps me step out of my underwear and tosses them to the side. I hiss as she runs her hands up my thighs, her nails digging in hard enough to leave marks. Her eyes are locked on my cock and her tongue peaks out to wet her lips.

"Look at me," I demand and her eyes immediately flash

up to mine. I groan at the hunger I find there as she leans forward and licks the bead of precum.

"Fuck." I wrap her hair around my hand and tug so her face is angled up more. I push my hips forward and run the head across her lips. "Open," I growl.

"Good girl," I hum when she opens and a moan rumbles in my chest when she closes her mouth around my shaft. My head drops back as she bobs on my cock and I hiss when her teeth lightly scrape against the underside of me.

I open my eyes and start to look down at her, but my eyes catch on the reflection in the mirror. It's a perfect view of her sun tattoo, her muscles flexing with her movements.

I groan and thrust my hips forward, making her gag. "You are something else," I moan as I flick my eyes down to her.

Her eyes are already locked on my face and a triumphant gleam reflects in their blue depths. I feel her hands slide around my thighs and over the curve of my ass before she pulls me farther into her mouth.

"Fuck, yes," I hiss. "Think you can take me deeper?"

She moans around me and pulls back, slipping a hand off my ass and wrapping it around my shaft. She pumps me as her tongue swirls around the head.

With her eyes locked on mine and she slowly slides down, taking me farther and farther into her mouth. She gags when I hit her reflex, but her hand slips back over my ass and squeezes.

Taking the cue I place a hand on either side of her head and slowly thrust into her mouth. "Breathe through your nose, that's it. Look at you on your knees for your King, taking his cock down your throat like the good fucking girl you are. You love choking on my cock, huh?"

She moans and my balls tighten at the vibration. I push farther and her hands tighten on my skin, eyes closing in concentration. I ease all the way out of her mouth and she heaves a breath while I catch my own.

She licks her lips before running her tongue from root to tip and taking me in deep. A guttural moan leaves me when her hand slips between my legs to cup my balls.

"Fuck, love," my chest heaves.

Peeking up at me through tear soaked lashes, she slides off my cock, "Use me."

"You want me to fuck your face?"

She nods, "Please."

Blake slips me back into her mouth and places her hands on my sides. I wrap her hair tighter in my fist and pull her head farther down my hard as steel cock. I give a few tentative thrusts before her hands slip to my backside and her nails dig into my cheeks.

"Fuck," I yell and slam my hips forward to avoid the sting.

She moans around me and her eyes fill with lust. On a growl I begin thrusting faster, harder, until I'm doing exactly what she begged for.

I use her.

"Touch yourself," I breathe. "I don't come until you do."

Her right hand leaves me and I watch in the mirror as her fingers slip under the fabric of her thong. Her hips move and she moans around my shaft.

"That's it. Ride your hand while I fuck this pretty mouth of yours."

She whimpers as I thrust and the room fills with her muffled moans and my panting. "Are you close?" I ask through clenched teeth and she nods.

I thrust once, twice, three times before her body wracks with her release. The vibrations of her moans send me over and I come on a roar, unloading everything I have to give down her throat. She swallows down every drop.

I pull out of her mouth and wince at the sensitivity. She licks her lips and smiles up at me. I release her hair and cup her jaw. "You're going to be the death of me."

She giggles and I help her to her feet before we head into the bathroom to clean up. I'm about to wipe off the mask when a shrill ring causes her to jump.

I chuckle when she huffs and picks up my phone from the nightstand. "It's Jace. I'm going to change and head down, Sydney texted that she's ready."

"Okay, I'll see you later. Have fun." I bend and give her a kiss, watching as she prances out of the room. I lift my phone and swipe to answer the FaceTime call, only it's not Jace's face that greets me.

"Uncle Ryder!"

"Becks!" I double check that nothing above a G-rating is visible. "I thought you were with your mum this weekend?"

There's a noise in the background and Beckham brings the phone to his chest.

"Dude, who are you talking to?"

"Uncle Ryder."

Beckham uncovers the camera and Jace shoves his head into frame alongside his sons. He blinks and bursts out laughing, "Hey Shrek, where's Fiona?"

"What the hell are—" I glimpse at my reflection and groan, "Blake!" Her light laughter floats from the bedroom and I walk out to her waving bye on her way out the door.

"Oh! Woah, innocent eyes over here!" Jace calls out.

I look at the screen and the little box showing my face also shows the reflection of my bare ass in the floor length mirror behind me. I grumble out a curse and snatch my underwear off the ground before shoving my legs through them.

"Sorry," I mumble. "What's with the surprise visit from my favorite Collins? I thought Angie had Beckham this weekend?"

Jace sighs, "I need a beer for this one. Scratch that, I need a shite ton of Bailey's in a coffee the size of my head."

Thirty minutes later, Jace is guzzling down his extra large coffee with two servings of Bailey's as we lounge on the deck of our shared yacht. Lawson sits next to him, sipping on water while Beckham eats his treat I picked up for him at the table behind us.

Jace finishes off his cup and lowers his voice, "That bitch called me at three this morning asking where I was at. I was like, 'where the hell do you think I am'. Then she went off on me having an attitude and I was about to hang up on her when there was a knock on my door."

He sighs and rubs his eyes, "I open the door—mind you

it's three in the morning—to see my six year old son standing there, barely able to keep his eyes open. Alone."

My face twists. "What?"

"Yeah," he scoffs. "She gave me some fucking excuse that she has a last minute modeling job and won't be around for the next three weeks or longer."

"Remind me again how the hell she has joint custody?"

"I don't know man. I really don't know," he laughs but it's weighed heavily by exhaustion.

"I just thought with everything that happened, she would have wanted to be around him more, but it's like it did the opposite. I'm really trying here to be everything he needs but sometimes I feel like it's still not enough."

I lean forward. "You are an amazing father, Jace. That little boy is incredibly lucky to have you. But if you feel like you're struggling, lean on us. If you need anything Jace, and I mean anything, I'm here."

"Me too," Lawson nods. "I know you have that support group you can vent to but you have us too. We love that kid like he's our own."

"Support group?"

Jace nods. "It's something the doctors recommended. It's helped a lot and the people in it are actually really great."

My chest tightens and shame washes over me that I wasn't there for him when he seemed to need it most. Jace catches my eye and shakes his head slightly as if reading my thoughts, telling me I have nothing to be sorry for. It won't stop me from doing everything I can to make all of this up to him, to them.

"He even has a little thing going on with one of the mums." Lawson sips on his water with a smug grin, breaking me out of my thoughts.

"Oh really," I drawl.

Jace scowls at Law and mumbles, "I don't have a *thing* with her. Her son is Beckham's age and we were both new to the group. I thought it wouldn't be as daunting if we had each other to talk to outside of it all."

"Isn't that chivalrous of you," Lawson chuckles.

Jace shrugs and picks at his beer label, "It's nothing. I don't even know her name."

"You've been talking with this girl for over a year and don't know her name?"

"It's all anonymous and that's what sold me on signing up for the group in the end, honestly. When I'm talking to her or the others, I'm not world champion Jace Collins." He looks over to where Beckham plays. "I can just be a father learning how to navigate this new reality for his son."

I nod. "That's good. I'm glad you have that."

"Me too." Jace blows a raspberry and claps his hands. "Okay! Time to talk about less depressing shite. What are the girls up to today?"

"Sydney wanted to take Blake shopping for a 'proper' dress for the gala coming up."

Jace shivers. "Godspeed to her. I went shopping with Syd once and I'll never do it again."

"It's not that bad," Lawson drawls.

"She stopped in every store in that shopping mall. Every. Store. Even the ones that had absolutely nothing for her!

Watch, I bet Blake comes home with more than just a dress. I bet there will be at least five bags."

"I don't think so. She isn't that big on shopping."

"Sydney is very convincing."

Lawson points, "I have ten pairs of the same shirt all because Syd convinced me I needed every pair because 'what if they stop making it'."

"Beckham has a closet full of clothes he won't be able to wear until he's in high school. When I asked why she got them she told me it's because she thought they were cute and wanted to make sure he had them in case they weren't around by the time he was big enough. I seriously don't think I'll have to buy him clothes for the next twelve years."

I chuckle. "Blake wears the same ratty old t-shirt every morning and my luggage is bigger than hers. I'm telling you, she won't be swayed."

Jace smirks as I talk about my girl and shakes his head. "What?"

"You better not mess that up man."

"I'm trying my damndest not to."

"She's good for you. I mean, if you would have asked me before the beginning of this season if we would be sitting here right now and I would have one of my best friends back? I honestly don't know what I would have said."

"She's definitely changed things."

"For the better," Lawson muses.

"It's just good to see this side of you again, Ryder. You had me worried there for a while. I was honestly one more unreplied text or phone call away from breaking down your front door," Jace chuckles.

I sigh and lean forward, resting my arms on my knees. "I really am sorry. I just wasn't... here. I wasn't present and I didn't want that to bleed into your lives. I didn't want my problems to become yours."

"You're like a brother to us, we'll always be there for you. Just like you offered for me and Beckham, it's the same for you. Whatever you need, we're here."

"I know," I sigh.

"Good. No more disappearing. No more ignoring or shutting us out. No more or else I reserve the right to come over there and beat your arse."

"Deal."

We chuckle as Beckham comes racing over. "Who's ready to lose the cannonball contest?" We look around at each other before I swoop down and throw him over my shoulder, sprinting to the end of the deck.

Feet pound on the wood behind me as booming laughter and screeches fill the air. It's by far one of the best days I've had in a really long time.

Later on, I come home to Blake and her two shopping bags full of ripped jeans and band t-shirts. After a shower, I take her slowly and lay with her head on my chest. I think about how no matter what each day brings, it will be worth going through as long as she's right here at the end of them.

POST-RACE CONFERENCE TRANSCRIPT
UNITED KINGDOM GRAND PRIX

DRIVER GROUP 1 — Jace COLLINS, Blake STONE, Jean BEAUMONT

Q: Jean I'd like to start with you. It's been a difficult season so far for you and Onyx.

Jean BEAUMONT: Oui. There have been some electronic issues with the car, but my engineers have addressed those issues and we will see if it holds up to perform at the race this weekend.

Q: Two years ago, this was the race in which an altercation went on between you and Ryder King, who was your teammate at the time. The actions on that day are what put him out for the rest of that season and the following one. It's never been made clear what went on that day. Do you have anything to say about that and is there still tension between you and him for this upcoming race?

JB: I don't really have anything to say about that time, no.

Q: Do you have any reservations about this upcoming weekend and how it will go?

JB: I think it is a high pressure weekend with it being more than half the drivers home race. There will be a lot of competition, but I've trained and the team seems confident in the car. I think it will be a good day for me.

Q: Thank you, good luck this weekend. Jace, you're one of those drivers Jean spoke of with this being your home race. How are you feeling?

Jace COLLINS: I'm feeling good, great even. The nerves always run high when it's a home crowd, but we've had a good season so far. The team made some upgrades to the front wing for this weekend so we are honing in on those small changes to increase the capabilities of the car. All good things.

Q: You have a bit of history here as well.

JC: I do. I grew up not too far from here. I also got my racing license on this track. A lot of my karting years were spent here, including my first ever crash. And now Miller racing is based out of here. You could say I've grown up on this track.

Q: Does it feel good to be home?

JC: Absolutely. This is honestly one of my favorite tracks. More fluidity in the turns and room to really let loose. It's always a fun one.

Q: Plus, you get to sleep in your own bed.

JC: *(laughs)* Yes, there's that too.

Q: Well welcome home and good luck to you. Blake, let's finish up with you. You have yet to place back on podium since your shocking win in Miami. Do you think you'll be able to change that trend for this weekend's prix?

Blake STONE: Wow, going right for the jugular I see. I'd like to think it'll change this weekend. I mean, the goal is always to hit podium, but sometimes there are things out of our control preventing that. I'm not saying that I could also be performing better because I one hundred percent can, I'm just saying that no one experiences what we do out there and none of us experience it the same way another driver does. I'm doing my best and giving each race my all, but I'm also going up against some of the best drivers in history who have many more hours on these tracks than I do. It's tough competition out there, but my mama always said that nothing worth having is easy.

Q: How are you feeling going into this weekend? Just what can we expect from you and Nightingale here?

BS: I think as a team we are pretty confident. The goal is always to do the best and possibly hit podium, and we've taken the necessary steps to lead us in that direction. So we will have to see.

Q: You think we will be seeing you on the podiums this weekend?

BS: I'm going to do my best.

Q: Could you walk us through a little bit of how you prepare for these tracks and races as someone who hasn't been to each before?

BS: A lot of studying. Of the track and of old races. I practically memorize each. I'm also fortunate enough to have a very helpful team and teammate who work with me on, pardon the pun, getting up to speed.

Q: And how is your teammate going into this weekend? This is more than just his home race for him with the twentieth anniversary of his father's accident and the two year anniversary of his accident with Jean. Is there any worry amongst the team with his performance?

BS: No comment.

CHAPTER 26

RYDER

"THERE'S MY LITTLE RACE CAR," *Da growls as he scoops me up when I speed into the garage. I squeal as Mum laughs, entering the area at a much more reasonable pace.*

Placing me back on my feet, Da squats down with his hands on my shoulders. "You been a good boy for your mum?" *I nod before peaking over my shoulder to see her smiling.*

She walks over and fixes my hat. "That he has."

Da hums and shares a look with Mum before smirking, "Well then. What do you say to standing out there with me for the opening ceremony?"

"Really?"

"Really really."

"Best. Day. Ever!" *I yell as my parents laugh.*

An hour later, Da's hands rest heavy on my shoulders, squeezing every now and then as the British national anthem plays. When the opening ceremonies are over, he slips his team hat on my head and kneels.

"I've got to go now. You be good for Mum, okay? Don't leave the garage."

He pulls me in for a tight hug and a kiss on my head, "I love you, my boy."

"I love you too." He stands to his towering height and leans over, hugging and kissing Mum one last time before he strides off towards his car.

Less than an hour later, the best day ever turns out to be one of the worst as I watch a driver collide with Da. He's sent flying through the air, flipping and crashing into the fence lining the track. A scream pierces the air as we watch his car break in two and go up in flames.

———

"Ryder, please," a frantic voice calls out as hands shake me and I bolt upright, sending Blake scrambling back to avoid being headbutted.

My chest heaves and I splay a hand over the rings on my chest. She follows the movement and scoots closer, placing hers and over mine.

"It was just a dream." My throat burns and my eyebrows furrow when her eyes dip to our hands on my chest, tears building in her tired blues. "What is it?"

She shakes her head and blinks up at me. "You were screaming... for your dad."

My heart stalls. I glance at the clock and see that it's the middle of the night and sigh. I shift back to lean against the headboard and pull her into me. "I'm sorry."

"No. Don't you dare apologize to me. I'm the one who's sorry." Her fingers slide through the two rings on my chain. "I'm sorry you've lost so much."

My arms tighten around her and I drop my chin to the top of her head, watching her fiddle with the metals. "Those are their wedding rings," I murmur into her hair.

I slide the larger one off her thumb, rolling it between my fingers, "Da would always give his to Mum before he left for a race and she would wear it on a chain around her neck, keeping a part of him close to her heart while he was gone. She didn't take it off after he died, saying it felt like he was there with her."

She runs the tips of her fingers over the smaller silver band with inset diamonds, "Now you keep them both close to your heart."

"And I swear sometimes I can feel them, especially around this time of year."

She hums and smooths her hand over my chest, over my heart. "They are. Here, I mean. They'll always be here."

I squeeze her against me and bury my face in her hair, breathing in her calming honey vanilla scent. She's been the only thing keeping me from falling completely victim to the monsters plaguing my mind this week.

Hell, she's been doing it since she walked into my life five months ago, taking down my defenses one stone at a time, and setting them back up with her locked inside my soul.

When I pull away, she follows to make sure I'm okay. When I shut down, she powers on a movie and sits with me until I'm ready to talk. When I question if any of this is worth it, she gives me a reason to get up every morning.

She's everything I never thought I needed. She's more than I'll ever feel I deserve.

I brush my lips across her forehead. "Thank you."

"For what?"

"For everything."

"You deserve everything and more." I feel her body sag against me as her words drift into a yawn. I shuffle us down the bed until I'm lying on my back with her draped over me.

"Get some more sleep, love." She hums and tucks her face into the side of my neck, pressing a soft kiss to my heated skin.

Her breathing evens out and I slide my hand over hers, my parents' rings warming under her palm. I stare at the ceiling and cling to the woman who has single handedly changed everything for me this season.

A few hours later, I slip myself out from under her sleeping form and put on some joggers before heading downstairs. With a steaming cup of coffee, I stand at the back door and watch the sunrise over the rolling hills of my family's property.

The light hits the window just right and I get a flash of my fathers reflection, only instead of blue eyes, green ones look back at me. I blink and clench my jaw as I stare at the face that looks so much like him.

I'm a inch or two taller than he was, but our builds are identical. I have his dark, almost black, hair. His ears. His eyebrows. His jaw. I even have the same crook in my nose.

I look exactly like he did the day he died.

I'm the same age he was when he died.

And I'm about to race the same circuit where he died.

I love you, my boy. I blow out a shaky breath and brace a hand on the glass sliding door, bowing my head as the last thing my da said to me echoes through my healing mind. I suck in a breath when arms band around my middle and Blake lays her head on my back.

She doesn't say anything. She just holds me, taking everything I'm able to give her. I turn in her arms and pull her into my chest. She leans her head back and kisses the rings hanging there before looking up at me.

"I'm here for you. Whatever you need today, consider it already yours."

My jaw ticks and I lean down, sealing my mouth over hers. She stands on her toes, looping her arms around my shoulders and her nails scratch along the backside of my head.

As I hold her, the pain in my chest dissipates. The shadows tickling the corners of my mind recede. Air floods into my lungs and I take the first bearable breath I have had all week.

Pulling back I lean my forehead against hers and smooth my thumbs over her cheeks. "All I need is right here."

She smiles and pushes her soft lips against mine in a tender kiss. "We should probably head out soon," she whispers against my lips and I nod.

"Hey." She runs her finger over my scarred eyebrow

261

before placing her hand over the rings and my heart. "We do this together," she whispers.

"We do this together," I murmur.

Blake holds my hand the entire drive to the track and glues herself to my side as we walk through the back gates. My hands clench as we approach what Lawson calls the pit.

These are the reporters unaffiliated with the industry. They're gossip magazines, local news outlets, and bloggers. Since they aren't allowed beyond a certain point, they tend to congregate where they know the drivers have to walk by, waiting for their target of choice.

Today, that target is me.

"Ryder! How are you feeling today?"

"Have you seen Jean yet this morning?"

"Do you feel confident about today?"

"Any thoughts on the ceremony honoring your late father?"

Blake nudges my arm, pressing us forward and we pass the small crowd without a backwards glance. We keep our heads down and no one else tries to talk to us on our way towards the Nightingale pit house.

The team meeting passes with quick glances in my direction as we go over the plan for the race. Blake squeezes my hand under the table when the head of PR discusses the ten minute ceremony where a replica of my father's helmet will be presented as this year's trophy.

As everyone leaves, Nikolai lingers and I meet his dark gaze.

"I'm good."

"Ki—"

"You're not keeping me from racing today."

He watches me closely before nodding and standing, "This track has taken enough from too many people on this team. If it becomes too much, just say the word and we'll pull you out. The points don't matter today."

"Morozov," I call when he reaches the door. "The same goes for you."

I see the haunted look flicker across his face before he's gone.

We watch the empty doorway and I shake my head, "With the anniversary of my father and the ceremony honoring him, everyone's seemed to have forgotten that I'm not the only one here who lost something that day."

She squeezes my hand and I meet her comforting eyes. "Then we have a lot of people to go win this one for, don't we?"

"Yeah, we do."

I give myself over to the fog and fall into the routine of getting ready for the race, slipping on my gear, running through the track in my mind, and listening to her through the thin wall dividing our room as she hums to her pre-race playlist.

Movements blur as I stride through the garage and slip into my car. We go through the set up lap and climb back out of our cars, preparing for the extended opening ceremony.

I stand separate from the other drivers as they present my fathers helmet. I shake hands and nod in thanks to words of luck and condolences twenty years too late.

I'm securing the last strap of my five point system when a thought drifts through the cracks. My eyes shoot to my mirrors and my stomach drops. *Blake.*

My hands fumble with the clasp as I try to disengage the lock when a shadow falls over me. I look up into blue eyes and freeze. Blake reaches through the halo and tugs on my shoulder straps before smoothing her gloved covered hand over the middle of my chest.

Her eyes flicker between mine and I reach up, squeezing her hand. She nods and stands, giving me one last comforting look before heading off towards her car in the P5 spot, taking all the loud thoughts right along with her.

Tyson talks in my ear as we move through the formation lap and with every turn, I feel my muscles loosen as my mind clears. The lights begin their sequence above us and I flex my hands on the wheel. Closing my eyes, I let the memories wash over me one last time.

One. Sitting on Da's lap as he teaches me to drive my first kart.

Two. Watching Da twirl Mum around the living room.

Three. His laugh as I run around the garage in his team helmet.

Four. The last time I heard either of them say 'I love you, my boy'.

Five. This one's for them.

Holding my breath, I open my eyes and slam on the gas. I don't breathe through the fifty two laps or the congratulatory interviews or the presenting of Blake's third place trophy and Jace's second. I don't breathe until I'm looking down at my reflection in the visor of my fathers helmet. His signature sprawled across the paint.

I look over and Blake watches me with tears in her eyes, a warm smile on her beautiful face. "For them," she mouths before turning and waving to the crowd.

But I don't take my eyes off of her. Not as the champagne sprays or the cameras flash from our team pictures at the garage. I don't take my eyes off of her as we walk hand in hand to our rooms in the pit house or when I pull her into mine, locking the door behind us.

I don't look away as I set down the helmet and take her trophy from her to do the same before stepping into her space and framing her face with shaky hands.

"I love you."

She freezes, "What?"

I swipe my thumbs against her cheeks, "I didn't think I'd be able to make it through today, Blake. There was a time I didn't think I wanted to. But I did it because of you."

Tears spring to her eyes and her hands wrap around my wrists.

"For so long, I didn't think I would ever feel alive again, let alone be happy. I accepted that maybe I was destined to be alone. That maybe all I was put on this earth to do was drive and I was okay with that reality. Made peace with it. Built my life around it."

She shakes her head and I lean my forehead against hers.

"Then you came in and for the first time in two years, the air felt a little easier to breathe. The weight on my shoulders didn't feel as heavy to bear. The torments of my mind ceased.

My heart jolted from the cold, dead, useless muscle it's become and threatened to beat out of my chest."

I brush my lips against hers and she sucks in a shaky breath. "You brought me back to life with your soft smiles, melodic laughs, and bright eyes. You make the hard days worth it and the easy ones feel like a dream. You've made me a better driver, a better friend, a better man."

I pull back and my eyes shift between hers. "You make me want to be worthy of you because you deserve everything. And I promise I'm going to spend every day for as long as you'll have me, trying to give you all that you deserve. To give you all of me. Because I love you and I won't ever stop trying to show you just how much."

She laughs on a cry and sniffs, bringing her hands to cup my jaw. "I love you too. I've loved you longer than I probably even know." She goes up on her toes as I lean down to fuse our mouths together in a desperate kiss.

Pulling back, her hands smooth over my face and her eyes dance between mine.

"Say it again," I whisper and she smiles.

"I love you, Ryder King."

And just like that, the day that has tormented me for years doesn't feel as harrowing.

CHAPTER 27

RYDER

My heart threatens to beat out of my chest, my palms are slick with sweat, and I think I've worn a path into the hotel suite's marble floor.

"Bruv, you're making me dizzy," Jace groans from the couch and I send him a glare. Beckham lounges back against his chest, playing some game on his da's phone. Lawson leans against the counter in the small kitchenette and looks to be testing his x-ray vision on the closed door across the hall.

"He's nervous," the big brute drawls without looking away.

Jace scoffs, "Why the hell are you nervous? It's not like it's your wedding day."

I turn towards the large floor to ceiling windows, giving them my back, so that he can't see the lack of fear his joke would strike in any other bloke.

Because the thing is, the idea of marrying Blake doesn't scare me.

When I woke up this morning and looked over at her, I knew there was no other view I'd want to wake up to for the rest of my life. With her, I feel safe. I feel loved, needed, and wanted. I don't feel like I have something to prove or like I have to work to keep her.

She's my best friend. My teammate. My inspiration. My driving force. She's the love of my life and one day I am going to marry her, but like Jace said... today is not that day.

A cadence of laughter brings me out of my thoughts and I turn back to the room. Jace stands up and puts Beckham down. "I'm bringing out the big guns, boys. It's time to send in the kid."

Lawson pushes off the counter, "Are you insane? Syd threatened to confiscate my nuts via dulled scissors if I knocked one more time."

"That was you. This is Becks. She loves him, shares blood with him... And he's cute, so he should be safe." With a pat on the butt, Jace sends his little man off.

Beckham timidly knocks on the door and looks over his shoulder at the three grown men too scared to do it themselves with hesitant eyes. The door flies open and Sydney's head pops out with a scowl.

"Hold your freaking—" her eyes drop to her nephew and the scowl vanishes underneath a beaming smile, "Spud!"

Walking out into the living area with his hand in hers, Beckham sighs, "Wow. Aunty, you look like a princess."

Sydney bends and kisses his cheek. "And you look like a prince."

Straightening, her eyes trail over Lawson. "Black on black on black. How on brand."

"You look good too, sunshine," he smirks.

"I know," she winks and walks over to me and Jace. He kisses his sister's cheek and she looks over at me with a smile, "Ready for your Juliet, Romeo?"

I nod, not trusting my words to be steady as my nerves rack up to an all time high as she calls out for Blake. When she doesn't appear, Sydney laughs nervously and walks back into the room. Whispered words float through the open doorway before there's a thud.

"Alright! I'm going! Stop pushing me or I'm going to fall on my face in these damn heels," Blake calls over her shoulder as she walks out.

My breath stalls and everything fades until there's only her. When she turns her head and our eyes catch, a brilliant smile spreads across her gloss lined lips. Her hair is styled with one side pinned back and soft waves cascading over her shoulders.

Her dress is a deep emerald green with straps hanging loosely over her arms from the modest neckline, exposing her collarbones. The fabric hugs her, flaring at the hips in a waterfall of silk.

As she walks, her leg peeks through a slit and the moment she's within reach, I'm wrapping my arms around her. Laughing, she stumbles into my chest and wraps her arms around my shoulders. "Hi."

"Love, you look," I huff and shake my head, "You look transcendent."

She meets me halfway in a gentle kiss and hums against my lips, leaning farther into my chest. Pulling away, she wipes her gloss from my mouth and looks up at me with glimmering eyes. "You are perfect. As always."

A throat clears to our right and we look over then down at the little man by our sides. "You look very pretty, Ms. Blake," Beckham blushes.

She giggles and crouches down. "And you look very handsome." She kisses his cheeks and his eyes go wide before he smiles and slowly walks backwards into his father's legs.

"The car's here," Lawson calls out, walking towards the front door with Sydney on his arm. Exiting the room, we load into an elevator and descend to the lobby floor. Blake and I take up the rear as our little group walks out into the warm Belgian summer evening air.

"So cool," Blake whispers, ducking into the open door of our limousine.

I slide in behind her, followed by Beckham, Sydney, Lawson, and finally Jace. "I feel fancy," he sings and we laugh as the driver pulls away.

I don't release Blake's hand the entire twenty minute drive to the museum and notice as we get closer, her fingers tighten slightly around mine. Leaning over, I kiss her cheek and brush my lips against her ear, "Nervous?"

"Slightly," she sighs.

I pull away and my eyes flick between hers. "I can't wait to tell the world you're mine."

She laughs on a shaky breath and leans over to kiss me softly. "I love you," she says against my lips.

"I love you too."

The car pulls up to the curb and Jace swings open the door, climbing out. One at a time, our friends exit until it's just me and my girl.

"Ready?"

She looks from the open car door to me and smiles. "More than."

Sliding out, I hold her hand in mine as she stands and guide her to the start of the paparazzi lined red carpet. Jace, Beckham, Sydney, and Lawson are already halfway down the line, posing and waving to the cameras.

With my hand on Blake's low back, I guide us forward to the first marked spot for pictures. Turning, I wrap my arm around her and she steps into my chest as we face the flashing cameras.

"Ryder! Is Blake your date tonight?"

"Blake! Are you with him?"

"What does your team think about you two together?"

"Are the rumors true?"

"Are you two together?"

"Is this a flavor of the season or something more?"

As questions fly through the air, she tenses next to me and curls her hand into the back of my shirt under my jacket. I turn to her and lift a hand, tilting her face to mine.

"Hey," I whisper.

"And here I thought the press lines at races were nuts," she laughs.

"I'm right here. I've got you."

Her eyes flicker between mine and she whispers, "You always do."

I bend down and take her mouth in mine, silencing the nerves. There's a beat of shock before cheers ring out and cameras flash. She smiles against my lips and I shake my head, leaning in to taste her again. Her hand slides up my back and she steps farther into me.

A whistle breaks us apart and I look over my shoulder to see our group of friends cheering us on. Nikolai stands next to them with his arms crossed and a small smirk.

I turn back to Blake and she watches me with flushed cheeks and love shining in her eyes. I brush my thumb over her cheek and then kiss her one last time before taking her hand and pulling her along with me towards the entrance.

Her heels click against the pristine marble floor as her laughs fill the echoing lobby. I turn and wrap my arms around her waist and lift. She squeals as I spin and her arms go around my neck. "We did it," she cries into my neck.

I put her down and pull away. "No going back now."

"Wouldn't want to even if I could," she smiles.

"Well that's good to hear because it's been five minutes and you two are already going viral," Sydney chirps as she holds up her phone to us.

"What? How?" Blake grabs the device.

"The internet never sleeps and some people never stop working," Sydney sighs.

"Including yourself in that statistic?" Lawson raises an eyebrow.

Sydney scowls up at him, taking back her phone and

sliding it into his jacket pocket. She pats his side and plasters a tight smile on her face. "Happy?"

"Exceptionally," he deadpans.

A slow clap draws our attention towards the doors leading to tonight's event. Jean stands at the threshold with his sidekick, Markum. "Wasn't that something?" His french accent floods with arrogance and I hold Blake closer to me, using her to ground myself.

"You know, I had a feeling something was going on." He walks closer and his eyes slide over Blake with disgust. "I always wondered why the great Nikolai Morozov never contacted my agent back about signing me to the team and if there was anything I could have done to get my spot back after new ownership took over."

He tilts his head. "But I guess there really wasn't anything I could have done was there? In the end I just didn't have the right 'assets' for the team, did I?" He steps closer. "Tell me. Did she get on her knees for you before or after she signed on the dotted line?"

I shove him out of my space and take a menacing step forward, but a hand lands on my arm. I look down into flaming blue eyes and watch as Blake steps forward.

"You know, I've had to deal with assholes like you my entire career. The guys who think they're Gods' gift to racing. Who believe women have no place on that track. That the only way we could possibly get here is by using our 'assets'." She takes another step. "It has been my absolute pleasure proving every single one of you wrong."

Jean's smirk slides off his face as she continues, "You were right, you didn't have what this team wanted. If you did, I would have seen more of you than just in the reflection of my mirrors. Don't think my lack of a penis has anything to do with you not being able to keep up."

Jean takes a step towards her but Nikolai steps between them, gently guiding her behind him. She doesn't take her eyes off of him as she backs away.

"I think it's time for you to go, Beaumont."

Jean's eyes flash to and around our small before settling on Blake. "You're going to be sorry you ever stepped foot on my grid, salope," he spits before stalking off towards the side exit.

We watch him go and the slamming door echoes through the empty space. Sydney steps up next to Blake, "Dude, I want to be you when I grow up."

"Blake—"

"I'm okay Nikolai, really. Nothing he says will ever get to me. This one though?" She throws her thumb in my direction. "Might want to keep him far—far—away."

Nikolai chuckles and nods before heading towards the ballroom, squeezing my shoulder as he walks by. Jace follows with Beckham and Lawson drags Sydney away from her new role model, leaving us alone in the quiet lobby.

I close in behind her and slide my hands around her middle. "You're amazing." She leans into my chest and spins in my arms, looping her arms around my shoulders.

"I really don't care what he or anyone else like him thinks. I know I've earned this seat. I know I deserve to be here. I worked my ass off to get here. I've proved myself—"

"You don't have to prove anything."

"I know, but I have and I'll continue to do it because, I'm sorry to break it to you, one day I'll be standing on that top podium with the championship trophy in my hands."

I chuckle and kiss her forehead. "There's no doubt in my mind that you'll do just that."

CHAPTER 28

BLAKE

"I don't think I can eat another bite," I huff, rubbing my overstuffed stomach. Ryder chuckles next to me and his fingers dance on my shoulder.

"Want to go check out the silent auction?"

"Oh, yes please!" I perk up out of my food coma.

We walk arm in arm to the side of the room where tables are lined with various items up for auction. We're halfway through the second table when one catches my eye.

"Disneyland?" He chuckles, as I read through the informational packet.

I hum and smile over my shoulder at him. "Mama always wanted to take me to the one in Florida when I was younger but we never had the time or money to make the trip. I think it could be fun. Maybe we could talk to Jace and cash it in around Beckham's birthday? Make it a whole trip with the group?"

"Beckham would be ecstatic, he's been begging Jace to go

for months," he smiles softly, kissing the side of my head.

"He's a good kid and deserves all the happiness in the world. So why not take him to the happiest place on earth?"

Ryder told me about what happened that day in Monaco and how Jace woke up to find his six year old son standing outside his front door at three in the morning. Alone. In the last two months, things haven't really improved and I can see it weighing on Beck's little shoulders.

Of course Jace is there to try and make up for her absence and keep his son's mind occupied, but there's only so much you can do with a schedule like ours. If I can help brighten that little boy's day, I'm going to do it and I think this might do the trick.

We finish looking over the last few items before making our way back towards the main event space. The live band plays a soft ballad and I smile softly, watching the dance floor. Ryder pulls at my hand and guides me out amongst the swaying couples.

"I thought you don't dance," I muse, looping one arm over his shoulder as he takes my other hand in his and lays it against his chest.

"For you, I do." He leans in and kisses me softly before pulling me into his chest.

We let the music sway us and I close my eyes, falling into the feel of him. I never in a million years would have thought I'd be standing right here, in this moment. With him.

I've idolized this man since witnessing my very first race. He's been my muse, my reason, the voice in my head telling me to keep going. Without knowing it, he's been there with me through the toughest parts of training and the sleepless nights. I have all this because of him.

"July 3, 2016."

We lean apart and he looks at me with furrowed eyebrows. "What?"

"Your first podium win on the Formula 1 circuit."

"I know that," he chuckles, "Why are we talking about my stats right now?"

"Because that was the first race I ever saw, sitting cross-legged in my living room with a bowl of soggy Froot Loops since I couldn't take my eyes off the screen."

His smile slowly drops and his eyes sear into mine.

"You say that I'm the one who brought you back to life," I shake my head, "But you got me here Ry. If it wasn't for you and that janky tv on a random Sunday morning, I wouldn't have fallen in love with racing. Without that, I would have never worked as hard as I did to get where I am today. Without you, none of this would have happened."

I lift both my hands and cup his face. "You did this." My eyes flicker between his. "You brought yourself back to life."

I breathe out a laugh and shake my head. "Mama always told me that whatever's meant to happen will and at just the right time. That I can't force things no matter how much I'd want to. Granted she usually said that after I'd rage quit."

He chuckles and I smile. "You came into my life at just the right time. Then eight years later, when you needed it most, I came into yours." His eyes shine as I tip up on my toes and brush my lips over his, speaking softly, "I love you, Ryder King."

I seal my mouth over his and give myself over to the feel of him. We pull apart as the music shifts into something more upbeat and he leans his forehead against mine.

"Let's get out of here yeah? I'm done sharing you with the masses."

I giggle and bite my lip as I nod.

———

"Ry, I've got little legs!" I call out as I trail him through the hotel lobby. A squeal bursts out of me when he turns and throws me over his shoulder before continuing on towards the elevator.

Ryder doesn't put me down until our door clicks closed behind us. The air whooshes from me when he swings me off his shoulder and cages me in against the wall. He pins my hands above my head and trails his nose over my exposed collar bone. "This dress—"

"Reminded me of your eyes."

He pulls away and stares down at me. The lights of the city beyond our window twinkle across his face. "God, I love you. It feels like my heart is on the outside of my body. Like I can't take a full breath unless you're with me. You've completely flipped my world on its axis and I don't want it to ever go back. I'm going to do everything I can to be worthy of you."

"You don't have to do anything but be you. I love you."

I drag him down and take his lips in a fierce kiss, punctuating my love for him. He leans down, lifting me with ease by the back of my thighs and my legs band around his waist.

He pulls away from the wall and walks us over to the bed, bending at the waist to lay me out on the fluffy comforter. I watch as he kneels and lifts my right leg, unclasping the strap of my heel and sliding it from my foot before switching to the left.

He slides off my other heel, his lips skimming up my leg as he lays it over his shoulder. Pulling the dress apart by the slit, he brings my other leg up before leaning forward and sliding the silky material up my waist.

"We left before dessert was served." His eyes flick up to mine as his finger pulls my thong to the side. "I guess I'll have to find something else to satisfy my craving."

My head falls back at the first swipe of his tongue and my fingers thread through his hair, pulling him closer. I bite my lip to hold in the moan threatening to burst out of me and he pulls away.

"Don't," he growls, "I want everyone in this hotel, this city, this whole damn continent to know who is making you feel this good. So be a good girl and scream my name."

He dives back in, sucking hard on my clit and plunging two fingers into me.

And I do as I'm told.

I scream his name.

I'm panting, squirming in his unrelenting hold as he takes me over the edge. He stands, heavy eyes scanning my silk covered body as he strips out of his suit, piece by piece.

The lights from the window dance over his sculpted form

and slide off the bed to stand in front of him. Trailing my lips over his chest, I turn us and push him down onto the bed.

His hands slide up my back before he slowly drags the zipper down. I step back and shrug out of the sleeves before letting the material pool at my feet.

His eyes darken as they drift over the lingerie. The corset style top plunges down almost to my navel and the entire bodice is see through with emerald lace detailings. It may not be the most extravagant set, but I feel beautiful in it and from the look in my man's eyes, I'd say it works all the same.

"You're so goddamn beautiful," he breathes, "And I'm one lucky bastard."

I step between his legs and his hands run up my sides. I cup his face and bend, taking his lips. He pulls me into him and I plant a leg on either side of his hips, moaning into his mouth when I brush against his hardness.

I lift up on my knees and position him at my entrance before slowly lowering down until I'm fully seated on his lap. He groans and pulls back to meet my eyes. "I love you."

"I love you," I whisper, rolling my hips.

His hands latch onto my sides and guide me up and down his shaft. I throw my head back and moan when he hits that spot deep inside me.

Banding an arm around my waist, he twists and shifts us up the bed. He pulls back and slides my thong over my legs before untying the corset and peeling it off my body until I'm lying bare beneath him.

He climbs over me and notches himself at my entrance. "Say it again."

I lean up and trail my lips up his neck and over his jaw until they brush the shell of his ear, "I love you."

His head drops back as a shiver wracks through his body. I toss my arms over his shoulders on a scream when he thrusts hard into me. Clinging to him, my nails score his back as he ruts into me, his groans filling the air.

Thrust after fierce thrust, he fucks me into the bed all the while whispering sweet musings into my ear. His hand slips between us and I jolt when his fingers work my sensitive clit.

"One more," he growls, "Give me one more."

Magic. That's what this has to be. Because no way am I now coming by his command. Honestly? I don't care. I just don't want this to ever stop.

"That's my good girl," he purrs in my ear as I come down from my high.

I push at his chest until he falls on his back and climb over him. His hands tangle in my hair, pulling my face to his as I slide over his cock.

"Fuck. You're so goddamn perfect, it's like you were made for me," he groans as I widen my hips, taking him deeper.

He trails his lips down my neck and over my chest before his warm mouth clamps over my nipple, tongue teasing. I jolt when his teeth graze over the hardened peak and feel myself building to another climax.

"That's it Blake. Ride me. I'm so fucking close," his lips brush against my skin as he moves to the other breast. His body tenses under me and he wraps an arm around my waist, widening his legs to thrust up into me.

"Fuck. I'm going to come," he pants, bursting up into a sitting position with his arms banded around me. I wrap myself around him as our hips roll into each other. His eyes bore into mine, unwavering and full of love.

"Come with me." He slips his hand between us and at the first stroke of his thumb, I set off like a firework. Stars burst behind my eyes and I moan his name so loud I'm sure the whole hotel can hear it. He roars his release, teeth scoring my collar bone.

We fall back against the bed in a tangle of limbs and heavy breaths, me sprawled across his chest. His hand lifts up and brushes away my wild hair and I look up into warm eyes.

"What?" I smile.

"I know what I want."

My eyebrows furrow and he rolls us so that we're on our sides facing each other. "Remember that little competition involving your swimming suit—"

"Bodysuit."

"And how we said that whoever wins gets whatever they want?"

"Yeah," I drag out the word, curious as to where he's going with this.

"Well I won and I know what I want."

"And what is it you want?"

His eyes roam over my face and the biggest smile I have possibly ever seen graces his lips before he leans in and takes my mouth in a soft, lingering kiss.

INSTAGRAM POST

@STONECOLDBLAKE

Carousel of images:

1. Image of Blake tucked under a blanket on a plane, smiling at the camera.

2. Image of Ryder shirtless in the kitchen with his head thrown back and lowering a piece of bacon into his mouth.

3. Clip of Blake and her mom hugging at the airport.

4. Collage of Blake, her mom, and Ryder sightseeing around London.

5. Clip of Ryder and Blake dancing in the living room at night as "Can't Help Falling in Love" plays in the background.

6. Image of Blake and Ryder facing a mirror and lifting weights in the gym.

7. Image of Blake cheering in victory with a gaming controller over her head and Jace pouting on the couch.

8. Image of Blake and Ryder cuddling in bed.

Caption: There's always room for a little fun, family, friends, and love.

Comments:

@blakeandryder4ever: Oh my god! He met her mom!

@f1forlife: better be ready for the next race.

@ryderkingfanpage: I want to be that piece of bacon.

@thejacecollins: Blake cheated at that game!

@thelawsonmoore replied to @thejacecollins: No she didn't, you just suck.

CHAPTER 29

BLAKE

I wake with a start, sweat coating my forehead as fear trickles down my spine. Ryder shifts below me, his groggy voice filling the still air, "Blake? Are you okay?"

"Just a bad dream," I croak. "I'm okay, go back to sleep." I lay my head back on his chest and lean into him when his lips brush my temple, drawing on his comfort to keep from shaking.

It wasn't a bad dream. At least, I don't think it was. I can't remember exactly what happened, but now I can't shake this feeling that something's wrong. Lightning flashes illuminating the room and I jump when a loud clap of thunder follows. "It's storming," I whisper.

He hums and reaches over, retrieving his phone from the charger. The dull light from his screen highlights his features and my lips twitch. He's got an imprint of the pillow on the side of his face, his hair is sticking every which way, and his lips are puffy from sleep.

Without thought, I reach up and trace a finger over his bee-stung lips. He kisses the tip of my finger but his eyes don't stray from his phone. "Radar shows that the storm should be over by the start of the race. Looks like we'll have a wet one today."

I hum against his chest.

"Hey." He shifts me until I'm looking up at him. "What's wrong? You're usually a ball of energy on race days."

"I don't know," I whisper. "Can you just... hold me?" I look up into his warm eyes and he pulls me to him.

"Always. Come here." I burrow into his chest and his hand runs over the back of my head, lightly playing with my wavy strands.

"That feels nice," I murmur, lips brushing against his bare chest.

He lulls me to sleep and I'm able to get another couple hours before it's time to head to the track. Today we will be racing the streets of the Marina Bay in Singapore.

I've always loved watching the street races and now I'm getting to experience them for myself. So far they've been everything I could have ever dreamed they would be, but I can't help feeling like this particular one is going to be different. Life changing different.

The anxiousness in my stomach doesn't dissipate as I get ready. It's there, in the way my hands shake, voice wavers, and my mind races.

Ryder watches me closely as we walk out the door, keeping a hand on my lower back. As we grow closer to the track, the feeling of dread seeps deep into my bones and

I'm a shaking mess by the time we pull into our parking spot.

He shuts off the car, leans over, unbuckles my seatbelt, and pulls me over the console into his lap. "You're starting to freak me out here. What's going on in that pretty head of yours, huh?"

"I just can't shake this feeling that something is wrong and I'm so freaking pissed about it," I groan, covering my face with my hands. "I should be excited!"

He doesn't say anything, letting me work through my spiraling thoughts. "I'm starting on pole today," I whisper, like if I say it too loud, someone will pop out and yell 'you just got pranked' in my face.

"You are," he murmurs, pride peaking through the concern in his eyes. "You have a real chance at walking away with a win today." His eyes search mine.

"You really think that?"

He nods and pulls me closer to him until our foreheads touch. His fingers brush mine, linking our pinkies together. His lips brush over mine gently and I lean into him. Into my safe space. Into my home.

A hand slaps against the driver's side window and I shriek, jumping back from Ryder. My ass hits the steering wheel and the horn blares. Ryder scoops me back towards him, scowling at a keeled over Jace.

"I—" heave, "can't—" inhale, "breathe!" He braces a hand on the window, trying to catch his breath through the cackling.

"Move back so we can get out, you fucking prat," Ryder growls.

Jace stumbles when Ryder shoves open the door and I climb off his lap. Ryder follows behind me and punches Jace's shoulder.

"Ow! What the hell?" he cries.

"Fucking peeping Tom," Ryder grumbles as he reaches back into the car, retrieving both of our bags. Jace walks over to me and slings an arm around my shoulder. "And how are we?"

"Good," I quip, ignoring the side eye Ryder sends me.

"I bet you are." Jace wiggles his eyebrows at me and I elbow him.

"You're a man child," I laugh.

"Didn't know your kink was exhibitionism."

"Nothing would have happened," Ryder cuts in.

"Tell that to your dick. You've adjusted yourself three times in the past two minutes."

"Don't look at my dick."

"It's kind of hard to miss." Jace leans into me. "Get it? Hard to miss?"

I push his shoulder again and point up at him. "Man. Child."

Ryder's arm replaces Jace's across my shoulders and we walk through the back entrance. With every step, my nerves settle as Jace grumbles about how Sydney jacked Beckham up on sugar prior to bringing him back last night, leaving him with a six year old too wired to sleep.

He calls it sabotage. I call it comedy.

Lawson catches up to us with his earphones in, music blasting, hat pulled low, and eyes focused ahead—his usual pre-race routine.

The pair of Miller boys break off and head towards their team's building as we pass it. Ryder guides me farther until ours come into view, but I stop abruptly at the entrance.

The hairs on the back of my neck prickle and my shoulders stiffen. I turn and glance over the bustling paddock lane, feeling like I'm being watched.

I freeze when I lock with darkness. His lean figure, dressed in all black, stands just under the overhang of his team's garage. His arms are crossed and a deep hatred burns his features.

Refusing to show any sign of weakness, I don't back down from Jean's stare. His molten eyes pass over me from head to toe, briefly pausing on I and Ryder's joined hands before his lip curls in disgust and he stalks out of sight.

I blow out a breath turning to follow Ryder back inside, but run into his chest instead. I steady myself with a hand on his stomach and look up at his scowling face. Jaw tight, he watches where Jean once stood.

"Hey." I squeeze his hand and he slowly draws his eyes to me, features softening. "We should get inside for the pre-race meeting." Ryder nods and I follow after him with one last glance over my shoulder at the shadows.

The meeting goes by in a blur and I blink at the sound of shuffling chairs, locking eyes with the hazel ones across from me.

"You good?" Nikolai tilts his head, watching me closely.

"Mhm," I nod.

"Okay," he agrees but the hardness in his eyes tells me he doesn't believe me one bit. His eyes slide to Ryder for a moment, something passing between them before he gathers his things and strides out of the room.

The second he's out of sight, my chair is spun around and Ryder takes my hands in his hands. "I love you," he rushes out.

"I love you too?"

"Is that a question?"

"I don't know?" I laugh. "Why are you saying it like you're bursting at the seams?"

"Because I haven't said it today and I can see the nervousness that you're trying so hard to try. I just wanted you to know that I love you and I'm here for you."

I smile and scoot forward in my chair, brushing my lips lightly against his. "I know without you having to actually say the words."

"I'm so proud of you, Blake. You know that right?"

He tucks a piece of my hair. "I was so skeptical about this at first. Bringing in a kid with no professional experience? I didn't see it working out in anyone's favor, but you proved me wrong. You proved everyone wrong."

"You know you deserve the same praise right?" I trace his broken eyebrow. "To go through what you did and come back like this? No one thought you could do it, but you said 'fucking watch me' and did it anyway." He huffs a laugh and I smile.

"We're quite the pair."

"That we are," he agrees.

With one last lingering kiss, we gather our things and head to our rooms to get changed. After I have my gear on and helmet in hand, Ryder steps into my room and helps me fashion my boxer braids.

Together, we head out to the garage and he gives me that knee weakening wink before slipping on his helmet. Securing my own, I climb into my car and pull out into the pit lane.

Setting up on the grid, I take pole with Ryder staged in P2, Jace in P3, Lawson in P4, and Jean in P5. There's four cars between us, but I can still feel his eyes.

The opening ceremony passes in the blink of an eye and before I know it, Ryder is tugging on my harness before climbing into his own car for the formation lap. I catch glimpses of Jean's weaving car in my mirror as we drive through the streets and I struggle on the next breath when a fresh wave of dread washes over me.

Pulling up to the grid once more, I close my eyes and take three steadying breaths before I open them and lock in on the lights above.

One. Breathe in.

Two. Roaring engines drown out the thudding heartbeats.

Three. The current of the car washes out the trembling unease.

Four. The view of an open track ahead dissolves the memory of sinister dark eyes.

Five. Release.

I accelerate down the straight with Ryder and Jace right

behind me. Into turn one, Ryder's closer on the inside but I push harder to keep pace ahead of him.

We battle it out through ten laps, pulling ahead of the pack. Halfway through, Ryder gets called into the pits and two laps later I'm informed that his car is being retired after having issues with shifting.

Part of me dims, because I know he'll be upset about not being able to finish the race. The other part of me lights up at the higher chance to clench my very first pole position win with him being out of the race.

I make a mental note to make this up to him later as I shift into gear and push harder to extend the gap between me and the others. At some point I'm going to have to pit and I want to lessen the chance of being overtaken.

When I've built up enough cushion, I pull in for the seamless tire change. Entering back out onto the track, I get the lineup update that Jace follows behind me at two seconds with Jean right on his tail.

Lap after lap I build up my gap once again, but I'm pushing down the straight between turn fifteen and sixteen when white flags wave and Michael comes over the radio, "Big wreck in turn five, safety car deployed."

"Understood. Are they alright?"

"Both drivers are out. Team is cleaning up the area now."

"Who was it?"

"Lawson and Markum."

"Shit," I breathe.

"Hey. So when this safety car pulls off, you're going to need to push and push hard. We worked hard for those seconds but now it's level playing field. Jace came in right after you so your tire age is similar, but Jean is working on fresh ones. He's going to be breathing down your neck the minute we get the greens," Nikolai breaks over the radio.

"Understood."

The safety car pulls off and green flags wave as we roar down the track. Jace and Jean battle it out behind me as I push my car to its limits.

We enter into lap sixty when I check my mirrors and see their cars gaining on me at an alarming speed. We weave between each other into the tight thirteenth turn, but I'm able to hold them off.

Nikolai barks in my ear and my heart rate increases as Jean grows closer with each turn.

We're neck in neck, the three of us, into turn sixteen. I put everything I have into holding them off leading into turn eighteen. I glance in my mirror in time to see Jean's car swing wide and accelerating around Jace, creeping up on my side.

I downshift, preparing for the turn. The pounding of my heart rings in my ears as the foreboding feeling that's been lurking in the shadows breaks free, dragging me under.

One. Nikolai yells out my name.

Two. There's a flash of Jean's car on my right.

Three. My scream pierces the air as my world turns on its axis.

Four. My lungs seize when I'm tossed against my restraints.

Five. Everything goes black.

CHAPTER 30

RYDER

"Fuck!" I rip my helmet off and watch as the crew wheels my car into the garage.

Fixing a hat on my head, I jog across the lane and step up next to Nikolai at the pit wall. He turns as I slide on a pair of headphones and claps me on the back. "We'll get it figured out and have you back out there for Austin."

I nod and use my towel to wipe sweat from my face, deciding to focus on the other Nightingale car and the girl blazing down the track in it.

A cheer breaks over the garage when she increases her gap time, almost effortlessly, and my lips tip up as I watch her eat up the track.

Nikolai calls for her to come in for new tires. The crew is ready for her and within the blink of an eye, her tires squeal as cheers follow her back out onto the track.

"Oh shit," Tyson breathes on my right a few laps later

and I glance at his screen showing a collision just outside turn five.

"Who is it?" I step closer.

"Looks like Lawson and one of the Onyx boys, has to be Markum. Last I checked Jean was foaming at the mouth for second."

"Sucks for Moore, but he can join the club," I joke after I see him settle into a car that'll bring him back to the garages.

Flags wave for the deployment of the safety car and Nikolai gets on the radio with Blake to work out a game plan. She's so close. She just has to hold them off for a few more laps.

The safety car pulls off and she shoots off down the straight. By lap sixty, my shoulders are tense as I watch her fight to keep the lead. Jean's driving becomes aggressive, reckless and my breathing picks up when he almost collides with Jace into turn thirteen.

"Nik."

"I know. I see him."

Nikolai warns her and frustration rolls over her radio when she replies. They slip into the straight leading to turn eighteen and my heart stops when Jean pulls out wide, speeding past Jace. I slam my hand on the button to open the line when I see Jean pull to the left, cutting her off too early into the turn.

"Blake!"

My voice cracks as squealing tires pierce the air before that all too familiar crunch of metal on metal vibrates through my head, shutting down my senses. I stand helpless and watch as my entire world goes up in flames.

Smoke spills out from her tires as she slams on the brakes to avoid contact with him, but Jace is right behind her, ramming into her from behind. The collision sends her forward and her car collides at an angle that propels her up and over Jean.

Her screams filter through the drumming of my heart as she flips.

The radio goes silent by the second flip.

The car explodes through the pit lane entry by the third.

Everything stills as what's left of her car hangs upside down, dangling from the fence, with what would be the front wing scraping the ground and mangled engine in the air.

Three agonizing heartbeats go by, but she doesn't move. My eyes peel off the screen, searching the varying camera angles for any sign of her.

I vaguely register Nikolai throwing off his headphones and grabbing my shoulder. He tries to talk to me but her screams echo through my head at deafening volumes.

"Ryder!" *She's okay.*

"Get him out of here!" *She has to be okay.*

"Move!" *Please.*

"King!"

I suck in a desperate breath and my eyes focus on a frantic Nikolai in front of me before I twist to the sound of sirens. *Move.*

I twist out of his hold and sprint down the pit lane,

ignoring his strained yelling and pushing through anyone who tries to keep me from getting to her. "Blake!"

A man in a bright yellow uniform steps out in front of me, "Stop!"

"Blake!"

"Sir! You can't go over there!"

"Get your hands off of me."

"Let—"

"Blake—push me back one more time, I fucking dare you."

"I need help over here!"

"Blake," my voice breaks as two other crew members come to help hold me back. "Help her!" I shove a man in her direction and take a step forward, but everything in me seizes when her engine bursts into flames.

My skin lights on fire from the heat, but my veins turn to ice and a scream barrels out of my soul as I take a step closer. A body slams into me from behind taking me to the ground and pinning me to the asphalt.

"Stop," Lawson pleads in my ear. "You have to stop."

I scream out in agony as I watch the flames rise.

"I know. I know," his voice drops to a whisper.

"I got her!"

People move in a blur around us and work to get her out, all the while Lawson keeps me pinned to the heated asphalt. It isn't until they have her loaded on a stretcher and are sprinting her away from the growing blaze that the weight on my back lifts.

I push up and race towards the ambulance as they load her in. One of the EMTs steps back and places a hand on my chest, "Sir—"

"She's my wife!" I yell and the man blanches before stepping aside.

I crawl into the ambulance and take her limp hand in mine, bringing it to my lips. She's wrapped in a fireproof blanket with her helmet still on and visor shattered on the right side.

We pull off and I glance out the back window at the chaos beyond. Jace stands with a bawling Sydney as she clutches on to a stony Lawson. Nikolai jogs up behind them and says something before they all take off towards the garages.

I shift my eyes back to Blake as the tech works and the machines around her come to life with her vitals. I drop my head and bring her hand to my forehead. *Please, don't leave me too.*

Eight minutes later we pull up to the hospital's emergency entrance and the hospital staff takes over. I'm held back as they swap her over to a hospital bed when we enter an exam room.

"Hi, how do you know the patient?" A woman in blue scrubs steps into my line of sight and I side step to regain my view as they rush around Blake.

"Sir." She places a gentle hand on my arm and I jolt back.

"I'm her husband," I croak.

Blake has single handedly healed me from the inside out.

She's made it easier to breathe. She's given me a reason to wake up every day. With her, I feel alive. I feel loved.

I can't lose her when I just got to secure forever with her.

When I told her that I wanted forever as my prize for winning that ridiculous competition, half of me expected her to laugh it off because it's so soon. But she didn't. Tears ran down her face as she held my face in her hands, whispering yes over and over again against my lips.

Two weeks later her mom stood at her side holding a small bouquet of flowers while Nikolai was the one to hand us the rings as we said 'I do' in a small courthouse wedding during the summer break.

That night she asked for me to finally tell her what the weirdest thing was I'd ever signed. She said it would be my wedding gift to her. I'll never forget the twisted look on her face when I told her it was a toilet lid before she burst out in a fit of giggles. I wrapped my arms around her and twisted my mother's ring that now decorated her finger as she did the same with mine.

That day was the happiest of my life.

But today, I watched that happiness go up in flames.

"Your wife's in good hands. How about while they take care of her, I take care of that cut? Check you out to make sure you're all good for when she wakes up, does that sound okay?"

I take a step away from her and shoot my eyes to the room where Blake lays horrifyingly still on the bed while the medical staff flutters around her. Fear of being separated from her right now racks my body.

The nurse in front of me steps closer. "We won't go far, I promise. I just need to get the cut on your hand cleaned up so it doesn't get infected." Her eyes search our immediate area and she steps to the side. "Here. We can sit right here."

I look from the exam area to Blake to the nurse and back to Blake. Hesitantly, I sit on the edge of the bed and wince when the nurse prods my cheek. I don't take my eyes off of Blake's room the entire time.

"Where is she?!"

"I'll be right back," the nurse rushes off. "Sir? How can I help you?"

"Blake Stone, they just brought her in. She's the driver from the accident at the track."

"And you are?"

"Her father."

I'm off the bed in a flash, rounding the corner and trip over my own feet when familiar blue eyes lock with mine. "Callum?"

"Ryder." He rounds the counter and pulls me into a fierce hug. One I don't return.

"How is she?" he pulls away.

"I don't know," I say numbly as my mind races over what I just heard. "They haven't come to update me yet."

"Ryder!" Sydney cries, flying through the emergency room and colliding with my chest. Unlike Callum's embrace, I lean into this one and wrap my arms tight around her shivering body.

Nikolai, Jace, and Lawson jog over. "Updates?" Jace asks.

"Blake Stone?"

We all turn to the deep voice and I step forward. "Yes."

"They're taking her for some scans now. She doesn't have any broken bones, and the only major laceration is on her right temple, above her eyebrow."

"Is she awake?" Callum asks, stepping forward.

"No. There are concerns for a major concussion, but we'll find out more with the scans. If you could all move into the waiting room, we will come get you when she's settled into a more private room."

He steps forward and holds out a fist with a thin silver chain and ring dangling from the end. "I thought you may want to hold onto this."

I numbly take it from his hands and tighten my hold around it. With that, the doctor walks off and our small group shuffles into the waiting area. Jace and Lawson take a seat on either side of Sydney, Nikolai steps away when his phone rings, and Callum paces in front of the windows.

"I need to call her mum," I mumble.

"I can do it," Nikolai says as he walks back towards us.

I shake my head. "No, I'll do it." I pull out my phone and walk outside.

Taking a deep breath, I dial her number and she picks up on the first ring.

"Ryder," she cries.

We talk for ten minutes and I confirm my card info with her so she can get the first flight out. With one last goodbye, she hangs up so she can pack and get to the airport.

I collapse against the brick wall and suppress a scream

with my arm as the tears flood my eyes. My body racks with agony and I flinch when heavy arms wrap around me.

"I've got you," Lawson's deep timbre breaks through my sobs. "I've got you."

He holds onto me until my eyes have dried up and my voice has grown hoarse. He holds me until a nurse comes to find us. He stays close when they show us to her private room. He stays until I shower in her room's bathroom and comes back after having one of his own.

Hours later, I listen to the machines beeping around me that let me know she's still alive, that she's still here. Nikolai reclines in the corner, sleeping with his head leaning against the wall. Sydney is curled into Lawson's shoulder as they watch something on his tablet. Jace stayed back at the hotel, keeping Beckham distracted, with the promise of hourly updates.

Callum left to handle the media and hasn't returned since, but I haven't forgotten about what he said earlier. I just don't have it in me to confront him on it.

Not right now.

Right now, she is my main priority.

She will always be my priority.

I lean forward in my seat and raise her hand to my lips, brushing my lips against each of her delicate fingers. I reach up with my freehand and take off my chain. Sliding off the small silver band, I gently slip it onto her ring finger before laying my head down on top of it.

As the machines drone, I repeat the same pleas over and

over in the hopes they will eventually drown out the sounds of her screams.

I love you.

Come back to me.

Please don't leave me.

CHAPTER 31
BLAKE

My scream cuts off as the sound of squealing tires, crunching metal, and a crackling radio with panicked voices fills the air. I grit my teeth as restraints bite into my shoulders and close my eyes as the world turns upside down.

For a moment everything fades and I'm weightless. All I hear is my shallow breathing through the steady beat of my heart as I blink open my eyes in time to see the ground close in.

———

I jolt awake and blink into the dimness of an unfamiliar room. There's an incessant beeping to my left and I turn my head, wincing at the tightness in my neck. My eyes adjust to the dark room and I watch as the machine next to me ramps up in speed.

"Wha—"

"Blake." I peel my eyes away from the vitals monitor and

turn my head to follow the urgent voice filled with relief coming from my right.

Mama sits forward in her chair, her tear filled eyes rove over my face and she heaves out a shaky breath. "Get the doctor," she calls over her shoulder as she takes my hand and I hear shuffling before the door opens and closes.

"Mama," I whisper.

"Hi, sweetheart," she laughs through a stilted sob.

"What's happening?"

"We should wait—"

"Move!" A voice bellows from the hallway. The door bursts open and I take in his disheveled form. Jeans hang off his hips, a wrinkled shirt stretched across his heaving chest. His hair sticks up in every direction as if he constantly ran his fingers through it. The stubble lining his jaw is thicker than I remember and dark circles line under his tired green eyes.

"Ry," I croak.

He rushes into the room, rounds to the other side of my bed and takes my face in his hands. "I'm here, love. I'm here and you're here," he whispers, brushing hair out of my face.

"You're here," he repeats, his voice wavering.

"What's happening?" I ask shakily.

The door opens before anyone can answer and Nikolai walks in, followed by a tall brunette in a white coat. "Ms. Stone, hi. I'm Dr. Ryes."

"H–hi?" I say wearily.

"Can you please tell me today's date?"

"Um, it's September 22, 2024. Sunday."

The doctor hums and types out something on her tablet. I

slide my eyes to Ryder and he watches me closely, hand holding onto mine. "What?" I look at Mama and she gives me a sympathetic smile. "What is it?" My voice rises in panic and Ryder's hold on my hand tightens.

The doctor looks up from her tablet, "Today is actually September 24, 2024."

"What?" I laugh but it's filled with nerves. "No it's not," I glance between Mama and Ryder, "Right?" My body locks up when I'm met with nothing but solemn faces.

"What's wrong with me?" My shoulders slump and Ryder pulls my hand up to his mouth, running his lips over my knuckles while his eyes flicker across my face.

I turn back to the doctor and she steps forward, "You were in an accident on Sunday during the final lap of the race. You sustained some head trauma, but there's nothing showing up on the scans, so it's more than likely you have a major concussion. Now that you're awake, we can move forward with a couple more cognitive tests to get updated results."

"What kind of tests?" Ryder finally looks at the doctor.

"What's the last thing you remember?" Dr. Ryes asks.

"Uh," I glance at Ryder, "the last thing I remember is falling asleep."

Please don't ask me to—

"Can you be more specific? What happened before you went to sleep?"

Do that.

I nibble on my lip and Mama reaches for my hand,

307

squeezing. She smiles reassuringly at me and my cheeks heat as I dart my eyes away.

I meet Ryder's concerned face and clear my throat, "Um, well. Before that, we had a quiet night in after qualifying with spaghetti and a movie. I fell asleep on the couch and Ryder carried me upstairs. I took a shower and—" his eyes widen and he coughs.

"Okay! Yes! That," he clears his throat, "She remembers. She remembers everything up until going to sleep Saturday night."

A wave of giggles takes over me as I watch him fidget, chancing glances in Mama's direction. *Is he? Oh my god, he's blushing!*

"I'm not blushing," he grumbles but I see his eyes light with humor.

My laughing stops, smile along with it. "Did I say that out loud?"

"Are you surprised?" He squints and I giggle at the 'you'll be paying for that one later' look he sends me. *Bring it on, big guy.*

His eyes widen and Mama leans back in her chair, cackling. "Good God, love."

Dr. Ryes clears her throat and I see her lips twitch. "You're on some pretty powerful medication right now for the pain, so you may be a little out of it for a bit."

"Oh, joy." I drop my head back and close my eyes. *Wow, I'm exhausted all of a sudden.*

"That's to be expected. Your body went through something traumatic and is working overtime to heal, that process uses a lot of energy. Expect to be tired over the next couple days."

"What about the day of the race? Will she eventually regain those memories?" Mama shifts forward, taking my hand again.

"It's not uncommon for those involved in accidents—especially as severe as the one Blake was in—to mentally block out the events leading up to the incident."

"So I have the memories, my brain just won't let me access them?" I ask.

The doctor tilts her head. "If you'd like, we can have one of the therapists come up and talk with you. They can help you work through any question you may have about accessing those memories."

Do I even want to remember the accident? Do I want to relive that?

"Could I maybe think about it?" My eyes slide over to Ryder and he gives my knuckles a kiss before smiling softly against my skin.

"Yes, of course," Dr. Ryes nods as the door opens and a male nurse pushes a wheelchair into the room. "Ah, okay. We're going to take you for those last rounds of tests and if nothing pops up, then you'll be able to go home as early as tomorrow morning. Sound good?"

I hum in agreement as Ryder and Mama step aside to let the nurses closer. They unhook me from all the machines except my IV and help me from the bed to the wheelchair. I tip my head back and close my eyes once I'm seated, waiting for the lightheadedness to fade.

"We'll be right here when you get back okay?" Mama steps up and kisses my forehead.

"Uh huh," I breathe as I blink open my eyes and gaze up at Ryder. He squats down in front of me and my hand reaches up, cupping his jaw. He turns his head, his lips brushing against the palm of my left hand. "I'll see you in a little bit, yeah?" he murmurs against my skin.

"I love you."

He turns my hand and kisses the woven silver band on my finger. "I love you." Sliding the ring off my finger, he sighs, "This is the last time you're taking it off for anything other than racing."

I squeeze his hand, "Deal."

With a single soft kiss, he steps back and the nurse wheels me out of the room. Two hours of scans and tests later, I'm struggling to keep my eyes open as we approach my room.

We roll through the doorway and I jump as a room full of people cheer. Immediate regret flashes across each of their faces and Ryder sends them a glare as he meets me by the side of my bed. "I told them not to act like idiots," he grumbles.

"It's okay," I whisper as he kneels in front of me.

"Let's get you back into bed, yeah?"

I nod and he stands, asking the nurses if it's okay that he helps me. Upon their approval, he takes my hands after they lock the wheels and together, they guide me back over to my bed.

He steps out of the way when Mama pulls the blankets

up to my waist and leans in, kissing my forehead gently. Her finger runs over the bandage covering my right eyebrow and I take hold of her hand. "I'm okay Mama."

"I know, sweetheart."

"I'm really happy you're here," my lip wobbles.

"My baby needed me. I wouldn't be anywhere else," she runs her hand over my hair.

I lift my hand and trace over the bandage, my heart rate spiking. My fingers fumble as my breathing picks up and I claw at the wrap around my head. "Get it off."

"Blake—"

"Off, I want it off," I cry.

"Blake, stop." Mama takes my hands and I twist, trying to break her hold.

"Love," Ryder soothes as I throw my head back, tears streaming down my face.

"Ry," I sob, "Please, I want it off. Please."

"Okay, okay," he nods and reaches for the nurse alert button.

A young woman in blue scrubs comes bustling into the room, "You summoned," she chirps but her smile drops when she sees my panicked state.

"She'd like to take the bandage off, please," Mama says, stepping aside.

The nurse fills her space and smiles cautiously down at me, "Hi, Blake. I'm Liz." She pushes a button, inclining the bed so that I'm sitting up more. "Let's get this off, shall we?"

"Please," my voice breaks.

I hold tight to Ryder's hand as the nurse works. "They

used dissolvable stitches, so you won't have to worry about getting them removed," Liz says, pulling off the cloth wrap and adhesive bandage. "Let me clean up the area real quick and then I'll get out of your hair. Unless you need anything else?" I shake my head slightly and she finishes up before leaving.

Slowly, my eyes track across the room. Lawson leans against the wall. Jace stands with his arms on Beckham's shoulders by the window. Sydney inches closer to my bed white knuckling her phone. Nikolai sits on the small couch with his arms propped on his knees.

Each of them watches me with cautious expressions and I clear my throat. "Does anyone have a mirror?"

Mama digs through her bag and pulls out a small compact, handing it to me. Taking a deep breath, I open the container and lift it up to my face.

"I think you look badass," Sydney blurts out.

The room erupts in agreement as she smiles. "I know plenty of people who do things to look like that on purpose."

The room quiets down as I study the two inch cut dividing my right eyebrow. I lift my hand and, without actually touching, trace the area. My eyes flick to Ryder and he steps forward, "Loved mine so much, you just had to go and get one yourself, huh?"

I stutter a laugh as he perches on the edge of my bed, brushing my hair out of my face. His eyes roam and a small smile slides into place. "Still just as beautiful," he whispers.

I sniffle and lean into his touch, eyes dancing across the

room and loved ones here. My eyes settle on a weary Beckham and I tilt my head. "Hi, Becks."

"Hi," he whispers, leaning back into his father's legs and clinging to a small gift bag. Jace nudges him and Beck's nervous brown eyes glance up at him before landing back on me. "I—um—I brought you something."

"You did?" I wipe away the remaining tears and shift on the bed.

He nods and fiddles with the handles of a small gift bag. "You going to give it to her?" Jace chuckles, guiding him forward.

I scoot over on the bed and pat the empty space beside me. He shuffles over and Ryder lifts him up, cautiously depositing him on the bed. I take the shyly offered gift bag and remove the tissue paper. Reaching in, I pull out a small golden dog stuffed animal.

"His name is Gears," Beckham whispers.

"Is he yours?" I ask, running my hand over the soft fur.

"Mhm. Da got him for me when I was sick."

My eyes flash up to Jace and he watches his son with a soft but haunted look.

"He helped make me feel better and I thought maybe he could do the same for you."

I wrap my arm around his small shoulders and pull him in for a gentle hug. "Well thank you, that is very sweet of you." I hold the plush dog as he picks at the fur, lights twinkling off his small silver medical bracelet.

"Know what will make me feel even better?" I mutter into the silence.

"What?" His small voice perks up.

I share a look with Ryder and mouth my idea. He walks over to Jace and leans in, whispering. I watch as he smiles when Ryder pulls back and he nods.

I lean back slightly and Beckham looks up, "What would you say about if after the season, we all go to the happiest place on earth?"

His eyes widen. "Where's that?"

I lean in and whisper, "Disney."

He gasps and glances at his smiling dad before wrapping his arms around my neck. "Yes!" he cheers loudly.

A laugh bursts out of my chest and the room fills with lightness, chasing away the unknown of what happens next.

PRESS ROOM TRANSCRIPT
FOLLOWING SINGAPORE GRAND PRIX

Nikolai MOROZOV: Afternoon. Thank you all for being here on such short notice. A lot has been going on behind the scenes following the accident on Sunday involving Blake Stone, Jean Beaumont, and Jace Collins. We are not at liberty to comment right now on how the crash happened or why it happened. I am here to answer your questions, because it has been brought to my attention that there are certain rumors, misconceptions, and opinions going around and I would just like to clear the air. Let's start with you.

(Nikolai points to a reporter in the first row)

Reporter 1: Is there any investigation going into the wreck and who was at fault?

NM: Yes. Our focus is to figure out why this happened to ensure it doesn't in the future. Whether that is on my team or not.

R1: So you don't think it was a malfunction on your car or driver's part.

NM: No comment.

(Nikolai nods to a reporter in row two)

Reporter 2: What is Blake's status? Last we heard this morning, she has yet to wake up and it's been two days.

NM: You might want to double check your sources next time before speaking because as of two this morning, she has regained consciousness. As of right now she is set to make a full recovery. Next.

Reporter 3: Will this affect her contract with the team?

NM: Absolutely not. Blake is an excellent driver, this was something out of her control and in no way reflects on her ability to perform at this level.

Reporter 4: You said she is awake and responding. How is she feeling?

NM: She's feeling good. She's tested well and is already giving the nursing staff hell for not letting her go home.

R1: Were there any other injuries sustained in the crash?

NM: Some bruising and a sprained shoulder, but both are minor.

R1: It's hard to believe someone could walk away from what she experienced with a simple bump on the head.

(The room fills with chuckles)

(Nikolai stands and slams his hands on the table before bracing himself and glaring down at the crowd)

NM: Let me be very clear here. The next one of you that tries to downplay or make a mockery of what occurred on Sunday to my driver, will be stripped of access to everything. You won't even be able to attend your own children's karting races.

(The room falls silent and reports shift in their chairs)

NM: We are talking about a life. A life that could have easily ended way too soon but by some grace of God, she survived.

She. Survived. She is safe. She is healthy. She will be coming back to drive for us for the rest of the season and if I have anything to do with it, she will do so for as long as she wants. Blake Stone is a rare talent and quite frankly has the makings to be one of the greatest drivers I've ever seen step foot on the grid. This is just the beginning for her. Congratulations, you are all witnessing her origin story.

(Nikolai sits down and readjusts the mic)

(Reporter clears his throat)

R1: I apologize Ni—

NM: Apology not accepted, do better. Next question.

CHAPTER 32

BLAKE

"You know I can walk, right?"

"You know I don't care, right?" Ryder quips as he strides up the front porch stairs of my childhood home, carrying me bridal style.

"Let the man be jellybean," Mama says, unlocking the front door before stepping aside. "If I were you, I'd take full advantage of this caregiving while it lasts."

"Yeah, jellybean. Listen to the smart woman."

"You know you can stop sucking up now right? We're married. You got the girl."

He chuckles and I wiggle in his arms. "Okay, I'm safe and sound in the house. You can put me down now."

"Where's her room?" he asks Mama, ignoring my protests.

"I'll show you," she winks at me and I throw my head back groaning in defeat.

"Ryder, seriously."

"Blake, seriously. It's late, we've been traveling for over twenty-four hours, and I know you're exhausted. I'm putting you to bed."

"This bossy Ryder is boring. Let the other one come out to play, I like him better."

"Not something a mother needs to hear from her daughter," Mama laughs and I tuck my face into his neck, giggling.

She opens my bedroom door and without turning on the lights, he strides across the small room and bends to lay me on the bed. I shift and feel something move next to me.

"What the—"

"I said get out me swamp!" a voice screeches and shoves me out of the bed.

I scream, stumbling to my feet before clinging to Ryder's arm.

"What the hell," he bellows.

"What's wrong?" Mama shrieks, clicking on the light.

I blink against the assaulting brightness and laugh, "Cassie!"

My nutcase of a best friend sits up and rubs the sleep from her eyes. "Oh. You're home." Her face lights up and she throws her arms above her head in a cheer.

"And you're in my bed," I mock.

She rolls to her feet and rushes over to me, pulling me into a crushing hug. "And you're okay," she murmurs into my hair and I wrap my arms tightly around her.

"I'm okay," I echo.

She pulls back and looks over my shoulder. "Thank you for taking care of our girl."

Ryder slides his arm across my chest and kisses the side of my head, "Always." He grunts when he's suddenly yanked forward and stumbles into my back.

"I—" Cassie grabs my hand and lifts it to her face. "This —" Her eyes bounce between us. "I can't—"

"Spit it out woman," I laugh.

"I still cannot believe you married your childhood celebrity crush. Like what lottery did you play and where can I buy my ticket?"

I shake my head, laughing and pull her into a hug. "I've missed you," I sigh.

"I've missed you more, chick."

She leans back and her blue eyes roam over my face. "So. How are we feeling?"

"Exhausted."

"Besides that?"

"Spent."

"That's the same thing."

"Downright knackered," I mock in a horrible English accent.

"What are you? A thesaurus?"

"Well it's how I'm feeling," I smile.

"Point taken," she nods and claps her hands. "You heard her, champ. The lady needs her sleep. Out with you. Don't worry, the couch is mucho comfortable." She pushes at his shoulders until he's on the other side of the doorway.

"Can I—"

"Nope. You get her for the rest of your life. Don't be greedy." She slams the door in his face.

I gasp, "Cassie!"

"What?" she turns, "Oh, he'll be fine! It's girls night!"

She walks over and looks me up and down, eyes catching on the cut through my eyebrow. Humming, she nods once, "Syd was right, you do look badass."

I laugh and shake my head. It's good to be home.

———

It's been two weeks so we arrived in Georgia and I've been resting for every second. We have one more week until the race in Austin and the doctor has finally cleared me to return to training alongside Ryder. Just in time too because I have officially gone stir crazy.

He hasn't let me lift anything heavier than an empty dinner plate.

Cassie keeps yanking the laundry out of my hands.

He sits outside the shower to make sure I don't slip and hit my head.

Mama only allows me in the kitchen to watch her and him cook.

He barricades me in his arms to make sure I get a full eight hours of sleep every night.

And none of them will let me go with him to his training sessions, even when I promise not to do anything.

I love them, but I'm also on the edge of throttling them if I'm told one more time not to do something because 'I need to rest' or 'I need to let the healing process do its thing.'

It's been fourteen days, 336 hours, 20,160 minutes of Ryder mother henning me along with my actual mother and hopefully now, with the doctor's confidence that I'm fully healed, they will both be the ones doing the resting.

I wake with a smile and toss the blanket off before shuffling across the hallway to the bathroom. Yawning, I flip on the light and pick up my toothbrush.

The minty foam fills my mouth and I'm about to spit when I hear the one thing no person wants to hear their parents say to a significant other. "I know I may be biased but wasn't she the cutest baby?"

With wide eyes, I bolt down the stairs, toothbrush in hand, and slide into the living room. "Wha ay ou oing?" I rush out around a mouth full of toothpaste and suds.

"What did you just say?" Mama laughs.

I growl and roll my eyes as I move into the kitchen, spitting and rinsing out in the sink. Wiping my face with a hand towel, I speed back into the living room to see Mama holding a photo album up for him.

With a yelp, I throw myself across the room and slap a hand over the open page, not caring what I'm covering up because he doesn't need to see any of it anyway.

"What are you doing?" I squeak, my voice cracking as my eyes dart to Mama.

"We were just looking at—"

"Nothing! We are looking at none of these. He doesn't need to see baby me dressed up as a pumpkin, or the bubble

322

baths with fohawks made of soap, or the detailed documentation you got of me with braces."

"Pardon me for finding it interesting to see all the little changes your teeth went through," Mama lays her hand across her chest, gasping dramatically before smiling and winking at him.

"I too find that interesting. Where's that album?" He points at her, looking over the shelf packed full of my childhood and I backhand his chest.

He reaches for my high school yearbook and I swat his hand. "Please don't. Not all of us were blessed to always look as perfect as you do. Seriously, you completely bypassed the awkward phase. I, on the other hand, grew up stuck in it."

"It can't be that bad," he chuckles, reaching for another book.

"Let's not and say we did?" I wrap my arms around his and pull it to my chest.

He smirks down at me, "Let's do so we aren't lying?"

"Ry—"

"Blake—"

"King—"

"Mrs. King," he smiles.

"You can't keep using that to make me do whatever you want."

"I'll stop using it when it stops working."

"Well, that would be now!" I laugh and yank on his hand, dragging him away from a lifetime's worth of embarrassment.

"Don't worry, I'll slip you some of the best ones later," I hear Mama whisper to him and whip my head around.

"Mama! You're such a little traitor," I laugh.

She smiles and shrugs her shoulders. "This is what mamas are for sweetheart." Trailing behind us into the kitchen, she opens the fridge and pulls out some bacon and eggs. "Let me whip you kids up some breakfast real quick before you go."

I step up next to her and kiss her cheek. "Thank you."

She smiles, "Go on and finish getting ready, the burritos will be ready for you to grab on your way out. I'm going to head out as soon as they're done, so good luck today and don't push yourself too hard, okay?" She pulls me in and I lean into her comfort.

"Yes ma'am."

Pulling away, she steps around me and grabs Ryder's arms. "That goes for you too." She pulls him down to her height, and into a hug.

I watch as his body stiffens a second before his arms wrap around her. She speaks low into his ear and his head bobs before he stands back up his full height. Her hands take his and she squeezes before turning around and continuing on with breakfast preparations.

I slowly walk up to him as he watches her move around the kitchen with a look I can't quite decipher. "Hey," I murmur and his eyes slide to mine. "Come on big guy, let's go get ready. I've got things to do, weights to lift, and a very handsome husband to beat in a foot race."

His face breaks into a smile as he chuckles and shakes his head. Thirty minutes later I scoop up two aluminum foil wrapped burritos on our way out the door, following behind him as he carries our gym bags to the car.

He drives fifteen minutes to a small private gym that the team was able to rent out while we're here and I'm bounding out of the door as soon as Ryder puts the car in park. His low laugh follows me as I grab our bags and head towards the entrance.

"Oh sweetheart!" Maeve calls out, almost tackling me to the ground the second I step through the door. "I'm so glad you're okay," she rubs my back.

"I'm okay." I squeeze her back. "And I'm ready for whatever you have to throw at me."

She laughs and steps away. "Well, today we'll start off slow. Ease you back into the routine since you've been out of it for a little bit."

I nod along and she glances over at Ryder. "You can keep up with what we've been working on and then we'll meet at the end for cardio."

"Remember what you promised your mum," he points at me, walking backwards towards the free weights.

"Yes sir," I roll my eyes and immediately blush when his eyebrow lifts.

I watch him walk away and Maeve clears her throat, watching me with knowing eyes.

"What?" I laugh and she shakes her head.

"Nothing. It's just good to see him smile again. He looks really happy. You both do."

I smile. "I am."

"Good," she claps her hands, "Now! What do you say we get to the torture?"

"Don't you mean workout?" I laugh and she waves me off.

"Yes. Yes. Workout. That's what I said."

Maeve leads me over to the weight area and we get to work. For three hours we move through the many sequences and machines, setting up a jumping off point for the rest of the week. While I wouldn't say it was 'torture', it still wasn't a walk in the park.

By the end of our session, I've sweat through my hoodie and am ready for a nice refreshing shower. Preferably one where a certain tall dark and handsome man is there to soap up my already increasingly sore muscles.

I'm currently regretting all the gloating I did this morning about kicking Ryder's ass in the cardio portion we are about to do. I'm walking like a newborn deer, using machines to hold me up as we walk by. Meanwhile, the man glides across the floor like I didn't just watch him and the leg porn of a lower body workout he just finished.

"Okay, I want a mile run out of each of you. After that, you're free to go and I will see you tomorrow." Maeve claps and I clamber up onto my treadmill. "You did good today. Tomorrow we'll bump it up and start focusing on the areas needing a little more improvement."

"Goody," I breathe. She smiles, tapping a hand on the machine with a 'see you tomorrow champs' and walking off.

"How are you doing?" Ryder asks as he ramps up his speed to a steady jog.

"Good." I take a deep breath and wiggle out my legs before turning on my treadmill and increasing the speed. "It feels good to be back. Moving around," I peer over at him, "Getting to act like I'm not made of glass."

"I have not treated you like you were made of glass."

"Maybe not to that extent but, Ry," I laugh, "You refused to even let me walk for the first few days. Not even the ten steps from our bed to the bathroom."

"Well, you have historically been very clumsy. I wasn't taking any chances."

"I am not that cl—" I stumble when the tip of my shoe catches on the moving mat, catching myself on the side railings.

"Shut up," I mumble when he lifts an eyebrow that screams 'you were saying'.

We power through the last of our cardio and clean off the machines before waving goodbye to the lingering staff members on our way towards the front.

"Hold on, I had to pee that entire run. I feel like my bladder's about to burst."

He chuckles as I take off towards the bathroom, my legs moving faster than they did for that run. When I'm done, I exit the bathroom and am about to round the corner when I see Callum walk up to Ryder with hesitant steps. *Huh, I didn't know he was here.*

"Ryder."

There's a pause and I watch Ryder's head slowly raise from his phone. "Callum."

The older man slips his hands into his pockets. "How is she?"

"She's good. Glad to be back."

Callum nods. "That's good. That's good. And you?"

Ryder's shoulders stiffen and he crosses his arms. "What do you want, Brennan? I know damn well that you could get your updates on how she's doing from Nikolai. I don't have time nor the patience to deal with this twenty questions game, so ask the one you really came over here to ask me." *Whoa, why the hell is he talking to him like that?*

I throw myself back against the wall when Callum looks around and try to quiet my suddenly heavy breathing. There's a sigh before he says in a low voice, "Have you told her?" *Her? Her who? And what has he or hasn't he possibly told her?*

CHAPTER 33

RYDER

"No," I answer, carefully watching the man in front of me.

Callum Brennan was someone I grew up idolizing right alongside my father. He was actually one of his best friends. They raced together, grew up together. They were practically brothers.

When my parents got married, he stood at my da's side. When I was born, he was the first of their friends to hold me. When my father died, he was there and through it all, he stayed.

He guided me through those angsty teenage years. He gave me the birds and the bees talk when I was too nervous to ask Mum. He taught me how to drive. He attended every race my first year on the circuit and trained with me in the off season.

He was there when Mum was diagnosed and stayed with her when I couldn't. He was there, hand on my shoulder, as we buried her.

I thought I knew who this man was. I thought he was honorable, good.

But a good man doesn't leave his child behind.

A good man doesn't leave Blake behind.

He drops his head and blows out a breath before slowly meeting my eyes. "Thank you. I just... I need to talk to B—"

"And why haven't you? We've been here for almost three weeks now. Why haven't you reached out to her? You know where she is."

"I don't know what I'd say."

"Maybe say 'I'm sorry for abandoning you to raise my kid alone for the past twenty one years?' or something along those lines," I seethe and his eyebrows furrow as he frowns.

"I don't think you understa—"

"Do you not understand what walking away did to them? She was shunned by her entire family. At eighteen—barely even a legal adult—she left home with nowhere else to go and anything she could carry packed away in her car."

Callum's eyes widen and he opens his mouth, but I cut him off. "How could you walk away from her, from them? Don't you know how incredible they both are? Breanna got her degree in nursing, worked two jobs, and raised a child, all by herself. She's loving and compassionate and kind. She has all the gentleness a mother should have, but also an unmatched fierceness when protecting the ones she loves."

I shake my head. "And Blake," I sigh.

"Blake is extraordinary. Her strength and determination is staggering, but the light that emits from her soul would bring anyone to their knees. She's passionate and selfless and believes there is good in everyone, some just have more than others. Being around her is like breathing fresh air after the darkest storms. Getting to love her is the best thing I will ever do and nothing can measure up to how thankful I am that every single day she chooses me."

My eyes bounce between his, "So tell me how you could ever walk away—"

"I didn't know!" Callum bellows, cutting me off and blowing out a heavy breath before lowering his voice. "I didn't know she was pregnant," he shakes his head. "I didn't even know her last name," he mutters, almost to himself.

I clench my jaw at his defeated stature. "I feel disgusted with myself, with you. Because instead of being the father she needed, you tried to be the one that I lost."

"Ryder, I—" he steps forward, but his eyes move over my shoulder and his face blanches.

I whirl around and follow his eyes to see Blake standing with her bag loosely held in her hands, her face pale, mouth parted, and eyes glassy.

"Blake—" Callum starts but she cuts him off.

"Don't," she raises a shaky hand in his direction. "I-I-I need... I don't know what I need, but I-I can't do this right now." She rushes out and bolts for the exit.

With a glance in his direction, I take off after her.

"Blake!" I call, pushing through the heavy front doors. The wind has picked up and dark clouds loom in the distance.

Blake paces in front of the car and when I put a hand on

her shoulder, she jolts back with a yelp. "Sorry, I didn't hear you," she mumbles.

I watch her fidget with the hem of her shirt and take a steady breath. "How much—"

"All of it," she whispers, her tear filled eyes meeting mine. "How long have you known?"

"I didn't—still don't—know for sure, but—"

"How long Ryder?"

"Since the hospital," I sigh.

Her mouth closes, jaw hardening as she watches me. "Take me home."

"Blake—"

"I need to go home. I need to figure out what the hell to say to Mama. And I need to get answers from someone who won't keep secrets from me."

My stomach drops as she steps around me and my chest caves in with the slamming of her door. I glance through the windshield at her but her eyes are drawn out the passenger window. On shaky legs, I get behind the wheel and drive the short distance back to the house.

Blake doesn't move to get out after I shut off the car. We sit in silence, staring out the windshield as rain begins to sprinkle.

"Why didn't you tell me?" she whispers.

"Blake," I turn and she faces me with red rimmed eyes, "I had just watched you—the love of my life—almost die and there was nothing I could do to stop it. I stood there, helpless, as your car was decimated and went up in flames."

My jaw clenches. "I thought I'd lost you," I whisper.

"For days I didn't sleep because all I would hear were your screams and all I would see was the fire swallowing your rig. I stayed by your side until your mum had Nikolai physically force me out of the room to go get some fresh air and change out of my racing gear. All of my focus was on you, nothing else mattered in that moment except you waking up."

She nods, "What about after we got home? Ryder, it's been three weeks!"

"I know."

"So why? Why haven't you said anything?"

"I wasn't going to tell you something that I didn't know was for certain. I wasn't going to upend your life like that, especially when all you needed to concentrate on was healing. I needed you to concentrate on that because the thought of you not being okay was slowly destroying me."

Her eyes flicker between mine.

"I'm sorry I didn't tell you. I should have and I know that. But you have to understand that nothing—and I mean nothing—over the past few weeks has mattered more to me than making sure you were okay and healthy." She nods in understanding, her lip quivering.

"I love you, Blake. I'm sorry I didn't tell you," I breathe.

"I love you too," she whispers, "but it's going to take a little bit for me to stop being upset with you about this."

"Take all the time you need, love. I'm not going anywhere."

She sighs and looks out the window. "We better get in there."

I reach over and take her small hand in mine. "We do this together."

Nodding, she looks over at me and blows out a shaky breath. "We do this together."

We walk through the front door as the sound of pots and pans clattering echo from the kitchen. "Blake? Ryder? Is that you?" Bree calls out.

"It's us Mama."

Her mum walks into the living room, wiping her hands on a towel and smiling, "Hope you're hungry, I'm making enough lasagna to last us through the win—what's wrong?" Her eyebrows furrow and she rushes over to Blake.

"Is everything okay? Did you hurt yourself? I told you not to push too hard, sweetheart. Come on, let's get you off your feet." She guides her over to the couch.

"What's wrong, jellybean?"

Blowing out a breath, she takes her mum's hands, "Can you tell me about my dad?"

"Oh. Well," she says hesitantly, "You know a little bit already, but we met while my family was vacationing in Italy after my graduation. I was reading a book one day on the beach and some guys ran by me, kicking up sand. It got all over me and my stuff, and caught me so off guard that I screamed. The guys yelled out apologies but when I looked up, one of them was looking back over his shoulder, caught my eye, and tripped."

She blushes and a small smile spreads across her lips. "I jumped off of my lounger and ran over to see if he was okay, only to trip over his long legs and onto him." She laughs and Blake's lips tip up as she listens.

"I started apologizing, rambling more like it, and his body started to vibrate. I thought he was in pain or crying, but I sat up to see him laughing. His deep full body laugh was so contagious that I snorted one out myself. I was mortified." She shakes her head.

"Then he sat up and opened his eyes," she smiles. "And I was hooked. One look into his brilliant ivy blues and I didn't want to look anywhere else again. He introduced himself as Cal, but never said his last name. So I did the same and when he smiled as he said our names together, I swear my heart skipped a beat." She places a hand over her chest, eyes light with memories of that day.

"We spent every single day together for two weeks. Three days before we were set to return home, Cal and I were laying in bed when I told him that I didn't want it to end. He wrapped me in his arms and said that maybe it didn't have to."

"You were going to run away with him," Blake whispers. "Why didn't you ever tell me everything, Mama? You sound like you loved him."

"I did," she tears up. "I think I fell in love with him the second he opened his eyes."

"What happened?"

Bree shrugs, "I waited in the lobby for over two hours, until my parents came to find me after reading my note. He never showed." Her eyes bounce between us. "What brought this on?"

Blake looks at me with hesitant eyes and I scoot closer to her while speaking, "Do you remember the name of our team owner?"

Bree's eyebrows furrow. "Uh, I'm sorry. I don—"

"It's Callum Brennan," Blake rushes out and pulls out her phone. Taking a breath, she shakily hands it over to her mum. She brings the phone up and sucks in a breath, her free hand covering her mouth.

"Oh my god," she whispers, her tear filled eyes rising. "H-how?"

"I found out today. I didn't really stick around to ask any questions," Blake whispers.

"He didn't know, Blake." Bree reaches out and lays a hand on her forearm. "I didn't find out about you until three months later. I didn't know his last name or what he did or where he lived. I had no way of contacting him. And then eventually I just kind of gave up, I guess."

"What do we do now?" Blake asks.

Bree looks back down at the picture before handing the phone back. "Right now, we go eat this lasagna that I've been slaving over for the past hour. Maybe if you're lucky, there's a pint of Ben & Jerry's in the freezer for you. And all of this can wait until tomorrow, or whenever we're ready to face it."

She stands and bends down to kiss the top of her daughter's head. "I love you, sweetheart. We'll figure all of this out, okay?"

Blake gives her a weak smile before she sweeps out of the room and into the kitchen. Her eyes linger on the doorway before she slowly meets my eyes. "You said he walked out on us."

"I thought—"

"You really didn't know anything except that he claimed to be my dad?"

I inch closer and gently cup her face. "I didn't know anything. I didn't want to know anything because if anyone was going to hear his side of this, it was going to be you and your mum." Tears roll down her cheeks and I thumb them away.

"I'm not mad at you anymore," she whispers.

I breathe out a relieved sigh and lay my forehead against hers. "Whatever you or your mum needs, I'm here. I'll always be here."

"We do this together?"

I brush my lips across hers, "We do this together."

CHAPTER 34

BLAKE

"Blake, it's your first race back since the accident, how are you feeling?"

"Well, it's everyone's first race back, but I'm feeling good. I'm at a good spot with the P4 starting position and overall can't wait to get back out there."

"Good! And who's this with you?"

I smile, "This is my mama." I loop my arm through hers and lean my head on her shoulder.

The reporter standing in front of us lights up. "Wow! Welcome!"

"Thank you. I'm really excited to be here and see this all in person. There's a lot more going on back here than I thought," she laughs.

"So, this is your first time at a race of Blake's?"

"I went to the majority of them when she was back in the other league, but this is my first Formula 1 race, yes."

"This is a whole other monster right?"

"Oh definitely," Mama laughs. "But I'm proud of her. She's an amazing driver and I honestly tear up every time I watch her out there."

"Does she get it from you?"

Her smile dims, but she quickly recovers and shakes her head. "No. That's all her father."

I squeeze Mama's hand and intercept the reporter's next question because that is a road we aren't ready to go down. "It was nice talking to you, but we should get going."

The woman smiles and nods. "Of course, it was nice talking with you and meeting you. Good luck out there today."

"Thank you," Mama and I call over our shoulders as we walk away from the press line. Ryder leans against a pole at the beginning of the pit area, his eyes bouncing between the two of us with concern.

"How are you feeling?" he asks, dropping a kiss to my hair.

"I'm feeling good," I turn to Mama, "And you did amazing."

She waves me off, "That was not nearly as bad as I thought it was going to be."

I lean into Ryder's side as we walk down the pit lane and smile at Mama's wide eyes as she looks around. "I can't believe they built all of this in what? A couple days?"

"It takes about a week, I think. Longer in the cities where we take over streets, but with tracks that are established like this, it's pretty smooth."

She gasps and clutches onto my arm, "Oh my god."

"Ow! Nails!"

"Is that Matthew McConaughey?" her voice cracks at the high pitch.

I follow her line of sight and—*holy shit, it's Matthew McConaughey.* "Well, would you look at that," I laugh.

"Do you want to meet him?" Ryder asks with a smirk.

"Oh I don't—"

"She would love to," I cut her off.

"What? No," she yells before lowering her voice, "Okay maybe. Do I look okay?"

"You're beautiful," a deep voice sounds from behind us.

Mama's smile slowly drops as she meets my eyes. She takes a steadying breath before squaring her shoulders and slowly turns. Her chest heaves when she lifts her eyes and her hand comes to her mouth, holding in a sob.

"Cal," she whispers.

Callum sighs and eyes shine. "Bree."

"Hi," her voice wavers and she laughs through tears.

"Hi." He reaches for her and she unglues her feet from the ground, barreling into his arms. "God I've missed you," he murmurs into her hair.

Ryder steps up next to me, pulling me into him so my back is flush with his front. I latch on to the arm banding around my shoulders as I watch my mother hug someone who she never thought she'd see again.

I saw it in her eyes last week when she talked about their time together. She loved him with her whole being. And as I watch her shoulders shake and her arms hold onto him a little tighter, I know she probably still does.

Pulling away he reaches up and brushes her wild auburn hair out of her face. "Can we go somewhere and talk?" His eyes slide over her shoulder to me. "All of us?"

I nod wordlessly and we follow him to our team house a few trailers down. "Clear the room please," he calls as we enter the common area and the lingering crew immediately vacates.

When the door closes, Mama finally gets to ask the question that has plagued her for twenty one years, "Why didn't you show up?"

Callum blows out a breath and sits down on the small couch in the center of the room. "The night before we were supposed to meet up, a man and woman approached me. They told me that they knew who I was and that if I ever went near you again, they would go to the press saying I seduced and abused their seventeen year old daughter."

"What?" she gasps, plopping down onto the couch.

"I called their bluff." He raises his eyes to hers. "I still sat there that morning, waiting for you. I even got there early." His shoulders drop. "About thirty minutes after I got there, the same man showed up and handed me an envelope with pictures of us. Some of them out in public... most of them not."

His jaw ticks. "He said that he loved his daughter and that he wanted her to be happy, but she'd never have that if she came with me. He said his wife wouldn't let her. That not only would she take me down, but she would destroy your chances at truly living. She would take everything away from you. When it was just me being threatened, I could take it.

341

Risking all that I was to be with you was no question. But when the threats turned to you... I couldn't risk your future and happiness being ripped away because of me."

Mama chuckles but it's filled with hate and disbelief. "She did it anyway."

He stands and moves over to kneel in front of her. "I'm sorry I didn't try harder. I'm sorry you had to raise our daughter alone."

Mama cups his face. "I'm sorry my parents are the reason you missed out on that amazing daughter."

"You have to believe me, Bree. It leveled me to walk away from you but I thought that if I did then you would have been safe," he pleads. "But if I'd known," he turns his head, eyes meeting mine, "There was no way I would have been able to walk away from both of you."

My heart shatters and if it weren't for the man behind me, I would have crumpled to the ground. It breaks for Mama because of her parents' betrayal that cost her the love of her life. It breaks for Callum and the years he lost with the woman he loved and his daughter.

And it breaks for me because all this time I thought he didn't want me, but if he knew then he would have given up everything to be there. He would have wanted me.

I don't realize I'm crying until Ryder reaches up and wipes away the tear before kissing the side of my head. "I love you," he whispers against my skin and I lean into him.

"I can't believe you're here," she whispers, sliding her hands over his. "I can't believe our little family found each other."

"Did you know who I was?" I ask and he shakes his head.

"No. When I first saw you, it was a bit shocking because you favor your mother an incredible amount. I shook it off like I was imagining it because over the years I swear I'd seen her face pop up in the crowds. Every time I wished it really was her," he faces her. "I always search for her in the crowds." His thumb brushes across her cheeks.

"It wasn't until your workup at the medical facility that I started questioning things. Your birthdate and the timeline matched up. I'd watch you drive and see how similar our styles were. I'd listen to you talk in interviews and every once in a while, if I closed my eyes it was like I was listening to Bree."

He shifts to sitting on the couch, Mama's hand clasped tightly in his. "I built up enough courage to finally order a paternity test after the Australian Grand Prix."

I blow out a breath. "They took our blood right after to make sure we were all good to travel to Japan."

Ryder's eyebrows furrow. "No they didn't."

"What?" I turn to him.

"He's right," I face Callum as he sighs. "It was Maeve's idea. I told her I didn't want to do that, but you try telling that stubborn old woman she can't do something."

"Oh my god," my eyes widen, "Maeve's—"

"You're grandmother," he shakes his head but his lips tip up. "She says she knew the moment she saw you. That it was your eyes and dark hair that gave you away. 'That's Brennan traits if I'd ever seen them' she'd said."

I laugh in disbelief. All this time...

"I'm sorry we lied about what the blood work was for. And I'm sorry I didn't come to you sooner. I just didn't know what to say," he turns to Mama, "to either of you."

She smiles up at him, "It's okay. You're here now."

"I'm here now," he whispers, leaning his forehead against hers.

The shattered pieces of my heart mend together as I watch them together. *My parents.*

I've never seen her with someone like this. She's never brought dates home, she's never introduced me to a "friend" or talked about having someone like that. Sometimes I'd catch her lost in her thoughts as we watched a romance movie and I'd hoped that one day she'd find something like that for herself.

Little did I know, she'd already had.

"What do we do now?" she asks, her eyes meeting mine.

"How about we take it one day at a time?" He glances between us and I catch the relief in his eyes when I nod. "Right now, you two need to go suit up."

"Okay," I sigh and step over to Mama. "I'll see you after."

"She'll be in the garage with me," he turns to her, "I mean, that's if you—"

"Yes," she nods her head frantically and we all chuckle.

"Okay then," I give her cheek a kiss, "I'll see you in the garage."

Ryder takes my hand as we walk from the common area to the side of the building that houses our individual changing rooms. "Hey," he pulls me to a stop before I can open my door. "What's going on in that beautiful head of yours, huh?"

I sigh and drop my head back, "Too much."

His hands frame my face, "What can I do?"

"Kiss me?"

He chuckles, leaning in and murmuring against my lips, "You never have to even ask."

His lips brush mine softly once, twice. He presses in on the third pass and I sigh when his tongue teases the seam of my lips.

My arms wrap around his shoulders and I go up on my tiptoes to get closer. With every swipe of his tongue and every soft moan he pulls from me with his wandering hands, the suffocating worries about my parents, about this race, everything fades until all that's left is him.

We crash into my door and my back hits wood before it disappears and I'm falling. A muffled shriek leaves me as I wrap myself around Ryder. A grunt vibrates through his chest when he turns, taking the brunt of the impact.

"Oh my god, are you okay?" I push up off of him, eyes and hands roaming over his body.

"I'm fine," he chuckles, peaking open his eyes. "Just wondering how you could possibly be one of the most skilled drivers on the grid, yet I'm constantly saving you from your own clumsiness outside the car."

"Hey," I point towards the door, "That one was your fault. Let's stick to walls from now on, agreed?"

"Agreed," he smirks up at me and I lean down, balancing

my chin on my palms with my elbows braced against his chest.

"Thank you," I whisper.

"Feel a little clearer?"

"Mhm," I reach up and trace his scar. His hand slides up my arm and cups my face, his thumb brushing against my matching eyebrow. My breath hitches at the first swipe and I close my eyes. "Maybe we can, um. Can we do a lap?"

"Yeah. Of course." He scoops me up and positions us with his back against the wall. I lean back against his chest and fall into the comfort of him and the calming of the track behind my eyes.

When we're done, he kisses the side of my head and whispers against my hair, "Now let's go show them that they can't keep you down."

And I do.

As I stand up on the tallest podium, I look out over the sea of cheering fans and crews until my eyes land on the couple about midway back.

The man cheers out with a beaming smile and eyes full of pride, his arm is banded around the shorter woman's chest as she stands with her back to his front, much like Ryder does with me. The woman clutches onto his arm as tears fall freely down her face.

The champagne sprays and when the last drop is gone, Ryder wraps me in his arms and I hold on to him tight. With my husband holding me tight and my parents cheering me on, I let my own tears fall.

This is a moment I thought I'd never get to experience. This is a moment I'm never going to forget.

THE GRID GIRLS

EPISODE 245: WHAT HAPPENS IN VEGAS...

(Elvis Preseley's Viva Las Vegas song fades)

Zoe: It's Vegas baby!

(the girls all laugh)

Leah: Okay then. Hi, I'm Leah.

Zoe: I'm Zoe.

Tess: And I'm Tess.

Leah: We're three Formula 1 junkies who sit down twice a week to talk to you and sometimes with you about all the happenings on and off the grid.

Zoe: And boy has there been a lot of things going on this season.

Leah: You may have caught on, but if not, this week we've got the Vegas Grand Prix.

Tess: I've been looking forward to this one.

Leah: Oh yeah?

Tess: Definitely. I'm a little biased, but I have to say that the US races are my favorite.

Zoe: Is it because you don't have to be up at the ass-crack of dawn?

(the girls all laugh)

Tess: Well, there is that, but I just like seeing this sport—that has been historically not as popular in the States as it has everywhere else—become this whole celebrated thing. And boy do they know how to celebrate it in Vegas.

Leah: It really is like no other circuit.

Tess: But I'm also excited to see what our girl is able to do here. She has dominated the two previous American tracks, and I think she'll do the same here.

Zoe: Do you think it's the fact that these are her home races that helps?

Leah: I think we talked about this before the Miami race and Zoe, you said that you think the pressure of a home crowd would drive her to push harder. I think that continues to be the case. I wouldn't be at all surprised if she takes the win on this one.

Tess: It's interesting that you say that because a lot of people didn't really expect her to return to the track at all after Singapore.

(Zoe shivers)

Zoe: I honestly still have nightmares of that crash just from watching it. Kudos to her for being able to get back in the damn thing.

Tess: It's definitely something no one wants to see.

Leah: I have to hand it to her though, she's one tough chick. I don't think I could have come back, let alone win the first race back and place on podium for the following ones.

Zoe: And she doesn't seem to be slowing down if their social media has anything to say about it. This past week they did a day in the lifestyle video with her and I think I broke a sweat just watching her workout routine.

Tess: She's a beast, that's for sure.

Zoe: I think I want to be her when I grow up.

Leah: Zo, you're older than her.

Zoe: Your point?

(the girls all laugh)

Tess: Honestly, I'm right there with you. This girl has seriously blown this industry away. We're getting into the three final races of the season here and I don't think there were many people out there who expected her to make it past the first ones.

Leah: She's held her own and even showed some of the veterans how it's done.

Zoe: And even though she won't be walking out of this season as the world champion, she's given those boys one hell of a fight to get it.

CHAPTER 35
RYDER

"IN THE SPIRIT OF VEGAS, let's say we make this interesting, yeah?" Jace rubs his hands together as we walk to get set up for the opening ceremonies.

"What are the stakes?" Blake raises an eyebrow and mine furrow.

"Haven't you learned yet that gambling is not for you?"

"Maybe this time I'll win," she smirks.

Jace cheers, "That's the attitude! Okay, the person with the fastest lap time gets to decide where we go tonight, the person with the quickest pit time gets to decide what embarrassing thing the rest of us do, and the person who overtakes the most people gets to decide what they wear."

"This sounds like a fucking trap," Lawson grumbles. "What the hell do you have cooking up in that big head of yours, huh? Why not first, second, and third? Why those specific things?"

"Gotta keep you on your toes, bruv," Jace pats him on the chest.

"I'm in," she shrugs her shoulders before smiling up at me and I roll my eyes.

"I guess I'm in too." Her and Jace hiss out 'yes' and high five.

We all turn to look at our residential dark cloud and he huffs, "Fuck. Fine."

"Fuck yeah!" Jace wraps his arm around his teammates neck.

She cracks her knuckles and rolls her neck, "Hope you boys like glitter." She winks and struts down to our team's display box. The three of us stop and stare after her.

"What the fuck did you just do, Jace?" Lawson growls.

I chuckle at his wide eyes.

"I might not have thought this through completely."

Clapping him on the back, I follow behind my competitive girl, calling out to the guys as I go, "May the odds be ever in your favor!"

Jace whistles the *Hunger Games* tune and holds up three fingers. Lawson rolls his eyes and steers him towards the Miller team box.

Catching up to Blake, I lean in to kiss her head and she leans out of reach. "Uh, excuse me. What the fuck was that?" I laugh and she peers up at me.

"No good luck kiss for you. I need all the advantages I can get."

"Huh. Okay. Hey, your chain is sticking out."

"Oh, really—Hey!"

She squeals when I use the act of helping her tuck the chain with my ring back under the collar of her suit, but instead wrap my hand around the back of her neck and pounce, peppering her face with kisses.

"Okay," she laughs, "One more kiss and I'm going to make sure you get the g-string."

I choke on air and step back, "What the hell are you going to make us do?"

She smiles up at me, "You'll see when I win."

Calling her bluff, I bend down and slam my lips to hers. Pulling back she stares up at me with heated eyes and flushed cheeks. "You're going to regret that later," she breathes.

"I'll never regret kissing you."

———

I regret it.

She wasn't bluffing.

She also didn't lose the bet.

Nope, she had a clean sweep of each category. She had the fastest lap by a tenth of a second. I swear she worked something out with the pit crew because I've never seen them move so fast. And even though it was a risk, she dropped back just to beat Jace by one extra overtake.

Oh, and she won the race.

To say my sweet, caring, competitive, only humble to anyone but our group, wife is riding a high right now is putting it mildly. Because she's currently standing in the dressing room doorway of a popular male strip club, holding out a pair of red satin boxers for the guys and a matching thong for yours truly.

"You're serious."

"I'm always serious when I collect on my wins."

"Blake, come on."

"That's correct, put these on," she shakes the scrap of cloth at me.

"Love—"

"Nope, you will not sweet talk your way out of this."

"Hey! What's taking so long?" Sydney's head pops up around the doorframe and she frowns. "Why aren't any of you dressed?"

"I'm not going out there in that," Jace grumbles, eyeing the thong. Blake separates the fabric and holds up the briefs, "These are for you two."

"Oh! Why didn't you say so!" He happily takes the offered costume and struts off towards the small changing area.

Sydney slips in, snagging the other pair, and holds them up to Lawson. "Come on Hades, red looks good on you."

He growls and snatches the satin from her fingers, "You may very well be an only child by the end of the night." He stomps off towards the other

Sydney squeals and claps before dashing out the door, telling Blake that she'll save her a seat in front. She doesn't take her eyes off of me the entire time. Pushing to my feet, I walk over and her head tips up so she can keep her eyes locked with mine.

"You're lucky I love you so much and apparently have the annoying compulsion of never telling you no."

A triumphant smile spreads across her face and she presses up on her tiptoes, speaking against my lips, "I love you too."

After a brief kiss, I take the thong from her fingers and step back as she hands me three satin robes. "Don't forget the body glitter," she yells over her shoulder on her way out.

Thirty minutes later I'm following Jace out onto the dimmed stage, Lawson stalking behind me in our matching robes.

"Can't be too bad right?" Jace whispers. "It's just a bunch of strangers."

"I'm worried now that you're nervous," I glance at him.

He shrugs and the music starts before he can get another word out. The crowd goes wild and the lights dance.

"Take it off!"

I smile as Blake's voice pierces the air and the guys chuckle next to me. We glance at each other and nod. With a deep breath, we untie our robes sashes and let the fabric slide off our shoulders to the beat of "Smack That" by Akon featuring Eminem.

We begin the basic dance routine that Jace and Sydney came up with an hour ago. I'm so concentrated on not fucking up the choreography that I miss Jace and Lawson's curses when it's their cue to turn towards the crowd. I whip around and sling off my robe seconds after the guys and freeze.

Blake sits front and center with a cackling Sydney on her

left, a keeled over Cassie on her right, and all of our crews from both teams surrounding them. The crowd goes wild, and Nikolai shakes his head but amusement sparks in his eyes.

Jace jabs his elbow into my side and I jolt out of my shock, stumbling through the routine as we make our way across the stage. Women along the sides start throwing dollar bills and Jace even stops to let one slip a few into the band of his briefs.

Lawson scowls when Sydney stands and slaps his ass when the chorus rings out but even the dim setting can't hide the small smirk on his face as she dances along.

Cassie cheers when Jace stops in front of her and leans over, pulling her up onto the stage. I look down at a beaming Blake and hold out my hand. She hesitates and Sydney pulls at her arm as she climbs up. I help her stand on the shiny walkway and pull her into me.

She laughs when she pulls her hands away, now covered in the glitter we slathered our chests with. Cassie calls out to her and the girls begin their own little routine, strutting around us.

I jolt when her hand smacks my bare ass and look over my shoulder to see her head thrown back as she shakes with laughter. The song comes to an end and we take our bows to a screaming crowd. The guys on the crew go nuts and dollar bills rain over us as I pull Blake into a hard kiss.

Was that possibly the most embarrassing thing I've done in my life?

Absolutely.

Would I do it again if it meant that the woman I love would be this happy?

Abso-fucking-lutely.

"You always say you can't dance, but I'd say that just proved you can," she says as we walk out of the venue thirty minutes later and I shake my head.

"I just followed what the drill sergeant told me to do," I nod towards Jace.

"Well these hips," she squeezes my sides, "Don't lie." She breaks off laughing as she runs to catch up with the girls.

"Where are we going now?" Lawson grumbles next to me.

I shrug as Jace calls out, "I have a brilliant idea." The girls turn around and we circle up. "Let's go to a wedding?"

"What," Sydney laughs, "Who's?"

"Theirs," Jace wiggles a finger between us and I scoff.

"We're already married."

"Yeah! Without us," he laughs. "The only one here who was there was this arsehole," he throws a hand out towards Nikolai. "I've been cheated of my best man duties—"

"Oi! Who said you'd be the best man?" Lawson backhands his chest.

Jace waves him off, "There's a chapel around the corner."

"Please," Cassie grabs onto Blakes arm, "I know Mama Bree recorded the last one but I'd really like to see my best friend walk down the aisle in person."

Blake smiles, "I mean, it could be really fun." Her eyes slide up to mine, "What do you think, big guy?"

"Whatever you want, pip. I'd marry you a thousand times over if you wanted me too."

Forty-five minutes later I'm standing next to Elvis with Jace and Lawson beside me, Cassie and Sydney on the other side, as Nikolai walks Blake down the date pink aisle.

"Oh lordy, that's a pretty lady you got yourself there," Elvis murmurs.

"Yeah, I'm one lucky bastard."

The ceremony is short and filled with laughter and some tears on the girls' part. We kiss and walk out to "I Want You, I Need You, I Love You" by Elvis, Blake giggling the entire way.

We spend the rest of the night hopping from bar to bar and celebrating life with the people who mean the most to us. It's almost four in the morning when Blake leans against me and whispers in my ear, "Wanna get out of here, husband?"

I turn and brush my lips over hers, "Absolutely."

Thirty minutes and one frisky limo ride later, she squeals as I pick her up bridal style and step over the threshold of our suite. Closing the door behind us with my foot, I kiss her as I walk through the spacious room and over to the bed.

I follow as I lay her down, covering her body with mine. Trailing my lips down her neck, I continue over her body while I softly bunch up her skirts.

"Ryder," she gasps when I rip her underwear from her body and flatten my tongue against her center. Wrapping my arms around her thighs, I press down on her lower abdomen as I push a finger into her. Within minutes she's coming on my tongue.

Coming down from her high, she leans up and rips at my suit until there's nothing left. We slide the silky white material off her shoulders and down her legs. When we're both bare, she wraps her hand around the back of my head and pulls me with her as she falls back on the bed.

We're a mess of groping hands, clashing tongues, and needy moans. With my forehead pressed against hers, eyes locked, she notches me at her entrance and I thrust in. Her mouth opens on a moan when my hips meet hers and I drop down, swallowing it. Her hips roll into mine and her nails dig into my back.

"Fuck, I'm never going to get tired of this. Of you," I breathe.

"Ryder," she gasps when I slam in hard, "I need—"

"I know what you need." I pull out of her, grab her by the hips, and flip her so she's on her hands and knees. Yanking up, I position her ass higher in the air and thrust into her so hard that she jolts on a scream.

"Fuck you're so tight like this," I grit through clenched teeth. "Grab the headboard."

Her hand reaches up, bracing like I instructed and my fingers hold onto her with a bruising force as the room fills with the sound of colliding flesh.

I throw my head back when she flutters around me and groan, "Touch yourself. Come on my cock, love." Her body locks up when her fingers brush against her clit and I smirk down at her, "That's my good girl."

"Yes," she moans, turning to peer at me over her shoulder with heated eyes.

My hand slides up her spine and my fingers tangle in her loose waves. Pulling, she pushes up and flattens her back against my chest as my arm wraps around her chest, hand wrapping around her neck.

Her fingers don't stop moving and her hips roll into mine on each brutal thrust. "I'm going to come," she breathes against my lips and my balls tighten.

"Come with me," I whisper, diving in to take her lips.

I nip at her mouth and she ignites, shivers wrack her body as she comes. "King," she screams and I follow her over the edge. We collapse onto the bed and I roll so I don't crush her under my weight.

Pulling out, she rolls in my arms and lays with her head on my chest, fingers dancing across my abs. "We should get married more often. I quite like you ripping me out of wedding dresses," she murmurs against my skin and I chuckle, knowing full well I'd do it however many times she'd want.

CHAPTER 36

RYDER

"Okay! Let's go out there and wrap this season up shall we?" Nikolai stands and everyone around the table follows.

Blake and I walk hand in hand towards our rooms, pausing outside her door. She turns and loops her arms around my neck, smiling.

"I'm so married to the next world champion," she murmurs against my lips.

"You don't know that. It's been a back and forth between me and Jace all sea—"

She presses her fingers against my lips, "I know it. You know it. Jace has been shaking in his boots all week because he knows it too."

My eyes flicker between hers and the never ending confidence there. She's been doing this for the past two weeks, calling me her world champion every chance she gets. Talking me out of my spiraling thoughts about coming so close but not being quite enough before they can manifest on the track.

Pulling her into my chest I press my forehead against hers and breathe in her warmth. She hums, threading her fingers through my hair, nails scratching my scalp.

"You got this," she whispers.

"We got this."

After changing, we walk towards the garage and nod as other drivers pass. Crew members pat our backs as we move through the crowded garage and her eyes go wide when she spies a few celebrities standing next to Callum. He catches her eye and mouths 'good luck' with a nod and she returns it.

Just like Callum said in Austin two months ago, we've all been taking this new relationship one day at a time. Blake was worried at first with not knowing how to act around him outside of the garage, but we've had a few dinners with him over the last couple weeks and with each passing entree I can see the hesitancy on both sides fading.

He's stopped being afraid of asking about her childhood, she's no longer hiding behind her polite smiles, and they've both made an effort to reach out to the other.

Bree's since opened up more about their time together with Blake and I don't miss the small smile on my girl's lips when she hears the love hanging heavy in her mum's words.

Bree's been a big part of constructing that bridge between them, between all of us. I've met up with Callum a few times since Austin and slowly we're moving forward.

I've tried to apologize for jumping to conclusions. He's waved me off every time, telling me he was thankful that his daughter was with a man willing to go to war for her like I was, a man willing to defend her happiness even if it meant severing his own.

We'll find that happiness again one day, the four of us. Together.

His eye catches mine and I return his nod as I slip my helmet on before hopping into my car. My hands flex on the wheel and my mind runs through the game plan for the hundredth time.

When I hop out of my car at the starting grid for the opening ceremonies, Jace and Lawson link up with us at the front line. We settle into position for the trophy presentation and anthems, with the guys on my right and Blake on my left.

I turn to her, but my eyebrows furrow at her tense shoulders and shallow breathing. She stares straight ahead, jaw working and hands clenched so tight her knuckles turn white.

My eyes slide above her head to the figure standing on the other side of her. Jean is leaned over saying something low into her ear and his eyes meet mine as he smirks.

I grab her and pull her behind me, stepping into his space. "What the fuck do you think you're doing?" I growl.

There's a scuffle behind me but I don't take my eyes off the man who put my whole world in the hospital for four days. "I'm just telling her good luck, King. Even threw in a little friendly advice in there. She really should work on corner preparations if she's going to drive alongside the professionals."

"You son of a—"

"Now. Now. We don't want to have another scene for the world to see, do we? I'm not sure you remember how well that ended for you last time, but I'm not too opposed to remind you."

Hands wrap around my arms, tugging me back, but I lean farther into his space and lower my voice, "I know there were no mechanical issues with your car because if there were, they would have found something by now."

"I don't know what your trying to insin—"

"I know you cut her off on purpose. Others might not see it, but it's the same shit you pulled with me two years ago. Only difference is there wasn't another driver to ram into my back, sending me flying over you."

His jaw ticks and I grit my teeth, "You're lucky she's okay. Because if she wasn't? I would have risked more than my career to end you."

I shake my head. "I'm not going to stop until what you did is brought to light. It's time this entire industry sees you for the poison you are."

"Ryder," Jace hisses and I glance around at the immediate crowd watching us closely. Blake catches my eye from where she stands behind Lawson and I send a silent thanks up to whoever's listening for giving me two best friends who are just as protective over my girl.

She gives me a small shake of her head with pleading eyes. I nod and turn back to Jean, "Go near her again and you'll see just how far I'm willing to go to make sure she's safe."

I let Jace pull me back this time and meet Blake on the

other side of them. We stand hand in hand, now on the other side of the Miller boys and hold our heads high throughout the entire opening ceremony.

When we're given the thumbs up to load into our cars, I follow Blake to her P4 position and tug on her harness for the last time this season. She smiles up at me and slides her hand over my heart, where her ring dangles from the chain on my neck.

———

Two hours, fifty eight laps, one pit stop, and a photo finish later, I pass under the checkered flag as crews line the fence and Jace hot on my tail.

"Hey mate, I got someone here for you," Tyson's voice crackles over the radio before Blake's cheers break through and I smile.

She's the first one jumping into my arms the moment I hop out of my car.

Her cheers are the loudest from the sea of crews, teams, and fans when I hold the final first place trophy of the season above my head.

It's her chants of 'I told you so' that brings out my smile as we walk down the pit lane.

After a night out with our friends, it's her that shoves me down on the bed and proceeds to show me how proud she is of me all night long.

And it's her hand clutching mine that keeps me from shaking as the announcer's voice echoes through the venue

365

two days later, "And now, this year's world champion, Ryder King!"

The crowd goes nuts as I stand and lean over, kissing a teary eyed Blake. "Go get 'em, big guy," she smiles, swiping her thumbs across my jaw.

With one last kiss, I make my way up onto the FIA Prize Giving Ceremony stage and shake hands with the presenter before carefully taking the offered trophy.

I nod and lift the trophy up as family, friends, and other teams applaud. Stepping up to the mic, I clear my throat, "Thank you." My eyes roam over the sea of faces. "There's a lot of people to thank so, I'm going to go ahead and get started because I know my wife's ready to drag me out on that dance floor."

Chuckles ring out and I smirk when Blake rolls her eyes.

"I want to thank my team for all the work they did this season, we wouldn't be able to do what we do without you. To my team principal and owner, Nikolai and Callum, thank you for giving me this chance. To the fans, each and every one of us wouldn't be here without all of your love and support, so thank you for the ungodly hours you wake up to watch the races."

I drop my eyes and take a deep steadying breath, "I wanted to thank my parents. My dad for instilling my obsession with this sport; I have no idea what I'd be doing today if it weren't for him. I've only ever wanted to be just like him. Now I hold the same amount of championships he collected during his career. I know if he was here, he'd probably tell me 'okay, that's enough'."

The audience chuckles. "But I'm sorry Da, I can't do that. Because I know you would have gone for more, so I'll just have to do it for the both of us now."

I shuffle from foot to foot. "My mum—" my voice cracks and I clear my throat. "She was the heartbeat of our family. She'd wake up before the sun every day to make sure I'd get to training. She'd give up her weekends to take me to races. She kept me going when sometimes all I wanted to do was quit. Without her, I never would have made it as far as I did."

I pause as the crowd claps and my eyes settle on the beauty in an emerald dress, wiping away her silent tears. "And lastly, I'd like to thank my wife. Blake Stone." Her eyes meet mine and she laughs through a fresh wave of tears.

"For so long my world had turned dark. I'd lost everything that was important to me and very few were in my reach to get back. I eventually found comfort in the silence, and after pushing away the loved ones I had left, I learned to survive alongside the monster that replaced them instead. I dove head first into the routine of eating, sleeping, and training, and slowly became a shell of a man with one purpose, one single focus. I didn't think I'd need anything else. That maybe I was destined to this life I'd created in the shadows."

I huff a laugh and smirk. "Then you came in and flipped the switch, eviscerating all of them with your loud music, bright smiles, contagious laughter, and nervous rambling. You blew me away with your heart, your drive, and your unrelenting need to leave it all out on the track. You made me enjoy this sport again, feel alive for longer than when I'm just behind the wheel. Somewhere along the way, it stopped being about carrying on my father's legacy or proving to the world that I still had what it takes."

I shake my head, "Driving alongside you made me fall in love with this sport all over again. You pushed me to be better, showed me that it doesn't matter if you come in first or last as long as you went out there and gave it your all."

I lean into the mic and lower my voice, "So thank you. Thank you for knocking me down a few pegs when I was just the arsehole who wanted nothing more than to win, for ignoring me and sticking around when I said I wanted to be alone, and for your patience while I worked to get my head out of my arse." Blake mouths 'I love you' as chuckles ring out through the crowd. "Thank you. I love you."

"We love you too," Jace calls out and everyone laughs as I shake my head smiling.

"Thank you." I raise the trophy and wink at my girl as the crowd stands and the room fills with their cheers.

Ten months ago all I wanted was to continue my father's legacy, to get back out on the track, and to gain back a part of my life that I'd almost had ripped away. I thought that's all I'd want, that it was all I'd need. I came into this season intending to leave with one thing, but I'm walking out of it with so much more.

FULLY THROTTLED ARTICLE EXCERPT

ENDINGS AND BEGINNINGS (DECEMBER 20, 2024)

Investigations into the cause of the crash involving Blake Stone (Nightingale Racing), Jace Collins (Miller Racing), and Jean Beaumont (Onyx Racing) that occurred during the Singapore Grand Prix, has concluded as of December 18, 2024 and we suspect the upcoming holiday season won't be so jolly for a certain Frenchman.

Sources say that he was paying off multiple crew members on the team to falsify his car's records to show mechanical malfunctions leading up to the accident. It wasn't until individual interviews where one of the members broke, confession after shocking confession spilling out.

During this enlightening interview, it was brought to the investigator's attention the malicious intentions Beaumont had towards Stone. There are a multitude of documented interactions between the two where Beaumont alluded or even went as far to threaten that Stone wouldn't cut it in this industry. Mentions of hushed conversations between Beaumont and the second driver for Onyx Racing, Markum Volkov, where the two would discuss ways to force retire her car from races.

The mysteriously missing dash cam footage from Beaumont's car that day has since been found and was the final nail in his coffin. In the footage you can see him deliberately down shift and turn into Stone's line. It was later noted that the footage was corrupted by the same member who was the one to finally step forward.

When asked about the investigation, Jean Beaumont has refused to comment on the allegations, findings, or his departure from the team.

Since the investigations closing, Onyx Racing has not only released Jean Beaumont from his contract, but also Markum Volkov. The crew members who accepted the payment from Beaumont were, in the end, also asked to leave. There is currently no word on who will be replacing the members of the team or driver positions.

Stone has stated that she will not be pressing charges against Beaumont for his role in the accident that day.

"I'm leaving that accident in the past, where it belongs. I still have not recovered any memory of the accident itself, and I'm honestly thankful. I would rather not relive the

day that could have ended my life. Instead, I'm looking to the future and the opportunity to come back next season," she said in an interview.

News broke yesterday morning of Stone's five year contract signing with her current team, Nightingale Racing, alongside her —now husband and this year's world champion—Ryder King. When asked about their partnership on and off the track, King replied with a smile:

"I get to spend every day doing the thing I love with the person I love most in this world. She's an incredible driver and I'm confident that it'll be her holding up that world champion trophy one day."

EPILOGUE
BLAKE

I PULL into my designated spot and shut off the engine. Leaning my head back, I close my eyes and let out the breath I've held captive as my shoulders shake with disbelief.

Taking one last grounding breath, I unclasp my harness and climb out of my car. The crowd surrounding the winners area goes wild as I hold my arms over my head.

A squeal leaves me when strong arms lift me up and over my car's halo before crushing me into a solid chest. Pulling back he leans his helmet against mine and I look up into emerald green eyes.

"Did that just happen?" I whisper.

"Need me to pinch you?" Ryder chuckles and I playfully slap his chest.

"No," I laugh, "I just... I can't believe that just happened."

"Believe it, love," he pulls me back into his chest, "You did it."

Mama squeezes my hand as we watch Dad climb up the stairs to the podium. He turns and leans into the mic, "Good evening. I have the distinct honor of presenting this award tonight to someone none of us saw coming. Over the past five years they have made their mark on the industry, headed the opening of a new driving school program, and continue to challenge those around them to do better both on and off the track."

He lowers his voice and holds up the trophy, "It is with immense pride that I present the 2028 World Champion trophy to Nightingale Racing driver and my daughter, Mrs. Blake King."

The room explodes with applause as I stand, hugging Mama before turning and kissing Ryder softly. He smiles against my lips and repeats the words I've told him for every title he's won, "Go get 'em, pip."

I carefully make my way up the stairs and Dad pulls me into a crushing hug before handing me the title trophy and stepping to the side.

Looking down at the trophy in my hands, I slowly approach the mic and smile. "Sorry, this kind of still feels like it's all a dream."

The room fills with laughter and I shake my head, lift my eyes, and get swept away by the love and pride in my husband's eyes. Ryder smiles softly at me and I take a soothing breath.

"That's what this has been, what it always has been. A

dream," I look back down at the trophy in my hands, "But now it's my reality."

Sitting it down on the stand I face the audience and smile. "Just like all the other drivers, I have been working towards this moment since the first time I climbed into my kart. The road here hasn't been easy. I've fought against prejudices, sexism, and disbeliefs. I've survived accidents, some big and some small. I've found a network of loved ones to help me to keep going when I feel like giving up. I've made the dream of a twelve year old girl come true despite those who told me I'd never make it."

My eyes slide to Mama as she wipes away her tears. "I want to thank the woman who instilled that drive in me. A woman who didn't let her circumstances hold her back from what she dreamed for herself or her family. She showed me that if I worked hard enough, then there's nothing I won't be able to do." Dad leans in and kisses the side of Mama's head.

"To Nikolai Morozov and Callum Brennan, my team principal and owner, thank you for taking a risk on the amateur racer five years ago. I hope I made the investment worth it." The two men laugh and Nikolai nods.

"And finally, Ryder King. My husband. You've enjoyed making me cry every year for the past five years at this thing, now it's my turn." The crowd laughs and Ryder shakes his head with a smile.

"This is all possible because of you. It was your first Formula 1 race that broke through the static of our janky tv that Sunday, leaving me with my newest obsession and a bowl of soggy cereal. For years I dedicated myself to this sport because one day, I wanted to be just like you. I wanted to be a champion. I wanted to be breaking boundaries and making a name for myself. I wanted to make my mama proud and be the inspiration for future generations."

I shake my head, "For the longest time, I didn't think it would ever happen. But then I got my shot and found myself teammates with the one man who brought this all into my life in the first place. I was nervous meeting you, afraid that I would let you down, let the team down. There was so much pressure that I wasn't ready for and instead of calling me out on it, you helped me, you stood up for me, you believed in me."

I smile and take a shaky breath. "You've believed in me every step of the way and there aren't any words capable of expressing how much that meant to me. How much it still means to me. Thank you. Thank you for having blind faith in me when you had no reason to. Thank you for guiding me through the dark days and celebrating with me on the good ones. Thank you for loving me and supporting me. Thank you for everything because none of this," I gesture around us, "would have been possible without you."

Ryder mouths 'I love you' and I laugh through my building tears. "Well it looks like you still got me to cry this year." The room fills with laughter and I sigh.

"Thank you. Everyone. The crews, the fans, the industry. This is truly a dream come true and for all of you out there that doubt if you're capable enough, know that you are. You are capable of achieving so much more than you could ever think of." The room erupts in cheers as I say my final thanks and hold my trophy up high.

Ryder meets me at the bottom of the stairs and bends, brushing his lips over mine. I look up and laugh, swiping away a tear from his cheek.

"You got me," he chuckles and I smile.

"What now?" he whispers.

I shrug, "Whatever it is—"

"We do it together," he finishes.

I press up and kiss him softly, "We do it together."

THANK YOU

Wow. Thank you so much for reading my debut novel, Lights Out! It's been such a wild ride this past year from reigniting my love for reading during my spine recovery to the embarrassing amount of Post-it notes, scraps of paper, and even some gum wrappers with story ideas written on them to finally pulling the trigger and deciding to do the damn thing.

It's been sleepless nights of crafting and editing more words than I thought I even knew. I've built new relationships and made new friends along the way. I won't even try to tell you how many times I found myself laughing at my own jokes or crying right alongside my characters or gasping when even I didn't know what would happen next.

I've truly fallen in love with Blake and Ryder's story. Did it go anywhere near the way I originally thought it would? No, it absolutely did not. But am I happy with where it ended? Immensely. This may be the end of their story, but don't worry, you'll be seeing them again real soon. This is only the beginning! So, buckle up because there's so many amazing stories yet to be told.

COMING SOON

The Grid Series

Lights Out

Book #2: Jace's Story (Coming later in 2024)

Book #3

Book #4

ACKNOWLEDGMENTS

This has been a WILD ride and none of it would have been possible without the village worth of people I met along the way.

To my sister, Vanessa, thank you for your relentless texts, calls, and gifs bombarding my phone until I gave you more of the story. I'm beyond thankful for you pushing me to do this and I promise that the next series will be the one you've been begging for.

To my beta readers: Bryn, Carolyn, Eden, Fernanda, and Morgan, thank you for taking the time to read Blake and Ryder's story. Your feedback kept me going and silenced my worries.

To Kristen, my editor, I could not have done this without you. It was your words of encouragement that kept me going and your comments that made me laugh through the anxious tears. Thank you for the unhinged reactions, posts on instagram where I swear you could read my mind, and every single late night text telling me I could do this. You're the absolute best.

To my ARC readers, thank you for taking the time to read and review this story and for your support with Lights Out.

To Ellie at LoveNotes PR, thank you for all your work with getting those ARC readers. You saved me from yet another panic attack and I will forever be grateful for you.

For all my new author friends, thank you for any and all advice you gave me along the way. We're in this together and there isn't any other community I'd rather be a part of.

To my family. Thank you for your never ending support, I couldn't have done this without you. Now remember that when you get a special redacted version of this book. Sorry, not sorry!

To my dear sweet husband. Thank you for suffering through countless one-sided conversations and breakdowns where I talked you through all my chaotic thoughts for this. You've truly mastered the art of patience, smiling and nodding, and knowing when to yank my computer away. You kept me sane through all of this. I could not have done this without your love and support. Thank you and I love you with all my being. Now please remember that when I'm knee deep into book two.

Finally, to the readers. You all make the sleepless nights worth it. Thank you for loving this story, these characters, and being by my side throughout this entire journey.

ABOUT THE AUTHOR

Kayla James is a romance reader who is obsessed with happily-ever-after's, swoon worthy moments, epic book boyfriends, and those scenes that make you blush (you know the ones, you dirty girl you).

When she's not writing, she's spending time with her husband, binge watching their favorite shows or traveling all over the country. She's a graphic designer by day and dreamer... Well, all the time.

Books found her when she needed it most and hopes that one day her writing can be that for someone else.

TRIGGER WARNINGS

This book contains references of:

- grief/loss
- ptsd
- death of a parent (past)
- detail of racing accident
- on page sexual content